BREATHE

BREATHE

Lauren Jameson

NEW AMERICAN LIBRARY

NEW AMERICAN LIBRARY
Published by the Penguin Group
Penguin Group (USA), 375 Hudson Street,
New York, New York 10014, USA

USA | Canada | UK | Ireland | Australia | New Zealand | India | South Africa | China
penguin.com
A Penguin Random House Company

First published by New American Library,
a division of Penguin Group (USA) LLC

First Printing, December 2013

 REGISTERED TRADEMARK—MARCA REGISTRADA

LIBRARY OF CONGRESS CATALOGING-IN-PUBLICATION DATA:
Jameson, Lauren.
Breathe/by Lauren Jameson.
p. cm.
ISBN 978-0-451-46663-1
I. Title.
PS3610.A464B74 2013
813'.6—dc23   2013023715

Printed in the United States of America
10 9 8 7 6 5 4 3 2 1

Set in Arno Pro
Designed by Sabrina Bowers

PUBLISHER'S NOTE
This is a work of fiction. Names, characters, places, and incidents either are the product of the author's
imagination or are used fictitiously, and any resemblance to actual persons, living or dead, business
establishments, events, or locales is entirely coincidental.

*For my wonderful husband, Rob. See?
I'm finally dedicating one to you!*

BREATHE

CHAPTER ONE

The sculpture stood on a small marble table in the center of the spacious resort lobby. A perfect, slender column of emerald green glass rose in a straight line nearly three feet high before overflowing into streams of glass that sparkled like crystals. Some were as thin as a pinkie finger, looking delicate enough to snap off at the slightest breath, and some of the tendrils were as thick as a pillar candle. All varied in tones from the merest whisper of mint to the green of a dense forest.

This piece had been the manifestation of a desire that had been haunting Samantha Collins's dreams lately. Dreams that she wasn't entirely sure what to do with.

It had been a long time since she'd had sex, true enough, and her stress levels had been through the roof lately. But these needs that had been tugging at her had been growing stronger . . .

She'd half hoped that putting these urges into her sculpture would exorcise them.

It hadn't.

"Wine, señorita?" An impeccably dressed waiter in a black suit made an appearance at Samantha's elbow. On his hand he balanced a tray of crimson wine in sparkling glasses.

"Thanks." Gratefully she accepted a glass. The flavors hit her tongue as she sipped eagerly, and she recognized it was much finer than any of the wines she was accustomed to drinking.

"Quilceda Creek Cabernet, 2005." The waiter beamed as if he had produced the wine himself.

Samantha pasted a smile onto her face and nodded enthusiastically. "Yes. Very nice."

Samantha liked wine, but the ones she tended to purchase came in a box or, if she was feeling fancy, in a bottle with a screw cap. She'd never heard of Quilceda Creek, though it tasted nice enough.

"Ten-dollar bottle, hundred-dollar bottle, the end result's the same," she spoke quietly to herself before lifting her glass in a silent toast. As she sipped, she looked down at her sculpture, still hit by a sense of disbelief that it had been chosen for exhibition.

Indulgencia was a luxurious resort located in the tourist-saturated town of Cabo San Lucas. It was infamous both for its wealthy patrons and for Devorar, the small BDSM club that catered to the varied sexual predilections of its clientele.

Once a year Indulgencia held an art exhibit with an erotic theme. The owner of the resort, some wealthy tycoon from the States, flew in artwork from around the world to showcase for the event, and when Samantha had submitted her piece, she hadn't been hopeful about her chances.

Though the twists of glass had been created with one of her most erotic dreams in mind, the result was a million miles away from the human-sized copper penis, which was the next sculpture over in the exhibit.

Samantha hadn't been sure that the wealthy mogul, who'd organized the show and selected all of the pieces himself, would see what she did, even though it was the most erotic sculpture she'd ever produced. She had put all the sexual frustration she had been feeling in the last few months into the work.

Being at this show wasn't helping that frustration. Not at all.

"Lovely piece, isn't it?" The voice came from just behind her shoulder, startling her. Samantha whirled around to face the speaker, her wine sloshing in her glass.

When she saw him, she nearly swallowed her tongue.

The man was tall, at least six feet, and though he wore expensive-looking black slacks and a dress shirt, she could see enough of his physique to appreciate the muscular body beneath the clothing. Combined with his dark blue eyes, flaxen hair, and sexy-as-hell smile, his sudden appearance made it seem as if all of Samantha's heated dreams had just come to life.

That sexy dream man cocked an eyebrow at her, and she belatedly realized that he'd asked her a question.

"Do you like this particular sculpture?" he repeated helpfully.

"It's . . . Oh, yes, it's very nice." She wasn't about to tell anyone here that she was the artist. She wasn't ready for anyone to ask what had inspired it, especially this man, who discomforted her with his focused attention.

Deliberately she shrugged, and tried to catch one thin strap of her sundress as it slid down her shoulder. She tugged it back up and caught the man's eyes following the movement. "It's such a pretty color."

She almost bit her tongue as she said it. She knew, of course, the painstaking effort that had gone into creating the gradation of hues in the sculpture, the hours she had spent gathering the molten material on her blowpipe, rolling it into finely ground glass of different shades, then setting the colors in by sweating over the smaller of her two glass furnaces—but she wanted to take care not to tip her hand that she was more than a casual admirer of the artwork.

She assumed the man would simply nod in agreement. Instead, he reached out and ran one slender finger over a curling tendril of glass, much as she had done. The care and attention of his touch over the smooth surface made Samantha think of those dreams she'd been having lately, the ones that had produced a constant ache.

In fact, last night's had featured a man running his hands over her body exactly the same way this man was doing to the sculpture. The memory made her shiver.

"Would you like to know what I see?" His blue eyes pinned her with their intensity, and Samantha lifted her glass to her lips to give herself something to do with her hands.

"Yes, I'm curious." She nodded, her breath catching in her throat as his fingers closed around hers where they rested on the stem of her wineglass.

The man captured the glass from her fingers and handed it off to a passing waiter. He secured a fresh one and had it in her hand without ever once taking his eyes from her.

"I see a meeting of male and female." She felt herself getting lost in the deep, husky tones of his voice as he continued. "But more than that, I see a balance of two opposites, each feeding a need in the other."

Samantha's lips parted in surprise, and her heart began to pound.

That was exactly what she'd intended. How on earth had he known? No one else ever saw what she'd intended in her art.

"That's what I— I mean, yes. Yes, I see that as well." She worried her lower lip with her teeth as she spoke, afraid he would ask her about what she had started to say.

With her heart still beating double time against her rib cage, she turned from the sculpture to look up into the man's face. He looked vaguely familiar, as if she'd met him once a long time ago.

More than the familiarity, though, there was a sense of connection. He'd understood the meaning behind her art, and with that came a tug on an invisible rope that seemed to stretch between them, pulling them ever closer.

And God, he was sexy. There was something in his demeanor that attracted her, made her want something she couldn't quite articulate.

Liquid heat pooled between her legs and she held herself back from reaching out to touch him.

"What are you thinking?" The man's voice was low, but Samantha could hear him as if he were the only other person in the crowded room. His sharp gaze made her feel like the only woman in the world, and she had the insane urge to spill all her secrets to him.

If she did, would he understand that—more than anything—she yearned for a man who would be strong enough to take control for her?

Samantha started to speak, then shut her mouth tight as the rational part of her brain took over. She couldn't even admit these desires out loud to herself . . . she certainly wasn't about to tell them to a stranger.

No matter that the stranger was the most gorgeous man she'd ever seen.

"I'm Samantha." Swallowing back everything she wanted to say, she gave him the big smile that she used on the rare occasions when she poked her head outside her studio. Her name seemed to break the heavy tension between them, but the slight cock of his eyebrow hinted that he knew there was something else she wanted to say.

Then he took her hand in his, encasing her fingers in the heat of his palm, and she forgot all about trying to keep her thoughts to herself. The simple touch, the way he rubbed his thumb over the curves of her own palm, sent sizzles shooting through her arm.

If he wanted her, he could have her. It wouldn't even occur to her to say no. *Wait—where did that come from?*

"Elijah Masterson," he said, continuing to stroke his fingers over her hand, his eyes telling her that he wanted exactly the same thing she did. Overwhelmed by his sensual touch, she didn't register the name right away. After a beat, the light went on in her mind.

Elijah Masterson. His gorgeous face, with that devil-may-care grin, had been on the front page of the local paper several weeks earlier, for an interview about the erotic-art show he'd been putting together for his resort.

His resort. Indulgencia.

Good Lord, this man owned the entire place.

"Oh, ah, I mean . . ." Samantha tried to tug her hand free. She should escape this encounter while she could. But she felt she should thank Elijah for accepting her piece into his show, although that would mean admitting it was hers.

"What brought you here tonight, Samantha?" Elijah gave her fingers a firm squeeze that spread through her body before he let her tug her hand away. Those bright blue eyes stayed focused on her as if she were the most interesting woman he'd ever come across.

"I . . . I don't know." The lie left her feeling uneasy. The sculpture had just been the first piece to the puzzle. Once her work had been accepted into the resort's exhibit, she'd longed to know more about the erotic-art scene. From there she had made some subtle inquiries, asking around to see if anyone knew what exactly went on at Devorar, the club inside the upscale hotel. She'd looked online to educate herself, entering every search term imaginable, since she wasn't entirely certain what it was she was looking for.

Yes, she'd been curious to see what her sculpture looked like on display, wanted to see if its sensuality still shone when surrounded by the more overtly sexual pieces that made up this showing. But more than that, she'd thought she might get a glimpse into the lifestyle that had started to fascinate her so much.

Apart from the wildly suggestive art, however, there was nothing there that suggested anything other than opulence and luxury. She wasn't sure what she'd been hoping for—waiters in leather chaps? some whips and chains?—but none of Devorar's secrets were revealed in the posh lobby of Indulgencia.

"Don't lie." Elijah's tone was stern. Startled, Samantha looked up into his eyes. He didn't appear angry, but the look on his face made her feel guiltier than if he had been. "Tell me why you're here."

Samantha couldn't quite work up the courage to speak. She began to tremble with nerves, thinking about what to say, and was exasperated with herself for the anxiety.

With it came an unbidden memory, a face from her past. The man in her mind's eye was old enough to be her grandfather, with salt-and-pepper hair and cold, dark eyes. But he too had been rich, and commanding.

She was her own woman, and wanted to think she was strong enough to live her life the way she wanted, without painful memories overshadowing things. But the truth was, she just didn't know if she'd wind up hating herself for what she wanted.

"You won't find any judgment from me, kitten."

Samantha gaped for a moment. *Kitten*? He'd called her *kitten*? She'd just been insulted. She should have felt insulted.

She didn't.

"I . . . I'm curious," she finally admitted, feeling her cheeks flush the same color as the wine she was drinking. "I've heard about Devorar and I . . . I thought someone here might have some answers for me."

"Answers to what questions, Samantha?" As he'd promised, there was no censure in Elijah's tone. Instead there was heat—enough that Samantha felt herself start to burn as the flush spread from her cheeks through the rest of her body.

But she froze as thoughts of her mother came wending their

way into her mind. Another reason she had held herself back from going after what she wanted.

Her mother's . . . vices . . . had nearly ruined her daughters' lives. If Samantha weakened, gave up control, was she any better?

"I . . . I think I'd better go." Closing her eyes against Elijah's penetrating stare, Samantha pressed her hands to her temples and turned away. It was tempting, so tempting, to give in to what she was quite certain she wanted.

But the memory of her mother's mistakes was a reminder that giving in to temptation could lead to disastrous results. No matter how much she felt this need, deep in her very core, she shouldn't have come here.

"Samantha." Elijah's voice was firm as Samantha began to walk away. She turned back halfway, not enough to see the gorgeous man again, but enough that she was confronted with her own work of art.

The sensual visual overwhelmed her senses and made her ache.

"Come back anytime." There was a note of concern in Elijah's voice that made Samantha hesitate. Not all men were like the ones who'd flitted in and out of her mother's life. Rationally she knew that.

But this man was gorgeous, wealthy as sin, and likely into some very kinky things, given that he had opened a BDSM club in his resort. That was enough danger to send Samantha running, even as she nodded, acknowledging his offer.

Even though, rather than walk away, she found herself wanting to tangle her fingers in that messy golden hair. Wanting to tilt her head up to receive his kiss.

She said nothing, though she felt his penetrating stare on her back as he watched her. It caused heat to simmer low in her belly, a sensation she'd never felt before.

The sensation didn't abate, not even as she exited the resort and walked to her car, a ramshackle bucket of bolts she'd purchased two years earlier, when she'd first moved to Mexico. She sighed as she slid into the driver's seat, the image of Elijah's sexy-as-sin face and his interest in her warring in her mind with the memories of that other man.

Samantha twisted her lips together as she put the key into the ignition and turned.

It was going to be a long night.

Elijah was puzzled and horny as hell.

He had been part of the BDSM lifestyle for a long time, and over the years he had become incredibly adept at reading people, especially women. The slender goddess of a redhead walking away from him had looked him directly in the eyes, then had steeled herself and walked away.

Elijah wasn't overly caught up in himself, but he had never lacked for a woman when he wanted one. That woman, Samantha, had clearly come here looking for something. Yet the fact that she had walked away from him was not suggestive of someone with a naturally submissive personality.

And yet something about her pulled at him, made him yearn. He'd learned the hard way that he needed someone who was truly submissive to make him happy, and in the years since his divorce he had trained himself not to even look twice at a woman who didn't meet that one particular criterion.

But the combination of sass and fragility in this particular woman—Samantha—very nearly had him running after her.

When the application for the stunning green sculpture currently showcased in his exhibit had come in, he'd been immediately entranced. It was innately sexual, the artistic expression colored with a dark need. When he'd seen it in person he'd become nearly obsessed. It painted a perfect portrait, to his eye at least, of dominance and submission, and he'd known at once that the artist behind it must have had a perfect understanding of the lifestyle.

Now, after meeting Samantha Jane Collins—he'd done some research, for the biography that had accompanied the application had been woefully incomplete—he wasn't so sure. She'd been interested, had responded to his dominance—he was sure of it.

But though she had come to the exhibit, though she'd admitted that she had questions, he'd bet one of his properties that she was a neophyte.

It had been on the tip of his tongue to offer to teach her—he knew he hadn't imagined the heat that had sparked between them. But then she'd reached within herself for something— what, he had no idea—and had walked away.

"Damn it." Bad marriage or not, Elijah was a man accustomed to getting what he wanted—in the bedroom, at least.

Suddenly he wanted Samantha.

In his younger years he would have been arrogant enough to be certain that she would submit to him regardless of her sexual preferences. He'd since learned that it took a very strong woman to fully submit care of herself to another.

He'd yet to find that woman, and so he remained alone, limiting himself to sexual encounters here and at a few other clubs that he had part ownership in, particularly In Vino Veritas, the combined wine bar and club that he owned with two friends back home in Vegas.

He'd been with enough women that he'd learned a hard truth. Unless he could find a woman who would submit herself to him entirely, he would be miserable. But that didn't necessarily mean that he couldn't enjoy a diversion with the woman whose skin flushed so deliciously when he looked at her.

Elijah slid his hands into the pockets of his suit pants as he watched Samantha hurry through one of the open stucco archways in the lobby. The hem of her little sundress slid up her thigh as she got into the ugliest car he'd ever seen.

It was an affront to his senses—a woman that beautiful belonged behind the wheel of something sleek and sexy. Yet his eyes moved past the hideous vehicle and greedily took in the lithe curve of her leg, which ended in a strappy, high-heeled red sandal that made his mouth water.

Need pooled low in his belly. He was a sucker for sexy shoes on a gorgeous woman.

Hell. He wanted her, whether she was submissive or not. Maybe he was playing with fire—he had no desire to be proven wrong again, and something about their instant connection told him that Samantha had the potential to be more than a quick fuck. But the more he thought about further exploring his interest in her, the more he decided he had to have her.

Snagging a glass of wine from a passing waiter, he sipped as he contemplated. Mouton Rothschild. His friend Alex had introduced him to this one, and it was now one of his favorites. It added to the heat in his gut.

Damn it. He was going to pursue Samantha Collins. He knew it.

He just hoped he wouldn't be consumed in the fire that was sure to come with it.

CHAPTER TWO

Elijah's GPS took him to a small house on the outskirts of San José del Cabo. The town itself was a tourist draw, and this cottage was just far enough out to have a solitary feel. That, combined with the woman's awkwardness at the party the night before, had him wondering if she was a bit of a hermit.

It was another piece of the puzzle that was Samantha Collins. He smiled to himself as the first hit of adrenaline began to work its way through his veins. It had been a long time—years, in fact—since he'd had to pursue a woman. The fact that she'd walked away from him the night before had sent his predatory instincts into full gear.

Most of the women he knew were interested in his wealth, his status as a Dom, and his looks. He knew it—even used it when he wanted to.

But this woman was something different, and he was enthralled.

After parking the Carrera on a small pad of gravel in front of the house, Elijah shrugged out of his jacket and exited the car. The front yard of the cottage was covered in that same crushed rock, with the occasional dried weed poking its head out, gasping for a reprieve from the Mexican heat.

He strode up to the door, painted a vivid red, a startling color against the shabby green of the rest of the building. There was no doorbell that he could see, so he settled for several sharp raps. Peeling paint flaked away under the blows.

Damn it. There was no answer, but Elijah was sure she was home. He felt that same heightened awareness that he'd experienced when he'd first laid eyes on her.

Yes, she was here. Somewhere.

Elijah moved around to the side of the house. It was much the same as the front, lots of gravel and weeds, with the addition of two grumpy garden gnomes who glared at him with their pudgy arms crossed.

The gnomes made him grin. He appreciated whimsy.

He was so caught up taking in the scene that it took him a moment to register the sound. A rumble, like the dull roar of a low fire, disturbed the air. His eyes homed in on a small shack at the far end of the yard, its boards faded by the sun and nearly indistinguishable from the rocks and weeds that surrounded it.

That was where the noise emanated from. Elijah squinted and could see waves of heat undulating from an oven-sized window that had been propped open with a stick.

Found you. Elijah grinned once more as satisfaction flooded him. She was home all right—she was working.

His blood pumping hot and fast, he hesitated only a moment outside the door of the studio. He knew the polite thing to do would be to wait for an invitation. But he hadn't amassed his fortune by being polite. Rude as it might be to enter uninvited, it would also catch the woman off guard, which upped his chances of success.

The way she'd run out of the party told him that he wasn't going to be able to woo her so easily. He'd even conjured a backup plan in case she tried to deny the connection between them—one that would bind them together, at least for a while, so they could explore the attraction. It was one he was pretty sure she wouldn't be able to refuse.

Suddenly even more eager to set eyes on her, he knocked on the swollen wood of the door. As he'd expected, no voice rose over the roar of what he now saw were furnaces. Pressing his palm flat against the splintered wooden door, he opened it and went in.

The heat was a moist slap in the face. Even though he'd been in Mexico for a week, nothing could have prepared him for the inferno that raged inside the tiny building. Sweat beaded at the back of his neck within seconds and dripped slowly down his spine as he inhaled mouthfuls of searing air.

"I'm busy." Samantha had her back to him, but was instantly recognizable by the red curls that were piled haphazardly on top of her head. She wore black athletic shorts, which showed miles of the creamy, curvy legs that he'd admired the night before. The ribbed tank that covered her torso clung to her skin with perspiration, making the thin fabric transparent enough that Elijah could quite clearly see that she wasn't wearing a bra.

"Wow." When she heard his voice, Samantha stiffened noticeably, and Elijah couldn't quite hold back a chuckle. She'd recognized his voice, and the primal part of him was pleased.

Then she turned around, and he deliberately swallowed that smile. It was a wise move, to his way of thinking, since clutched in her hands was a long metal pipe tipped with hot glass.

He opened his mouth to say something—he wasn't sure what, since her very presence clouded his mind, a remarkable novelty for him. Samantha held up a hand sharply, cutting off his words before he'd even spoken them.

"I'm working." Her voice was firm, even reproving, as she turned away from him and back to the source of the noise and heat. He narrowed his eyes, held his tongue, but stayed where he was, watching with fascination.

She placed the glass on the end of the pipe back into the blazing furnace. She was seemingly unaffected by the heat surrounding her. Rather than wilting, she seemed to glow, to draw energy from it. *Fascinating*, Elijah thought, unable to tear his eyes away from her competent movements, the long limbs that moved so gracefully, the mass of red curls.

The fact that she seemed so entirely focused on her work, so completely oblivious of him, was more enticing than frustrating. What would it be like, he wondered, to have that complete and total focus on him?

An image flashed through his mind, of Samantha naked and bound before him, the beautiful flush of arousal on her cheeks. The image was shattered when she scraped the glass off the end of the metal wand and, leaning it carefully against the wall, turned to face him. Instead of a beautiful smile, she cast him a look full of irritation.

"You know, most people wait for an invitation to enter." Her voice was appealing, reminding Elijah of whiskey and caramel at the same time, even though her words were imbued with agitation. She cast an irritated glare at him, setting the pipe down and rolling her shoulders back.

The movement made her unbound breasts jump forward, and Elijah found himself trying very hard to keep his eyes on Samantha's face. In every aspect of his life he was in control—made it a point to be so—but this woman was like nothing he'd ever encountered.

It made him thirst for her submission even more.

She'd been so unsure of herself at the art show, but here ... here on her own turf she felt comfortable enough to tell him off. Yes, she offered a fascinating combination, Elijah thought, even as warning bells sounded in his head, telling him to get out before he got in over his head.

I'm not about to get in too deep with her, he reminded himself. If—*when*—they embarked on the steamy affair that he had in mind, he was confident it would be satisfying for both of them, but a temporary engagement.

"I'm not most people." Slowly he raked his eyes over her from head to toe, making no attempt to hide the fact that he was doing so. He'd never been the type to play hard to get—when he wanted a woman, he said so.

He would be a little more cautious with this one, in case she went running, the way she already had.

"No. You're not." Picking up a bottle of water that must have been horribly warm just from being in the small room, Samantha cast him a considering look, then opened it and took long, greedy swallows, draining the liquid.

"When we met, why didn't you admit that you were the artist of the sculpture we were talking about?" Elijah found himself watching the sensual pull of her lips on the bottle. Once she finished drinking, those lips pressed tightly together, as if she was debating something with herself, before she finally spoke.

"Why are you here?" She ignored his question and looked directly at him, and Elijah felt a stab of disappointment that there wasn't even a hint of submission in her gaze. He had no desire to alter even a single thing about this gorgeous creature. But he wanted her. He wanted to know her intimately, as a man was made to know a woman. His cock was already aching for her, just from being in the same room. And he was intent on having her—more than once.

He wanted—needed—a woman who would let him call the shots. In return he would treat her like the most precious thing in creation for the time that they were together, but he needed to be in control. And though he knew that made him sound like a knuckle-dragging Neanderthal, the popularity of his clubs like Devorar and In Vino Veritas had taught him that he wasn't the only one.

Hot as he already was for Samantha, he didn't think this would be anything more than an intense affair, one that satisfied their mutual curiosity. But he wanted her enough to not need to think beyond that. She intrigued him beyond comparison, and in the world in which he now lived—a world in which things were given to him before he even asked—the chase was too much to resist.

Eyes narrowing, Elijah watched as Samantha rolled her shoulders back once more, his eyes taking in the arousing sight of her nipples pressing against the thin cotton of her tank top.

He wanted her enough to ignore his own rules, at least for the moment.

"I want you." He answered her question bluntly, honestly.

"Cut right to the chase, don't you?" Her glass green eyes widened. "What if I don't want you?"

At that, Elijah smiled and raised an eyebrow.

"I told you last night not to lie to me." As he spoke he drew up straighter, pulling his dominance to him. He watched Samantha inhale sharply, looking *him* over this time.

But she didn't drop her gaze, didn't seem eager to please him. Instead she ran her tongue slowly over her lips, considering.

"All right," she said slowly, nodding thoughtfully as she spoke. "Fair enough. I'm . . . attracted to you. That doesn't mean I'm going to do anything about it."

Elijah cocked his head to one side as he studied her. He enjoyed the dance of seduction, but here she had him on uncertain footing. He didn't think she was deliberately trying to be a brat, something his ex had done quite frequently.

Most of the world didn't understand the needs that brought people to seek something beyond vanilla sex, and because of that they frowned upon it.

For years Elijah had felt a drive to help people work past those biases. His desire for Samantha gave him an even greater incentive.

She was searching for something, and he didn't think

she even knew what yet. He was more than happy to help her find it.

"What if I told you that I could answer the questions that brought you to the show last night?" Deliberately he took a step closer to Samantha, just barely invading what he figured she probably considered her personal space.

She eyed him warily, her fingers twisting in the hem of her tank top.

"Maybe I don't need the answers anymore." She thrust her chin into the air.

Elijah thought it was cute.

"Again with the lies, Samantha?" He reached out and ran his finger lightly over the curve of her cheekbone, savoring the resultant quiver. "Your pants are going to catch on fire any second."

Samantha narrowed her eyes at him. Elijah waited patiently, making sure his expression was calm but stern.

Those green eyes never wavered in their focus, never looked down, as he would have expected from a submissive. But finally she swallowed, and he saw acceptance in the stubborn set of her shoulders.

"All right. I want answers, but I'm not sure I'm ready for them." Her face showed him nothing but stark honesty, and Elijah felt a tug of pleasure.

It was a step in the right direction. Being a Dom, he was inclined to push her, but he was also a strategic businessman, and he knew that in that exact moment she would have dug her heels in and pushed right back.

"I'd love it if you showed me how this all works." He deliberately phrased his words as a statement, not a question. Samantha furrowed her brow, seeming to sense that he was maneuvering her, but finally shrugged in acceptance.

"Fine." Eyeing him suspiciously, she turned and picked up

the long metal rod that she had leaned against the wall earlier. Turning back over her shoulder, she shot him an exasperated look. "Since my concentration has been broken anyway."

Elijah bit the inside of his cheek to keep from smirking as he followed her across the room. The contrast between her somewhat sweet inquisitiveness the night before and her smart mouth today was delightful. Each new facet of her personality he encountered told him how amazing her eventual submission would be.

She placed a hand on her waist as she stood outside the door to the furnace, the metal rod still in her other hand. She frowned at him, and he was struck again by how pretty she was.

Then she opened the mottled metal door, allowing an inferno of orange light and heat to escape into the room. It bathed her face with an unholy gleam, made her silken curls shine like rubies, and Elijah's mouth went dry.

Had he seriously thought she was just pretty? That she was cute? She was the most beautiful creature he'd ever seen, a goddess of fire.

"Are you paying attention?" Again that slight frown furrowed the space between her eyebrows, and Elijah found that he wanted to reach out and smooth the skin with the tips of his fingers.

He didn't know how she would react to a simple touch like that, which wouldn't normally stop him . . . but she had a furnace full of molten glass behind her.

He wasn't stupid. He'd wait until he wasn't literally playing with fire.

"I'm paying attention." Though it might not have been wise, he moved a step closer to her than he suspected she was comfortable with. Her shoulders stiffened, but a sidelong glance also showed him that the brush of their arms made her nipples tighten.

He made her uncomfortable, but she also wanted him. He was immensely pleased with the combination.

Holding herself rigid, as if unwilling to give in to the urge to move away from him, Samantha held out the metal rod for Elijah to see.

"This is a blowpipe. And I just dare you to make a joke about that." She raised an eyebrow at him, and he gestured for her to continue. "This pear shape at the end is what I use to collect a gather of glass."

Elijah watched, fascinated, as Samantha placed the end of the blowpipe into the glowing orange interior of the furnace.

"This is called the melting furnace." She rolled the pipe competently, wrapping a thick substance around its end. "This is always kept hot, and it's always full of colorless liquid glass."

"Where do you get the glass from?" Elijah remained transfixed as Samantha removed the blowpipe from the furnace.

"I make my own. It's mostly silica, with some potassium and limestone as stabilizers." Samantha rolled the glob of molten glass against the edge of the oven, her fingers working with small, competent movements. "After twelve hours at twenty-two hundred degrees, it becomes liquid."

The red-hot glow of the glass was fading, the gather cooling, Elijah guessed, now that it was outside of the oven.

"Pick a color." Samantha looked at him, still twirling the pipe. Her eyes were bright, that snapping apple green, and in that moment it was the only color Elijah could see.

"Green." He watched as Samantha pulled a dish full of what looked like dark sand from a metal shelf.

"What's that?" He watched, fascinated, as Samantha rolled the glass in the powder.

"This is colored glass, ground down as fine as salt." Her biceps flexed with the effort of keeping her movements even as she moved to another, smaller furnace and opened the door.

"This is called the glory hole. It's a smaller furnace used to reheat. This will fuse the green into the colorless glass." Samantha removed the blowpipe from the glory hole, and Elijah was surprised at the jolt of delight he felt when he saw that the gather of glass was now a deep green.

Except . . .

"Can we make it lighter?" He was intent now, engrossed in the project. Samantha pressed her lips together as she looked at him.

"Micromanage much?" Her voice was tart. He grinned at her, pleased to see she couldn't quite control the quirk of her own lips.

Leaning closer so that his lips brushed against the lobe of her ear, he whispered, his voice husky, "You don't know the half of it."

She didn't jerk away, didn't try to deny the heat that sparked between them as their eyes met and held.

She kept her eyes on his face as she moved to a table, still turning the rod.

"The glass is the consistency of honey now." Her own voice had thickened with arousal, and Elijah inhaled deeply. A fine sheen of sweat covered her skin and made it glow as she finally looked away from him to her work, holding something that looked like a ladle against the glass.

"This helps me shape it before I start the glassblowing." Her eyes flicked from the glass to him, just briefly. "That's when you'll get your paler green."

"How?" Elijah watched intently.

Samantha rolled her eyes, then put the ladle aside. Seating herself on a low stool, still rolling the glass back and forth on the narrow table, she ran her tongue over her lips.

"Breath is the magic of glass art." Her eyes darkened, a small smile curving her lips, which sent a surge of need straight to Elijah's groin.

Magic indeed. As she placed her lips around the edge of the metal blowpipe and exhaled, her focus entirely on the glass, Elijah would have absolutely believed she was a witch if someone had accused her.

He couldn't look away.

She blew delicately into the pipe, turning it evenly all the while. The glob of glass expanded like a balloon, thinning and stretching and, as she had said, becoming a paler shade of green.

"There." Her voice was satisfied and slightly breathless as she removed her mouth from the pipe and stood, her tall, slender frame in motion the whole time. She picked up a flat paddle and held it to the bottom of the blown glass, flattening it. Then she picked up a thick stack of what looked like soggy newspaper and shaped the object some more, steam and smoke issuing from the paper as it rubbed against the hot glass.

She scored the green glass where it met the blowpipe, then picked up a nozzle and flicked a switch. "This is compressed air, to cool it."

Once she'd cooled it, she hurriedly carried the blowpipe to the first furnace.

"Now I put a bit of hot glass on the bottom of the piece." Removing the project from the furnace, she picked up a long metal rod and attached it to the piece with the hot glass. "This is a pontil. It's essentially a maneuvering rod."

Elijah found that he didn't want to say a word even though he had a million questions . . . He didn't want to disturb the rhythm of Samantha's work. She was clearly aware of him, spoke to him, but her attention was fully on her work.

It was the sexiest thing he'd ever seen.

He watched as she dipped a stick into a bucket of water, shaking it until a fat droplet landed on the glass.

Samantha then broke the glass off the blowpipe, picking up

another pontil and moving back to the first furnace. She used yet more hot glass to plug the hole that had resulted from breaking the glass off of the blowpipe.

Her breath was now coming faster, her breasts pushing against the thin fabric of her tank top. The sight, combined with her unholy beauty as she worked in front of the glowing furnace, had Elijah shifting uncomfortably, willing his cock to behave, lest he scare her off.

"Almost done." The tension in the air eased just the faintest amount as she used a small machine to polish the edge of what Elijah could now see was a simple, elegant vase. She aimed the nozzle with the compressed air at it again.

"There." Satisfaction rang true in her voice as she picked up the piece between stacks of damp newspaper and held it up for him to see. "That last blast of air was to equalize the temperature throughout the piece. Now it goes into this electric kiln. It will cool slowly for twelve hours, so that the glass doesn't crack." As she opened the kiln, Elijah, unable to stay away from her any longer, moved to stand just behind her.

She placed the vase on a shelf in the kiln, amid a forest of glass palm trees.

"These are quite different from your sculpture at the show." He reached out a hand to run a finger over the glossy trunk of one tree, and Samantha smacked his hand away. The movement caused her scent to waft toward his nose, and he inhaled the smell of wildflowers and smoke.

"Tourist tchotchkes are easy cash." Samantha closed the door to the kiln, then turned. She started when she looked up and found him right behind her.

Yet she didn't move away. Heat began a low burn in Elijah's belly, searing the thin ribbon of space between them. "How did you get started with glass art?" He didn't mind making small talk, if it meant he got to stand close and bask in her heat.

She eyed him warily, and he could see her pulse, a rapid beat under the line of her jaw.

"When I was eighteen I had a crush on someone who was a glass artist. I asked for private lessons." Her voice was breathy, and Elijah watched her lips part slightly beneath his stare. "Soon I was more interested in the glass than in him. It was . . . I found something that I'd always been looking for, even though I didn't know it—" She hesitated, clearly swallowing back the rest of her words.

He thought he knew what she was thinking but couldn't say: that now there was something else she was looking for. A desire she wanted to fulfill.

He waited for her to continue.

"You're involved in . . . You're a . . ." She worried her lower lip with her teeth, and Elijah had to clench his hands into fists to refrain from leaning forward and running his tongue over the place her teeth worked.

"Are you a . . . a Dom?"

Elijah cocked his head, studying her intently. She looked so nervous, he wanted to laugh and tell her that no one was going to tie her up and spank her for asking the question. But to laugh would be to diminish her question, so he swallowed the chuckle and instead nodded solemnly.

The image of her bound, quivering with need, was something he longed to see.

"Yes. I am." His voice was even. Her eyes widened a fraction, but she kept her composure. Afraid to discourage her curiosity, Elijah didn't voice the second half of his answer: that he wasn't at all sure Samantha was a submissive.

She ran her tongue over those lips again, and again he felt his cock begin to swell.

"Is BDSM something you're interested in?" Since she had

paused, her next questions seemingly stuck in her throat, he tried to nudge her with his words.

Her face reddened, a delicious shade of pink, and he reached out to graze his knuckles over the curve of her cheekbone.

"I don't know." The way she ducked her head as she spoke told him that she was evading. The little kitten was intrigued by the notion—that much was plain—but how far would she go?

"What I'm feeling right now . . . for you . . . Is it just because you're a Dom?" Samantha's eyes were huge as she stared up at him. Elijah suppressed a moan.

What was this intriguing artist looking for? What would he find if he pushed her?

"No," he said finally, bending his head a bit lower. "No, it isn't because I'm a Dom—or at least, not entirely. This . . . It doesn't happen between everyone, just like you don't feel a connection with every person that you date."

He waited, trying to appear patient, as she mulled that over.

Elijah wasn't often shocked, but when Samantha rose to her toes, clasped his upper arms, and pressed her lips to his, he found himself unable to do anything but react forcefully. He hadn't been expecting it—and, indeed, he didn't care for it when a woman took control.

But he couldn't deny the fever that surged through his entire body as she tentatively explored his lips with her own. Her nipples grazed his chest as she moaned softly and leaned in closer, and the slight touch made his cock harden to the point of pain.

Without thinking, he threaded one hand through the length of her ponytail and pressed the other between her shoulder blades, pulling her flush against his body. He rocked his hips forward, pressing his erection into the softness of her belly, asking her without words if this was what she really wanted.

"Elijah . . ."

He'd let her draw back enough to speak his name, and rather than hesitation or the innocent nerves that he'd expected to see on her face, he found determination.

Determination mixed with need—need as hot as the air that was scorching his lungs in the small, enclosed studio.

"Be sure, Samantha." His voice sounded rough, like shards of broken glass, even to his own ears. Deliberately he added a hint of meanness, and though she never would have believed it, it was because he was experiencing a twinge of guilt.

He wanted her, and if she continued using that wicked mouth on him, he'd have her. But if he could scare her off, it would be better for them both.

Tightening his fingers in her hair, he pulled roughly until her head tipped back and she was forced to look up into her eyes.

"Fuck," she whispered. Rather than nerves or indecision over his roughness, Elijah found that Samantha's lips had parted and that her skin was flushed with arousal.

She *liked* it.

It was his undoing.

"Come here." His voice stayed rough, just a bit mean as he pulled her flush against his body. This time when their lips touched, he took control of the kiss, parting her swollen lips with his tongue, tasting her sweetness, stroking in her mouth the way he was dying to do inside her pussy.

With a needy sigh of pure pleasure, Samantha melted against him, letting him take control of the kiss.

Sliding his hands down to cup her ass, he pressed upward until she wrapped her legs around his waist. As he carried her across the torrid glass studio, he contemplated setting up a small scene, an introduction to submission, to see how she reacted before either of them took this any further.

But when she eagerly began to press kisses into his neck and along the line of his jaw, each resonating in a throb between his legs, Elijah found that, for once, he didn't want the ritual or rules of a BDSM scene.

He wanted this woman, just like this.

He was going to have her.

She arched her pelvis forward and his body clenched. The space between her legs was hot, the dampness apparent through the thin shorts she wore. She rubbed against his cock relentlessly, and he braced her against the doorjamb to lean into the sharp ache of need.

"Too fucking hot in here." Elijah took her mouth again, working his hand up beneath the hem of her tank top as he tasted her. He pinched sharply, then rolled the taut nipple between his fingers, savoring the way she cried out and arched against him.

Sweat dampened them both, gluing their skin together. Heat shimmered in the air, tangible lines of it, lending a surreal quality to the moment.

"House. Bed." Letting go of him with the hand closest to the door, Samantha turned the knob, shoving against the swollen wood. It didn't budge, and with a moan of frustration against Elijah's lips she abandoned her efforts, sliding her hand between their bodies.

When her eager fingers traced over the outline of Elijah's cock, he felt pleasure coil at the base of his spine. Fuck, if her touch felt this good through the cloth of his shorts, his boxers, then it was going to be heaven to be skin on skin.

"Bed," she panted, curling her fingers around him. Cursing, Elijah wrapped his arms tightly around her and braced his shoulder against the door, shoving at it.

Beneath their combined weight it shuddered, then finally fell open. They staggered through the opening as if drunk, falling to their knees in the mosaic of gravel in Samantha's back-yard.

Elijah intended to pick her up, to carry her across the yard to the ramshackle cabin that she called home. But as she fisted her hands in the hem of her tank top and lifted it over her head, all he could think was that he had to have her *now*.

"Perfect." Ducking his head, Elijah licked a trail from her collarbone to her breasts. Cupping the heavy flesh in each hand, he worked the nipples with firm fingers, and at the same time sank his teeth into the softness that was the curve of her upper breast.

"Aah!" Samantha cried out and pressed herself against him, even as her fingers found and fumbled with the buckle of his belt.

She seemed as eager as he was. Though she didn't appear to have any neighbors, her backyard wasn't closed off and was clearly visible from the front of the house. He couldn't have cared less if someone saw them, but spared a moment to wonder how she would feel.

"Samantha—" He curved his hands under her ass and made a questioning look toward the front of the house.

She narrowed her eyes at him in defiance and, releasing his belt buckle, started in on the zipper of her own shorts.

"I can't wait." Her voice was hot and full of need.

He looked down at her, assessing. She was aroused, her lips swollen and damp, her breasts flushed from his touch. But she looked completely in control of her faculties.

She was a grown woman, and she wanted him. He wasn't going to try to convince her otherwise.

"Strip for me." Standing briefly, he worked his fingers over his own belt buckle. Her eyes followed the movement, but she did as he said, hooking her fingers in the elastic of her waist-band and slowly lowering the fabric of her shorts.

"Everything," he ordered. A thrill coursed through him when she pinched her fingers into the side of her panties—plain cotton ones—and tugged them down her hips along with her shorts as he'd commanded.

"On your hands and knees." His cock jerked as she worked her clothing the rest of the way off. The late-afternoon sun made the russet curls between her legs glisten, and his mouth watered to taste her.

There would be time for that later. With burning desire, he wanted, *needed* to be inside her.

"I want to taste you," she said. Rather than dropping to the ground as he'd ordered, Samantha reached out and took the base of his cock in her long artist's hands.

"I want you on all fours, little one." Deliberately, he made his voice authoritative, anticipation catching in his throat. What would she do?

He wasn't expecting her to glare up at him, temper hot in her eyes, and to stroke her hand up and down his shaft.

Dipping her fiery head, she closed her lips around the head of his cock, and Elijah couldn't swallow the groan of pleasure that escaped his lips.

She swirled her tongue under the ridge of his cock, then slid it over the slit in the fat head, and he found himself fisting his hands in her hair.

Tugging her back, he glared down into her face.

"Are you sure this is what you want?" He had to ask because he wasn't confident he could hold back much longer.

Uncertainty flashed over Samantha's features.

"Is this . . . okay?" Her hot breath misted over his erection, and it was all he could do not to thrust back into the warm cavern of her mouth.

Her next words floored him.

"I just want to please you."

Caught off guard, Elijah stared down at those glass green eyes for a long moment. She couldn't have had any idea how potent those words were to a Dom.

He loosened his grip on her hair very slightly—while they spoke, they weren't playing the game.

"I won't be easy on you if we do this again, Samantha. I've told you that I'm a sexual Dominant."

She nodded in response, and he watched as a hint of fear and more than a little anticipation flickered over her features.

"But for today, you may do what you want to do. I'll do what I want to do. And it's going to feel damn good." He knew his grin had a hard edge to it, but he couldn't summon anything light or playful in that moment—not when his cock was aching with need.

That same need was reflected in her eyes. She shifted restlessly on her knees, the sunlight playing over skin so pale that she looked like she lived in Alaska rather than Mexico.

"Suck my cock, woman." He watched her furrow her brow, the irritation quickly melting into need as he took his cock in hand and pressed it to her lips. She swallowed the head and he groaned with satisfaction.

"That's right. I'm going to be bossy, even if we're having vanilla sex. For now it's up to you to decide what to do with that."

Watching through half-lidded eyes, Elijah stared down at Samantha as she sat back on her heels, doing nothing more than running her tongue lightly over the head of his cock. The need to thrust down her throat was a tangible force, but he found he was enjoying letting her do as she wanted to.

Though that wouldn't stop him from issuing orders. It was just who he was.

"I said suck it." He pressed forward with his hips, slowly sliding his length through the tight, wet cavern of her mouth. She glared up at him, gagging a bit when he hit the back of her throat. Her body tightened, and he wondered if he'd gone too far.

Then wickedness spread over her expression, and he caught the slightest hint of a smirk around her mouthful.

"Christ." Elijah bit out a curse when, without warning, Samantha hollowed her cheeks and sucked him down with more force than he'd thought she possessed. His fingers pressed into her scalp, holding her head in place as she worked her tongue and lips around him.

What she lacked in technique and experience, she made up for in enthusiasm. Far quicker than he had thought possible, Elijah felt his body drawing tight, warning him that he was close to losing control.

Once more gathering her hair in his hands, he pulled until she had no choice but to release him. Elijah winced, feeling something very near to pain, when those full lips slid off the rigid length of his erection.

"On your hands and knees," he repeated, noting that she'd worked so hard on his cock that her lips were swollen and her eyes had teared. And still she looked excited, aroused, just when he'd thought that she would have been second-guessing their encounter.

It only made him harder.

Her lips were silent, but her eyes spoke volumes, sparking with dangerous heat as she slowly turned and did as he asked.

Elijah's palms itched to deliver a light spank to the perfect globes of her ass. But the roar of the furnace intruded into his thoughts, reminded him that they were outside, in the doorway of her studio, and that this wasn't a scene that he needed to plan meticulously.

He wanted to plunge inside her slick heat. There was no reason to draw it out any longer.

"Lower." Dropping to his knees behind her, Elijah smoothed

a hand over the curves of her behind, unable to resist touching that pale, perfect skin.

With a quick glance over her shoulder, Samantha did as he asked, shifting her weight from her palms to her elbows. It caused her back to arch, to present her ass and her pouting lower lips to him in a way that made him want to bury his face between her thighs.

Later. He couldn't wait any longer.

"Lower," he rasped out, and savored the shudder of her body as she pressed her weight into her shoulders, her face turning so that one cheek pressed into the dry grass of the yard. Removing a condom from his pocket, he quickly sheathed himself, then took her wrists together in one hand, holding them behind her back.

"Elijah," Samantha whispered as he took his latex-sheathed cock in his free hand, ready to slide it into her slick folds. He paused for a moment to assess her body language.

She trembled, but not with fear. She wanted him as badly as he wanted her.

He guided his cock to her entrance and pushed the head against her tight heat.

"Aah!" Samantha's back arched and she clamped down around him like a velvet glove.

"Shit, you're tight." Elijah ground his teeth together as he tried to give her a moment to adjust to his intrusion. But her heat massaged him, lured him like a siren's call, and he knew he didn't have the willpower to resist. "I'm not going to be gentle."

In response, she pushed back against him, taking him in another inch. Elijah's fingers tightened around her wrists, on the skin of her hip.

Then he inhaled deeply, savoring that scent of wildflowers and smoke that seemed to come from her very skin, and seated himself the rest of the way in one rough thrust.

Samantha cried out and pulled against him, trying, he assumed, to relieve herself of some of his length.

"Give it a minute." He fought the need to press her to the
ground and simply fuck her as hard as he could. The gyrations
she was doing on his cock as she tried to find a measure of comfort had his orgasm gathering at the base of his spine again. "It
will feel good in a minute."

He pulled back an inch, heard her exhalation of relief from
beneath him. But he drove forward again just as quickly, heard
her cry out as the head of his cock pressed against her womb.

"Open your legs wider," he commanded, and bent over her
as she did what he said. Working his free hand between her taut
belly and the ground, he pressed down, feeling himself moving
through her slickness, tightening the passage even further.

"I—I can't—" When he began to truly fuck, to move back
and forth hard and deep, Samantha shifted wildly beneath him.
He could feel her flesh gripping him, milking him every time
he filled her, begging him to claim her completely. He hadn't
even touched her clit yet, and she was as wet as the ocean, the
scent of her arousal warming in the golden sun that slanted
over the skin of her back.

"You can." He shoved in all the way and, at the same time,
slid his hand between her legs. Sliding through her wetness, he
lubricated his fingers, then moved unerringly to the hard, tight
bud of her clit.

"Elijah!" Samantha's cry echoed across the yard, and Elijah
couldn't hold back a grin. Years in the lifestyle had taken away
any inhibitions he might once have had about public sex.

But if he wasn't mistaken, the fact that they were outside—
that someone could drive by at any second—only excited the
hot woman beneath him even more.

"Come for me. Now. Now—while I fuck you as hard as I
can." Increasing the pace of his movements, Elijah began to

play his fingers over Samantha's clit, rubbing in a slow but firm circle around its edges, brushing the entire pad of his finger over the top every few strokes.

Her breathing grew more ragged; so did his. She vibrated around him as her climax approached, and Elijah felt the sensation all the way down to the base of his cock. When she cried out and he felt her inner walls clamp down around him, hot and tight, he had no choice but to follow her into the heat of complete pleasure.

"Fuck!" Her voice was high with need as her thigh muscles clenched tightly, pressing back against his as her orgasm played over her body like the lash from a whip. The waves milked Elijah's erection, buried deep inside her, and that tension at the base of his spine drew down into his testicles and he exploded.

He squeezed his eyes shut, letting sensation take him over as they rode out their orgasms.

When the pleasure finally faded away, Elijah found himself bent over Samantha, his cheek pressed against her shoulder blade. Beneath him she exhaled, her breath slow and steady, her body lax and spent.

"Wow." Moved to press a kiss against the stripe of her spine, Elijah released Samantha's wrists and massaged her hands to get the blood flowing again. He pulled her up, held her in his arms for a moment, unable to hold back a deep chuckle as he brushed gravel and dust off of her clothing.

"What's funny?" Worming her way out of his arms, Samantha looked back over her shoulder at him. Elijah found it interesting that the woman who had initiated this entire encounter, the one who had seemed so in charge of her own pleasure only moments before, now seemed unsure, even a bit embarrassed by her actions.

He cocked his head, curious, as she reached for her clothing and began to dress.

"I'm not laughing at you, Samantha." Unabashed in his nakedness, Elijah rose to his feet, stretching before stripping the condom off his semierect cock, tying a knot in the end, then reaching for his own clothing. He saw Samantha's eyes flicker over him, and he couldn't hold back a grin.

"I'm amused with myself, because I don't normally enjoy vanilla sex so much."

Bending to hitch his shorts back up over his hips, he nearly missed Samantha's incredulity.

"*That* was vanilla?" she asked, then blushed. As if trying to hide the reaction, she tugged her tank top over her head. Elijah scowled when her creamy breasts disappeared from view.

"Vanilla sex refers to sex without any of the trappings of BDSM." His eyes on hers, he pulled his shirt over his head, then stalked toward her, following her into the studio when she retreated.

"That doesn't mean it can't be mind-blowing. But adding other . . . things . . . can make it into so much more." Curiosity sparked in her eyes, and Elijah felt his cock pay attention, never mind that he was spent.

He moved closer, watched as arousal and wariness colored Samantha's eyes. She moved backward, and he followed her back into the small studio.

"Let me show you." He wanted her to say yes—needed her to. Whether she was submissive or not, if things were this good between them without anything but the two of them and a condom, he wasn't about to be denied the pleasure of her again and again.

He still wasn't sure what exactly she was searching for. But he wanted to be the one to answer her questions, to help her explore whatever hidden kinks she had.

Samantha closed her eyes, and he studied the creamy lids. When she opened them again, he could see that her fierce stubbornness was out in full force.

"I can't." Disappointment warred with irritation. Elijah had never understood—would never understand—why people felt the need to deny their true desires. Life was too short . . . And what had just happened showed that they wanted each other badly. Hell, he still had his ace in the hole. He hadn't thought he'd have to use it after they'd had each other once, but now he saw he would. Narrowing his eyes intently, he studied her face until she flushed under his stare.

"What?" Her tone was waspish, which only made Elijah grin.

When it came to getting what he wanted, he was more than willing to play dirty. He hadn't gotten as rich as he was by rolling over every time he heard the word *no*.

Again inhaling that smoky scent that was so uniquely her, Elijah dipped his head until their lips were only a whisper apart. This close, he could see the trembling inhalation of her nervous breath, could see the beat of her pulse against the delicate white skin of her jaw.

He pressed his lips to hers with a quick, brief touch like the flutter of butterfly wings. He could smell himself mixed with her, and a primitive sense of possession clouded his mind.

A choked sound escaped from her throat when he drew back, triumph flooding him at her response.

"I want to commission a piece from you." Drawing back fully, Elijah slid his hands into the pockets of his shorts. The whisper of a kiss had brought his cock to full attention again, and there was nothing he could do to hide it. So he accepted it for what it was: evidence of his unquenchable desire for her.

Samantha's eyes flicked down, then back up, widening as she met his eyes again.

"I don't do commissions." He found he was pleased when she drew up, raised her chin, and regarded him saucily. "I work for myself."

"I had an offer on your sculpture at the show last night." Elijah rocked back on his heels as Samantha inhaled sharply.

"I'm not selling that piece. It's mine." Her eyes practically shot green sparks, and he held out a hand to settle her.

"I'm responsible for relaying all offers." If she *had* been willing to sell it, he would have outbid anyone and claimed the piece for himself. "I didn't think you would sell such a personal piece. But I'm interested in commissioning another in a similar vein."

"I don't make duplicates." Her temper was up; he could tell. "Nor could I. Each piece of glass is completely unique."

"I said in a similar vein, not a copy." Her irritation brought a pretty flush of pink to her skin. "I would just request that you . . . keep the same thoughts in your head while you create the second piece."

He'd succeeded in shocking her; her mouth fell open in response. She quickly composed herself, glaring at him heatedly.

"You couldn't afford what it would cost for me to create a custom piece."

Elijah fought the urge to smirk.

He always used his not inconsiderable computer skills to find out some background information on women he was interested in. He knew that Samantha had a sister in Colorado to whom she frequently sent money.

She wasn't going to turn this down.

"The offer on your sculpture was ten thousand American dollars." A hint of smugness warmed him as Samantha gasped at the amount. He didn't think she was caught speechless often. "Since it's a commissioned work, I think it's only fair to offer more. If you'll create this piece, I'll pay you fifteen thousand."

Samantha couldn't breathe. This man—who had just played her body like a virtuoso, who had wrung more pleasure from her than she had ever thought possible with nothing but his hands and his cock—was offering her more money than she'd ever seen at one time in her life, and by all appearances seemed certain that she would accept it.

She thought that maybe she should have felt like a whore, with him extending this offer after he'd just fucked her senseless. But she thought that one had nothing to do with the other, that he had planned to offer this to her before the heat between them had threatened to incinerate them.

To make matters more surreal, he was wearing a pink polo shirt. He should have looked ridiculous. Instead he looked like exactly what he professed to be: a dominant male, facing a female he wanted.

Her eyes dipped to the erection that was plainly obvious through the light fabric of his shorts. Given the intensity of the orgasms they had just shared, it seemed impossible that he could be hard again. But he was.

He was hard for *her*. It might have been stupid, but she was flattered, and ridiculously pleased.

"Fifteen thousand up front?" Each of her carefully constructed defenses began to dissolve. So much money—she could pay off at least half of Beth's student loans, and could buy her more than a year's worth of her supplies as well.

"Half up front." Elijah nodded sharply, and she saw a hint of the tycoon emerge. "Half on delivery."

To ensure I deliver, Samantha knew. And it was so incredibly tempting.

But . . .

"I need to think about it." More, she needed to work through the nausea that roiled in her gut at the thought of accepting such an offer. She already knew she would—her personal feelings could be put aside if it meant some financial security for her sister.

But she wanted to be very, very sure that she could live with the decision.

And being paid that much money by a man who had been inside her—well, she wanted to be absolutely certain that he didn't expect her "services" in return. Though if she told the truth, she was mighty tempted to continue sleeping with him. But there couldn't be any money tied to it.

"Day after tomorrow, Samantha." Before she could protest, Elijah bent his head and pressed his lips to hers. The kiss was short, but hot and hard, as different as it could be from that soft brush of his lips by the kiln before they'd gotten naked.

She was gasping for breath when he pulled away and nodded with apparent satisfaction.

"You'll give me your answer by the day after tomorrow." With a smile so devastatingly sexy that she was pretty sure it was illegal, Elijah turned on his heel and walked to the door. As she slowly followed him she greedily inhaled the outside air that rushed in, air that held the heat of a Mexican afternoon but was still cooler, fresher than the air in the studio.

"Day after tomorrow." Frowning, she hurried after him. "How do I contact you?"

He already had a business card in his hand when he turned. "Call my cell. I'll answer." She took the card in fingers that were suddenly trembling.

"Samantha." She looked up to find all traces of the predatory businessman gone. The dominance was still there, and she wondered if he turned it on and off, or if it was an integral part of him, written into his DNA.

She wondered if submission manifested the same way.

"And call me if you have any other questions," he said. Samantha knew exactly what he was referring to.

Questions about things that weren't . . . What had he called it? Things that weren't *vanilla*.

"I won't." She did have questions, millions of them, but Elijah pushed her buttons in a way that made her stubborn streak come out.

"We'll see." There was that sexy grin again, and then he was gone, crunching across the gravel of her yard to a low-slung sports car that glinted in the late-afternoon sun.

"Samantha?" Elijah tossed her name over his shoulder as he opened the driver's-side door. She leaned against the frame of her studio door and raised a questioning eyebrow in response.

"I want that vase too. I'm going to get hard every time I look at it." He grinned smugly at her stunned expression, then left her to ponder that as he drove away.

He'd given her a lot to think about, and Samantha didn't think she was going to sleep any better that night than she had the night before.

CHAPTER THREE

Samantha took a large sip of steaming coffee from a thick glass mug that had been one of the very first things she'd ever made. Mexican coffee was more bitter than its American counterpart, a fact that couldn't be hidden even with copious amounts of sugar and cream, but she'd become accustomed to its taste.

Two full cups and she was almost ready for the phone call she needed to make. She dialed her sister's number as she tugged on the ragged hem of the T-shirt she slept in. She'd been up for a good chunk of the night, and was exhausted.

Being awake in the wee hours wasn't anything new for her—she often worked until her hands cramped and she couldn't see straight—but last night none of the creative spark had come to her. Instead she'd tossed and turned as images of bright blue eyes, of leather and chains and bodies straining haunted her waking thoughts.

She was going to accept the commission, though she cringed at the thought. She had two reasons for overcoming her hesitation.

One was because Elijah Masterson was the only man who had truly pulled at her, ever. The memory of his hands playing over her body had aroused her all night long.

He'd seduced her in her backyard, in the middle of the afternoon, while her garden gnomes watched with impish glee on their faces. He'd proven that what he wanted, he got.

It scared the hell out of her. And it also made her hot. She wasn't ready to refuse more time in his presence.

The second reason was answering her phone call with a voice blurred by sleep.

"Sam? Why are you calling so early?" Beth was only four years younger than Samantha's own twenty-six, but because of their upbringing, Samantha often felt that four was more like fourteen. She could hear in the ragged husk of Beth's voice that her sister had been out late.

"You weren't out drinking, were you?" Worry gnawed at her gut like acid. A younger sister out until all hours was worrying enough, but Beth had an adverse reaction to alcohol, one that less kind souls could easily take advantage of.

"I had two beers, Sam." Beth's voice sounded flat, and in that moment Samantha felt as if she was talking to her daughter rather than her sister. "I know myself well enough to know when I've had too much."

"I know." She didn't want to nag but, God, she worried. She wondered for the millionth time if moving so far away had been smart, even though she knew that if she hadn't, she might have lost her tenuous grip on sanity. "I'm sorry. But someone has to check on you."

She could hear the rest of her sentence hanging in the air: *Because we both know that Mom sure as hell won't.*

On the other end of the line Beth cleared her throat, and Samantha could see her sister in her mind's eye raking her fingers through her strawberry blond hair, as if her older sister had used up most of the red gene and left just a hint. She would be pulling her bright purple duvet around her as she snuggled up with the phone.

"What's going on?" Beth asked. Samantha frowned.

"Why do you assume something's going on? Can't I just call my sister?" Samantha knew Beth couldn't claim that she was concerned because she'd called so early, because Samantha rarely had a firm grip on the time, living and working by her own internal clock.

"I can just tell," Beth said, and Samantha heard a muffled yawn over the line.

She bit her lower lip; her sister knew her well.

"I'm just checking in." Her mind strayed to the astronomical amount of money that Elijah had offered her and she blanched.

She wanted it for Beth's sake, but her upbringing and her... relationship, for lack of a better word, with Elijah made accepting the commission a bitter pill to swallow.

"Did you make the payment on your student loan?" Samantha sucked a finger into her mouth and ran her tongue over a small burn she'd gotten days before. "Did you do it right when I told you to? If you don't pay before a certain date you get charged interest."

"No, I went shopping instead. Bought some lingerie, some killer red shoes." Beth's voice was airy, and sincere enough that Samantha's mouth fell open. Her heart began to pound with anxiety, stuttering back to normal speed when her sister began to laugh.

"Not funny," Samantha fumed. She knew Beth rolled her eyes at her a good chunk of the time, but what Beth didn't understand was how much Samantha actually fretted over these things.

She'd moved to Mexico to try to give her sister some independence.

It had worked... sort of.

"Yes, I paid the bill." Beth's voice held a note of long suffering, which irritated Samantha, but she held her tongue. "And before you ask, yes, I have enough supplies."

"How much of everything do you have?" As well as Beth knew her, Samantha knew that her sister would downplay it if she was short on something, not wanting her older sister to worry about money.

"I have another month's worth of insulin. A couple weeks of test strips and syringes." Beth was an insulin-dependent diabetic, and had been for nearly a decade. "And I have an interview today, so cross your fingers."

"Is there a health plan?" Samantha hated the nagging that she heard in her own voice, but she had to know. "I'll wire you some money anyway."

Wiring money from her already slim bank account would mean she'd be eating noodles until she sold another piece. But she'd done it before, and she'd do it again. It was the price she paid to work full-time on her art.

Beth's last job had had a great health plan, one that had covered the cost of most of her medical expenses. Since she'd been laid off, Samantha had been sending her money to help while Beth worked odd jobs and job hunted.

If Beth got a new job with a health plan, then Samantha wouldn't be in such dire need of quick cash. She wouldn't have to be like her mother, depending on a wealthy man to get by.

Elijah was smooth, but she wasn't an idiot. He clearly appreciated her art, but he appreciated her body more. He wanted her, and if she accepted his offer they would be thrown together for the length of time it took her to create a piece of that magnitude, usually about a month.

Of course, there was still the student loan that had funded Beth's college years to pay off.

"I don't know if it has a health plan, Sam." Beth's voice was testy. "I haven't even had the interview yet. It seemed a little early to start grilling them about benefits when they called to set up the meeting."

Samantha remained silent.

Clearly sorry that she'd spoken so sharply, Beth's next words were softer. "I saw Mom yesterday." Beth sounded hesitant, but then, she had to know full well how Samantha would react. As always, Samantha's spine stiffened instantly, as if a steel rod had snapped into place.

"What did she want?" Samantha heard the frosty tone of her voice and knew it would make her sister cringe, but she couldn't feel sorry for it.

"I stopped by to make her some supper, Sam," Beth snapped. Samantha ground her teeth together. Beth had made it clear on more than one occasion that she thought Samantha was too hard on their mother, that their mother was a victim of circumstance.

Beth had borne the weight of Gemma Collins's alcoholism just as Samantha had, and both women knew that the alcohol had been Gemma's escape after the final man in a string of wealthy lovers had discarded her.

"Did she actually eat what you made her?" Samantha sighed as she spoke. Her sister insisted on seeing the best in everyone. Samantha liked to think of herself as realistic.

There was a pause.

"No," Beth said softly, and Samantha felt her stomach clench. Her mother rarely ate anything, because more often than not she was passed out on the couch with an empty bottle of vodka in her hand.

"The money I'm going to send is for you, Beth. Not for anything else. Right?" Samantha hated having to reinforce this, but she knew her sister would be their mother's first target when she ran out of alcohol.

Beth didn't answer right away. Samantha knew how torn she was, but still couldn't muster up any pity for their mother. She knew Beth bought their mom groceries and occasionally paid her bills, but even her kindhearted sister knew better than to pass cash along to their mother.

And soon enough Stanley would show up again, as he was known to do. He would barge into Gemma's life, tempt her with his wealth and his lies, make her hope, and then he would leave yet again.

Samantha couldn't count how many times the pair had broken it off, only to get back together. She wasn't even sure it *counted* as a reconciliation, considering Stanley was married and likely had plenty of mistresses besides her mother.

"I love you, Beth." Squeezing her eyes tightly shut, Samantha pressed her fingers to her temples, where a headache was beginning to make its nasty presence known.

This was a point on which she and her sister would never agree, not unless Samantha told her what she knew about Stanley . . . and that was a memory she never intended to visit. Ever.

"Love you too, Sam," Beth whispered quietly into the phone. Samantha waited to hear her sister disconnect before she pulled the cell away from her ear.

Allowing herself to give in to the hurt for one long moment, Samantha put down the phone and rested her head on the scarred surface of her countertop. Closing her eyes, she pressed her cheek against the cool surface.

Was it any wonder that she wanted a strong man in her life, a man who would simply take control? Samantha had been in charge—had assumed the role that should have been her mother's—since she was barely a teenager. She'd had enough control to last ten lifetimes.

She wasn't about to give up control to a man who had no idea what to do with it, of course. She was a strong woman by necessity, and knew that she would never bend to someone who wasn't every bit as strong as she was. But the possibilities of a man who would make the right decisions, and who would take care of her, would cherish her in return . . .

No matter how she fought the idea, it had become a deep-seated need, coiled tightly inside her.

Samantha shifted on the countertop, searching for a cool spot to move her cheek to.

Elijah Masterson wore dominance the way he wore a suit: as if he'd been born for it. And Samantha suspected that he was the kind of man who took care of what was his.

Her knee-jerk reaction to refuse his offer to help her explore her sexuality came from her mother's "career" as a mistress—she knew that. She would have felt the same whether she'd already succumbed to her desire for him or not. But she was so damn tired of being in charge all the time.

Rising slowly, Samantha inhaled deeply, then stretched as she looked out the window. The sun was rising, a tangerine ball in a brilliant blue sky. She'd always loved Mexico—had felt more at peace here than she had anywhere else. It was the first place that had come to mind when she realized she needed to put some distance between herself and her mother to focus on her art . . . and her sanity. Pouring herself another cup of coffee, she sipped slowly, savoring the taste. She'd thought about submission long enough to know that it was more than a passing fancy for her. And she knew—deep down she knew—that she would work hard for the money that Elijah had offered her, which made it a different situation from Gemma's entirely.

But that didn't mean she had to accept easily. She had a term that she wanted to add to Elijah's offer, one she'd come up with in the early hours of the morning. One she suspected he would be both suspicious of and eager to accept.

She'd convince him. And she was very much looking forward to seeing the look on his face when she asked. She just had one thing to do first.

"*Preciosa!*" Samantha couldn't hold back the grin as she entered Dos Hermanos, the small café that sat on the edge of San José del Cabo closest to her cottage.

The man who rounded the counter with his arms open for a hug was only an inch or so taller than she was, but he was thick with muscle. He was handsome in a Latin-lover kind of way and flirted with every woman under the sun, from girls who were newly legal to elderly women with blue hair.

"Morning, Jorge." She let herself be enfolded in his hug, inhaling the comforting aroma of peppers and spice. "Got room for one for breakfast?"

He gestured around the largely empty café, then tilted his head toward the counter. The grill he cooked on was behind it, and those who sat at the counter could watch their food being prepared.

"Come, sit and talk to me." He took Samantha's hand in his as he led her toward the back of the café.

Samantha sat contentedly on one of the high stools. Jorge was the closest thing she had to a friend in Cabo, and she smiled at him as he placed a steaming cup of coffee and a glass of some sort of juice in front of her.

"You'll eat what I make you, yes?" Samantha's grin at his words melted into a sigh of pleasure as she took a sip of what turned out to be freshly made mango juice.

She'd never understood why the café wasn't busier. The thought was only reinforced when Jorge placed a plateful of eggs scrambled ranchero style, with jalapeños and tomato, homemade tortillas, and green sauce in front of her. She dug in eagerly.

"Still haven't learned to cook, ah?" Jorge chuckled as he leaned his elbows on the counter and watched Samantha devour her meal. She'd lost track of time since seeing Elijah yesterday . . . In fact, she was pretty sure she hadn't eaten since before he'd showed up at her house. She cringed. She would have given Beth hell for doing the same thing, so she really didn't have a leg to stand on.

Jorge was quiet as Samantha ate, which suited her just fine. She'd always been quiet, a bit of a loner. One of the reasons she preferred him to his brother Angelo, who co-owned the café, was because Jorge just let her be.

But Angelo was the reason that Samantha was there that morning. She had a very, very big favor to ask of him.

"Jorge—" She waited until he'd cleared her plate away and refilled her coffee cup. She felt slightly nauseous, but wasn't sure if that was a result of stuffing her face after unwittingly fasting for twenty-four hours, or if it was because of what she was about to ask. "I have a . . . question to ask about Angelo."

"About Angelo?" Jorge wiped the counter in front of Samantha with a white rag, and she caught the scent of lemon cleaner as he moved. "*Sí*, what is it?"

"Ah, well . . ." Samantha trained her eyes on the wall behind him as she gathered her courage. She hated that she felt embarrassed to ask about something she truly wanted, but she knew she was about to shock her friend to the core.

"*Preciosa*, you can tell me anything. You know that." Jorge caught one of Samantha's hands in his and looked into her eyes. She was startled when she found a flicker of something more than friendship reflected in the depths.

It threw her off guard enough that she blurted out what was circling her mind.

"Angelo is into BDSM, right?" She cringed when she caught Jorge's expression. Apart from one drunken night with the two brothers in which Angelo had mentioned that he was a part of the BDSM lifestyle, it wasn't something they'd talked about. She'd known that she would shock Jorge, but she wasn't prepared for the heat that crossed his face as well.

"*Sí.*" Jorge looked her up and down and Samantha squirmed under the stare. "He is—how do you say?—Dominant. He makes no secret of it. Why are you asking this, Samantha?"

Samantha picked up her coffee cup and took a long swallow to hide her discomfiture. This next question—this was the hard part.

"I want to go to Devorar, and I was wondering if he would go with me." She set her cup down on the counter with a sharp clack, felt the jolt reverberate through her wrist as Jorge studied her face.

"You are interested in such things?" The sexy Latin man pinned her with that intense stare, and Samantha felt like a fly pinned to a wall. "You have never gone to a club?"

"I . . . yes." Samantha wouldn't soften her true desires just to make them sound less shocking. "Yes, I am very interested. There are things I . . . that I think I might find there. And, no, I've never been to a club. That's why I don't want to go alone."

Jorge cocked his head, still studying her.

"I do not think you are submissive," he said finally. Samantha's pensive expression melted sharply into a scowl.

Just because she could be outspoken, just because she knew nothing else besides taking charge, didn't mean she didn't want to have that control taken away from her.

"How would you know?" she snapped, irritated enough that she didn't try to soften her voice. "It's not your thing, is it? That's why I asked about Angelo, not you."

Jorge nodded, his expression thoughtful. "This is true." He steepled his fingers beneath his chin. "I did not find what I was looking for in the dynamics of such a relationship. That does not mean I am ignorant of the lifestyle, however. My brother has practiced it for over ten years, and I dabbled in it when I was younger."

"You?" Samantha eyed the man incredulously, then cursed herself for making assumptions about him just as he had about her. Still, he hadn't mentioned it the one time they'd spoken of it, nearly a year earlier, so it caught her by surprise.

Jorge could be a bit domineering, but he'd never made it a secret that he liked bossy women who took charge—women like her, she realized with a sinking sensation in her stomach.

Oh, she was so blind.

The hand in which Jorge clenched her fingers tightened. She bit her lower lip nervously and looked up to find that spark of desire out in full force.

"For you, I would try it again. If that is truly what you want."

Samantha sucked in a mouthful of air. How had she not seen this coming?

When she'd first moved to Mexico she'd felt . . . free. But she'd also felt a bit lonely, homebody though she was.

Jorge had helped to fill that gap. She'd never thought of him as anything but a friend.

If she wanted to keep that friendship, she knew she needed to be brutally honest.

"Jorge, I appreciate the offer. I do." Gently she tugged her hand from his, placing it in her lap and out of reach.

His eyes followed the movement and resignation spread over his face.

"I . . . I think I've met someone." Elijah's image flashed through her mind—she could never forget the power and intensity in his blue eyes when they looked at her. In the space of moments he'd been able to make her feel like the only woman in the world.

"And this person you've met, he is dominant?" Jorge nodded as if in understanding, but Samantha knew her friend well enough to see that he was filing away his own emotions behind those expressive dark eyes of his.

"He is." Samantha shivered as she thought about it.

"You will not pretend to be someone you aren't for a man." Jorge was looking at her again, this time with an inscrutable expression. His words were a statement, not a question, because *he* knew *her* well enough to know that Samantha didn't pull her punches.

"This is something I want." Samantha's voice was soft. "I mean . . . I think I want it. That's why I'd like to go to Devorar first, to get a taste before I . . . before I dive in headfirst."

Jorge nodded, pulled his cell phone from the pocket of the apron tied around his hips, and tapped out a text message. A moment later the phone vibrated, indicating a reply had come through.

"He will go with you." Jorge slid his phone back into his pocket. "Though he would prefer to go to Pecado here in town. He prefers it there."

"Thank you." It felt as if a weight had been lifted off Samantha's chest. It was replaced by a heady sense of jittery excitement.

Finally, she would see if these needs she felt were real. For all she knew, she'd get one look at what happened inside the club and would run screaming into the night.

Somehow, though, she suspected the opposite would be true.

A thought occurred to her, and she looked up at Jorge with alarm.

"I don't have to have sex with Angelo if I go to the club with him, do I?" Angelo Aguirre was every bit as good-looking as his brother, but Samantha wasn't the type to jump into sex with just anyone.

Before Elijah, she could count the number of partners she'd had on two fingers.

Instead of laughing at her, or answering in the affirmative, Jorge again took Samantha's hand in his. His fingers rested lightly on the paper-thin skin of her wrist where her pulse pounded.

"If that was the case, I would absolutely be the one going with you." His voice was completely serious, and Samantha's mouth went dry. "But I never had a chance, did I?"

Samantha looked down at where her friend's tanned skin touched her own. Biting her lip, she shook her head slowly. "I'm sorry."

And she genuinely was. Life would be easier if she could fall for Jorge. Jorge, who never pressed her about her past, who would never demand more than she wanted to give.

Elijah, she knew, would not be easy.

The thought was exciting and arousing.

"Angelo will stop by your house later to talk to you about tonight." Jorge waved the money away when Samantha produced a handful of pesos from her pocket to pay for her meal. Heaviness weighed on top of her anticipation as she slowly rose from the stool, knowing that, somehow, this conversation had changed her friendship with Jorge irrevocably.

She accepted his hug before she turned to go. She could feel his eyes on her back as she walked away, and it made her self-conscious—something she rarely was.

She pushed the thought away. She wasn't a cruel woman, and she knew that she'd never led Jorge on.

He would figure out soon enough that they would never have worked. In the meantime she would give him some space.

And she would get a taste of a BDSM club before she dove headfirst and offered to Elijah what she was considering offering to him.

The thought made her belly quiver.

She couldn't wait for the evening to come.

CHAPTER FOUR

'm going to be down here for longer than I'd anticipated."
Elijah reclined in the leather chair at his desk as he spoke
on the phone, looking down at the orange sports sandals
he'd bought on a whim earlier that day.

Anywhere but in Mexico, he dressed in a suit and tie. One of
the reasons he so loved working from his Mexican resorts was
that he could shed the business wardrobe and relax a bit, even at
work.

"Everything going all right?" Alex Fraser was one of Elijah's best friends. He and Luca Santangelo had once been just
business acquaintances, but a shared interest in extraordinary
wine and the BDSM lifestyle had led the three extremely
wealthy men to a joint venture.

In Vino Veritas was an upscale wine bar combined with a
BDSM club, and the three shared ownership. They'd wanted a
place where they could explore their interests in a manner
that suited them.

"It's fine." Elijah knew his reluctance to visit Devorar that
evening was about more than missing the club back home . . .
and it had everything to do with one smart-mouthed redhead.
"But I would like your opinion on something, if you have
time."

"I've got a few minutes. Then I need to see Maddy before
she goes to work."

Unbidden, Elijah felt a flash of jealousy. He didn't begrudge his friend the love he'd found with his fiancée, nor was

he particularly jealous of the woman, though if he'd met her first, he would have pursued her relentlessly.

No, the jealousy came from the fact that Alex had found someone who both loved him and balanced him. In terms of dominance and submission, Alex and Maddy complemented each other perfectly.

That was what Elijah longed for. He'd thought he'd found it with his ex-wife.

He'd been wrong.

"We've both been in the lifestyle for a long time," Elijah began, shifting restlessly in his chair.

"Over ten years," Alex agreed. The men were the same age and had both discovered their interest in alternative lifestyles during college.

"How often do you read someone wrong? Have you ever been convinced that someone isn't submissive but it turns out that they are?"

Alex's end of the phone call was silent for a long moment, and Elijah could all but hear the thoughts turning around in his friend's mind.

"I can't say that I've ever been that off base about someone," Alex said finally. Elijah felt his spirits sink, though he fought against it.

He barely knew the woman after all. She fascinated him, true, but surely he'd get over it.

"Now you have to tell me why you're asking, E." From Alex's end Elijah heard a feminine voice—Maddy, telling her fiancé to hurry up. "Have you met someone?"

Elijah considered before he answered. He could always just cut things off with Samantha where they stood right at that moment. Or keep things confined to the business of the art commission and leave it at that.

The very idea made him grind his teeth together. Samantha

was inquisitive enough that he knew she would continue to explore, even if he were to cut her loose.

He'd be damned if some other Dom would have the pleasure of introducing her enticing sugar-and-spice self to the wonders of dominance and submission.

"There's a woman, yes." Elijah conjured up a mental picture of Samantha's lithe figure, those green eyes that sizzled with heat, the red curls that made her look like a goddess. He pictured those curls brushing over his cock, and felt himself stiffen at the idea.

"And you're unsure if she's truly submissive? Is she new to the lifestyle?" Alex probed further. "Why not just take her to the club at your resort? I'm sure you'll get a better reading of her once she's actually in a scene with you."

Elijah pondered that for a moment. He rarely visited Devorar even though he owned it. He had a competent manager who ran it well, so he didn't need to enter the club often. This pleased him, because he wasn't nearly as comfortable there as he was back home at Veritas.

If Samantha would go with him, though, he would make an exception. And perhaps Alex was right. He needed to know. Painful as it might be for him if she wasn't the kind of woman he needed, he couldn't ask her to change for him. He would be negligent in his responsibilities as a Dom . . . and he just wasn't that kind of man.

"When you met Maddy, she intrigued you from the start." This wasn't a question—Elijah knew that Alex had been infatuated with the woman from the moment he'd set eyes on her. He'd pursued her despite the fact that he avoided relationships at all costs. "But what if she hadn't been submissive? Would you still have pursued her?"

There was a long moment of silence before Alex replied.

"I don't know if I can answer that." Alex's voice was serious. "Because one of the things that first caught my eye about Maddy was how submissive she seemed. You're that serious about this woman? What's her name?"

"Her name is Samantha." The name was like honey on his tongue. "I don't know if I'd describe my feelings as serious. True, I haven't been able to stop thinking about her since I met her. The heat between us is . . . tangible. I want her again. But her personality, her mannerisms . . . She's curious, but I just can't picture her as a submissive who does more than play. I can't picture her giving herself fully to a Dom."

And that description had applied to his ex-wife as well. He'd been young, and had thought that love and the desire to play kinky games was the same thing as submission.

He'd been wrong.

As if reading his thoughts, Alex mentioned his ex in the next breath. "I don't need to remind you of what happened with Tara."

Elijah snorted out a harsh laugh, leaning back in his desk chair and raking his fingers through his hair. "No, you certainly don't."

"But if you don't give things a try with Samantha, will you always wonder?" Elijah heard Maddy's voice again, followed by a giggle.

He guessed what she wanted Alex's attention for. He certainly wasn't going to deprive his friend of the charms of his soon-to-be wife.

"Thanks, Alex. This has been helpful." They said their goodbyes and hung up, and Elijah pondered the conversation.

Alex hadn't told him anything that he hadn't already thought of, but it had been useful to talk it out. And his friend had hit one point square on the head.

If he didn't explore this connection that he felt with Samantha, he would regret it. And ultimately, wasn't his lifestyle all about exploring a person's true desires? Even though he had never felt fully satisfied by sexual relationships outside of a true Dominant/submissive relationship, Samantha seemed to be an exception that he wasn't ready to give up on.

What would be so wrong with exploring their connection further?

Decision made, Elijah felt anticipation begin to simmer.

He had given Samantha until the next day to give her his decision regarding the commission. He would honor his word on that matter.

But he hadn't said he would leave her alone until then.

The thump of heavy bass disturbed the warm evening air. The parking lot of Pecado was full, steam from the day's heat curling upward between the vehicles that were crammed side by side on the asphalt.

Anticipation was like a million little needles running along her skin.

She was about to take that first step—to see if her compelling dreams had been a manifestation of her actual desires.

Inhaling deeply, she strode toward the front door of the club on shaky legs. The outside of Pecado didn't look different from any other club she'd ever seen—the name spanned the building in glowing neon lights, a bouncer dressed in black guarded the front door, and the ear-shattering music spilled out into the street.

The only hint that this club might be slightly different was the couple chatting with the bouncer. The woman was dressed head-to-toe in black rubber. The man wore nothing but small leather shorts and a collar around his neck.

A leash was attached to the collar, and the woman held the end of it.

Samantha couldn't quite hold back a smile when she saw someone walking by do a double take.

Slowly she walked up behind the couple. The tall, curvaceous Latina woman caught Samantha's eye and smiled at her in a way that could only be described as seductive.

"Pretty outfit, honey." The woman eyed her up and down, then nudged the man she was with. "You new here?"

Samantha looked from the couple to the bouncer with wide eyes. Her confidence and excitement had vanished somewhere during the walk from her car to the door, and now all she could feel was her anxiety.

"I'm meeting Angelo Aguirre." Her mouth was dry, and she ran her tongue over her lips to dampen them. "I'm Samantha Collins. I'm his guest for the evening."

The black-clad bouncer nodded, then opened the heavy wooden door for her. "Angelo said to look out for a smoking-hot redhead." He gestured inside the club. "He's inside."

Samantha cast her stare through the open door with trepidation. This was it. She was really going to do this.

"Thank you," she murmured, forcing her suddenly stiff legs forward. A hand on her shoulder stopped her in place, and she whirled around to find the Latina woman looking at her with undisguised interest.

"If you get bored with Angelo, you just come find me, honey." The woman licked her lips with relish, leaving Samantha no doubt about what she was referring to.

"Umm. Thank you." Samantha wondered if she was quite up to this after all—dry spell and curiosity aside—but then the couple was entering the club behind her and then she was inside, the sights and sounds overwhelming her senses.

The club was big, one large room ringed around the top with a balcony on the second floor. But it wasn't so big that she couldn't see everything that was going on.

Her mouth fell open—she couldn't help herself. There were scenes unfolding before her eyes that she could never have conjured up even in her wildest dreams. And the sounds—oh, the sounds.

The slapping of flesh, screams and cries and moans of pleasure blended in with an energetic dance tune, creating one of the most erotic songs she'd ever heard.

The space between her legs heated and began to ache. She shifted uncomfortably, not sure how to react to the evidence that she had been aroused by the sights in front of her.

"Hello, Samantha." Spinning, Samantha came face-to-face with Angelo. She smiled, relieved to see a familiar face.

"Hi, Angelo." She twisted her fingers in the front of her cardigan sweater. The man was handsome like his brother, but stood several inches taller. He was dressed in nothing but black leather pants and a matching vest, opened so that she could see his firmly muscled chest and abs.

He was hot, and she appreciated the visual. But she couldn't stop the image of Elijah that crept into her mind.

The idea of Elijah, bare chested and ready to take her on a tour of a club like this—that made her skin heat with pleasure.

Angelo seemed to note the flush in her cheeks and was nodding with approval.

"You'll be a pretty sub, Samantha." He nodded toward the fingers that she still had clenched in the hem of her sweater. "You are a guest here tonight, so the dress code will be relaxed somewhat for you. But you have to take off the sweater. It is not acceptable."

Samantha bit her lip, tempted to tell him that she'd wear whatever she wanted. She'd wanted someone she knew to go with her to a club, but the idea of stripping down was a sticking point.

"The reason submissives are expected to dress as they do is to strip away a layer of their control, Samantha." She looked up to study him as he spoke to her. In his own dark eyes she saw a hint of that same dominance that Elijah wore so easily, and she suddenly found it hard to believe that this man in front of her was the same one who had cooked her tortillas and eggs on so many occasions.

Responding to the command in his voice was one thing, yet she still didn't feel the desperate desire for him that she had for Elijah. She'd assumed she would, that any dominant man would fill that hole inside her.

And that was something to think about when she was back home, and not surrounded by people who were either naked or dressed in fetish wear.

"All right." Slowly Samantha unbuttoned the front of her cardigan, slipping the knit fabric down her shoulders. Angelo reached out to help her. She blushed as his eyes raked over her.

"Very nice." Angelo's voice held more than a hint of appreciation. Samantha was mortified. She was now wearing nothing but a fawn-colored lace nightie that barely covered her butt and the same red high-heeled sandals she'd had on the night she'd met Elijah.

Angelo had told her that many clubs frowned on lingerie as club wear, but that Pecado would accept it for a guest new to the lifestyle.

When a woman wearing nothing but a thong and a blindfold walked by her, she wondered if she hadn't gotten off rather easily.

Then his fingers were under her chin, forcing her head to turn. She tried to shrug away with irritation, but the fingers held firm.

"When I compliment you—when I say anything to you— you reply, 'Yes, Master Angelo,' or 'Yes, Sir.' Understood?"

She wasn't nearly as comfortable with Angelo as she was with Jorge, and she didn't much care for him manhandling her.

He looked back at her, patient, and she caught her breath, remembering.

This was the reason she was here. Right now he wasn't Angelo her buddy. He was a Dom, and he was here to introduce her to this club because she'd asked him to.

She worried her lower lip between her teeth for a long moment before managing a reply.

"Yes, Sir." The words tasted strange on her tongue. She wasn't sure she liked it, and her eyes were wary as she looked at his face.

The fingers still holding her face tugged, urging her gaze down. She resisted reflexively, then forced her muscles to obey.

"Don't look a Dom in the eye unless you are given permission."

Samantha shifted uncomfortably. This wasn't exactly what she'd imagined, though if she was honest with herself, she hadn't had a concrete picture of what the evening would hold.

"Very nice." Angelo released her chin and circled her as Samantha stared down at her toes. He smelled much as his brother did, like spices combined with a hint of musky aftershave.

She had thought that just being in the presence of a Dom would offer her some relief from her ever present stress. But instead of relief, all she was feeling at that moment was uncertainty.

Angelo passed a clipboard into her line of vision. She started to look up to ask him what it was, then remembered that she wasn't supposed to look up without permission.

Feeling incredibly silly, she kept her eyes downcast, accepting the clipboard and pen from Angelo.

"These are the forms that all new members and guests of the club have to fill out." The name of the club was spelled out across the top of the form, and Samantha started reading, finding the usual personal information at the top: name, birth date, gender. Then the questions turned to preferences. Was she interested in men or women? Was she hoping to find a Dom or a sub? Was she open to encounters with couples?

Then she came to something called the Limit Checklist. Cocking her head, she continued to read—and sucked in her breath as she saw some of the items listed.

Violet wand? What the hell was that? Fisting? If that was what it sounded like, it was so not happening.

"If you mark something as a hard limit, it means that you will not participate in it. Any Dom that you partner with here at the club has to respect that," Angelo said.

Samantha found it incredibly frustrating not to be able to raise her head, to look at his face.

She knew that Jorge hadn't believed she could be submissive, and that he would have shared that suspicion with his brother.

She was determined to prove them wrong.

"And may I ask what a soft limit is?"

Angelo chuckled, and Samantha again thought of Elijah. She had enjoyed the sound of his laugh, had wanted to make him laugh again.

With Angelo she just noted that she had pleased him and was probably not going to be subject to the discipline items that were listed on the checklist in her hand.

"A soft limit is something that you're not sure about it." Angelo tilted her chin up, and Samantha sighed with relief when her eyes were again at a level where she could see her surroundings. Angelo smiled at her with pleasure. "Very nice. You may look at me now."

Samantha bit back a retort, then swallowed past the hint of disappointment that came with it.

Shouldn't she want to obey him? Shouldn't it be making her feel good?

She turned her head to keep studying the club, but Angelo cleared his throat, drawing her attention back to him.

"Most Doms won't appreciate a new sub looking at them, so it's best to keep your eyes on me."

Samantha felt her brows draw together. No, this was not going at all how she'd planned.

"I'd like you to finish filling out your forms. I'll read them over as I show you around the club." Samantha lifted the clipboard again.

She was going to see this evening out. She knew it was too soon to form an opinion about anything.

Still, she found that she was bitterly disappointed.

She thought of Elijah, and of how he made her feel sparks that she'd never felt before. From the very first meeting he'd woken parts of her that had lain dormant ever since her teen years, when all the bad things had happened.

Elijah had admitted that he was a Dom. So he would want a sub. What if that wasn't what she was, not really?

It would be over before it even started.

Angelo was speaking again and Samantha forced herself to tune back in.

"Remember as you fill the form out that a Dom will take a soft limit as an invitation to explore further, to push you." Samantha's eyes went wide.

Her pen had been hovering over "auctioned off." She hastily checked no.

Animal roles. Boot worship. Mouth bits.

She had no idea what any of those were, and drew question marks next to them. No way was she agreeing to something unless it had been explained in full.

Asphyxiation. Scat. Breath control.

Oh, hell to the no.

Just when she was wondering if there was anything on the

list that she *was* interested in—and if she had maybe completely misjudged her own needs—she came across an item that caught her interest.

Bondage.

She furrowed her brow at the paper. So many of the dreams she'd had had involved just that: rope, chains, cuffs, all holding her down, stripping away her control.

The image stayed in her mind as she worked through the remainder of the checklist. By the time she was done, the idea of being naked and bound, of someone kissing her until she was breathless while her arms tugged at the chains, had slickened the space between her legs.

"Ready for your tour?" Angelo asked patiently. Samantha nodded, feeling a tug of guilt as Angelo took the clipboard from her hands.

He was a nice guy, taking the time to introduce her to this lifestyle.

And yet as she followed him farther into the club, he wasn't the one she imagined caressing her bound body.

Bracing herself against the onslaught of images and sounds, Samantha found herself wondering what Elijah was doing right at that moment.

CHAPTER FIVE

The tires of his car crunched over the gravel as Elijah pulled up in front of Samantha's small cottage. Several small rocks flicked up, bouncing off his windshield, something that would normally have him cursing.

Now, however, he was too intent on seeing Samantha to do more than cast an irritated glance at the pane of glass.

Crossing the small pad of gravel that was Samantha's front yard, Elijah rapped on the brightly painted door.

Like the gnomes in her backyard, he appreciated the light-hearted touch.

There was no answer. Furrowing his brow, he took the chance that she'd be irritated and he peered through the front window.

The room was dim. Straining his ears, he searched for the sound of her glass furnace and came up with nothing.

She wasn't home. Damn it.

He knew it wasn't rational to be disappointed. He hadn't called; they hadn't had plans.

But he couldn't help wondering where she was. Who she was with.

Jealousy was a new emotion for him, and he wasn't quite sure what to do with it. It didn't seem to suit him.

Turning, Elijah realized that he didn't have much say in the matter. Samantha was an incredibly beautiful woman, and they had admitted a mutual attraction.

He hadn't asked her if she was involved with anyone. His

gut told him she wasn't, that she wasn't the kind of woman to start exploring the way she was if she had ties to someone.

That didn't stop the little green monster from perching on his shoulder and egging him on.

Elijah had his hand on the handle of his car door when he spied a hint of white, bright in the fading sun. It lay on the gravel by the indentations that marked where Samantha typically parked her car.

Moving closer, he picked it up. It was a thick rectangular piece of paper. When he turned it over and saw the logo for Pecado, his eyebrows shot up and his jaw clenched.

Why would she be going to Pecado? Was she there with someone else?

Crumpling the card in his fist, Elijah lowered his rangy build into his Porsche and shoved the car into gear. Didn't she know that she had to be careful about whom she gave control to?

BDSM clubs usually had a lot of safeguards in place. If she had been at Devorar, then he wouldn't have been worried, knowing that all it would take was a word from him for Antonio, his manager, to keep a close eye on her.

But Pecado—he didn't know much about that club, had been there only once. And he found that he didn't much care for the idea of an opportunistic Dom taking advantage of Samantha's inexperience with the lifestyle.

As he sped down the road that led back into town, barely noticing the buildings that were nothing more than a colored blur in his peripheral vision, Elijah thought of Samantha's stubbornness and her smart mouth and winced.

Many Doms would take that as an invitation to discipline her. And she likely had no idea what discipline even entailed—hell, he'd been worried that she wasn't into anything more than bedroom kink.

The woman had no idea what she was getting herself into.

Grimly, Elijah looked at the speedometer on the dash-board, then coaxed the pedal a little closer to the floor.

She may not like what he had to say, but he'd made up his mind. If Samantha wanted an introduction to the BDSM life-style, then she would get it from him and no one else.

"Would you like to try it?"

Angelo's question came after Samantha had felt his eyes watching her for several long moments. He'd shown her the up-stairs area of the club, where the private rooms were located, and around most of the downstairs space. They'd passed the bar, where she'd had a shot of tequila to ease her nerves.

Now they stood watching what Angelo had termed a "play-ful" scene. But as Samantha watched, she was feeling anything but.

In front of them, a man dressed in leathers similar to Ange-lo's circled a naked woman. Her wrists were cuffed and at-tached to rings high up on two thick wooden posts. Her ankles were similarly bound, and while she had a small range of move-ment, she was for all intents and purposes at the mercy of the man.

The woman's skin was flushed and sheened with sweat, and the hair that brushed her shoulders was damp.

The man who circled her wore a mitt lined with some kind of furry fabric on one hand. His other hand held something that looked like a small pizza cutter.

As Samantha watched, the man ran the small device in cir-cles around the woman's nipples. The woman jerked against her chains, crying out, and Samantha felt her own nipples pucker in response.

"That's called a Wartenberg wheel." Angelo had noticeably limited the amount that he'd touched her throughout their tour, but now he clasped her hips and pulled her back against him. Samantha stiffened in surprise when her ass nestled against the ridge of his solid erection.

"It doesn't cut. It just brings the nerves to life." Though he was obviously aroused, Angelo made no moves to touch Samantha anywhere else besides that light press of his fingers on her hips. As they'd walked around, she'd noticed that most Doms did this, touching the subs as they pleased, a hand on a thigh here, a delicate caress of a cheek there.

It seemed, somehow, to reinforce the notion that a sub didn't have control here. Samantha felt, rationally, that she should object to this.

Instead, it made her relax. It was as if her control was in the hands of every Dom who took a moment to care.

She still wished that it was Elijah who held her.

Finished with the Wartenberg wheel, the Dom in front of them tossed it aside, then rubbed the furry mitt over the skin that he had just teased. With his free hand he slid his fingers between his sub's legs, then inside her. Soon she bucked against his hand and cried out as she collapsed in what looked to be complete bliss.

As Samantha watched the other woman collapse in pleasure, only to be gently released from the chains, then taken in the arms of the Dom, she flushed and her skin suddenly felt too tight.

That was what she wanted. To be so lost in the other person that she couldn't even think. To be cared for by someone she trusted so she didn't have to do it for herself. Stress had been a monkey on her back for most of her life, especially during her teens, but it had eased a bit as Beth moved into adulthood.

But lately, with her sister losing her job, the stress had come back full force. With a growing unease that her life was spiraling out of control, Samantha had found it more and more difficult to escape the anxiety and fear that dogged her steps every waking moment . . . and sometimes haunted her dreams, too. If this . . . *lifestyle* could give her even a moment's respite . . .

It was incredibly tempting.

"Would you like to try?" Angelo asked again as Samantha returned her attention to the scene playing out before them.

"Yes." All of Samantha's senses sizzled with anticipation. She knew that Angelo wasn't the Dom for her, and yet she wanted to allow herself the experience.

Angelo held her in place for a moment as the Dom in front of them cleaned the equipment they'd just used. He had wrapped his sub in a warm blanket, seated her on the floor at his feet, and provided her with a bottle of water.

Tossing the cleaning cloth into a pail marked for that purpose, the Dom bent and picked up his sub, holding her close to his chest. The woman's eyes were open but gazing far away, and she smiled beatifically, looking for all the world as though she was high.

"It's all yours." The Dom nodded to Angelo as he carried his sub away.

"Come with me." Again that sound of dominance and possession in Angelo's tone as he released Samantha's hips and took her hand to guide her in between the posts. Samantha cocked her head, puzzled.

She responded to him a bit, reacting to the command in his voice. But he failed to waken her senses entirely, and she thought that there had to be more to it than this.

"Give me your wrists." One at a time, Angelo raised Samantha's arms and secured them into the upper cuffs. The metal was cool and solid against her hot skin, and she trembled as she realized that within seconds she would be incapable of movement.

"Glass," she blurted out as the cuff clicked closed around her wrist. "My safe word is *glass*."

Angelo cast her a disapproving stare. "I know that, Samantha. I read it in your paperwork." He gestured to the sheaf of papers that he had tucked in the back pocket of his pants. "The club safe word is *tequila*, and you can also use the word *red*. No Dom worth his salt would restrain you without knowing your safe word."

Samantha looked down, abashed.

Angelo tilted her head up, looked her in the eyes unwaveringly. "Trust is the basis of a D/s relationship, little one. You and I may not fit, but it's a lesson you'd do well to learn."

Samantha opened her mouth to apologize, but a voice sounded from behind Angelo, cutting her off.

"Get your hands off of her."

Elijah had never been more torn. Samantha was dressed in a little slip of a nightgown, a froth of pale brown more feminine and revealing than anything he would have imagined she'd own. It left her legs, her arms, the curve of her neck, the swells of her breasts open for his eyes to feast on.

Knowing what she looked like beneath that lace only increased his desire.

Her wrists were cuffed, chaining her to two tall wooden posts. Both times they had met she had taken his breath away with her beauty and the fierceness that radiated from deep within her.

To see her bound made him feel things he'd never felt so intensely before.

He wanted to touch her, clasp her by the hips, and seat himself inside her to the hilt.

He also wanted to ram his fist into the face of the man who currently had his hands around her waist. Elijah had never been the jealous type, but right in that moment he had to fight the urge to tear the man away from Samantha.

"Are you all right?" He looked to Samantha, saw that her face was flushed a deep red. He looked harder as she hesitated before nodding.

She wasn't flushed with arousal, he realized, but with embarrassment.

"I'm fine." Her words were tart, telling him she was annoyed.

But he didn't miss the way she oriented her body in his direction just the slightest bit. If the man with her truly commanded her submission, she wouldn't have even noticed Elijah.

"You can't interrupt a scene, man." The other man, a well-built Latino who looked to be in his early thirties, glowered at Elijah, his hands clenching into fists. "Are you new to this, or what?"

Elijah rose to his full height, looking down at the other man with every bit of arrogance that he possessed.

"I'm responsible for this sub's safety this evening," Angelo said. "She is my guest here." Elijah saw the acknowledgment in the other man's eyes, but Angelo didn't back down. Elijah appreciated the way the other Dom moved in front of Samantha, protecting her from the perceived threat, even as it annoyed the hell out of him that his view was now blocked. "She chose this scene. You don't have the right to interrupt."

"She doesn't know enough about any of this to choose a scene." Elijah's irritation boiled over, and he turned his scowl to Samantha. He wasn't happy that she was here with another Dom when he'd made his desires known to her.

Instead of appearing happy to see him, his redheaded goddess glowered at him.

"Excuse me?" Samantha yanked on her cuffs, anger flooding her features. "I'm here. I can speak for myself."

Angelo turned to Samantha, placed a hand on her shoulder. Elijah ground his teeth together at the sight of another man touching her.

"Samantha, give me a minute. I'll uncuff you, and then we'll find a dungeon monitor to get rid of this guy."

Elijah was momentarily gratified that Samantha didn't appear to like that idea, either.

"Angelo, it's okay. I know him." Samantha still didn't sweeten her expression for Elijah, though he noticed that her nipples had hardened beneath the thin material of her nightie. It seemed that she felt just as he did: that one taste had only led them to a desire for more. "What are you doing here?"

"I went by your house and found this card." Fishing the crumpled card from his pocket, Elijah waved it in front of Samantha's face. "And save the attitude. I was worried that you were getting in over your head."

Her face reddened further.

"You must think I'm a naive idiot." Her words softened, but Elijah could still hear the upset in her voice. "I would never come to a BDSM club for the first time by myself. Angelo is a friend. He's doing me a favor. Helping me . . . helping me test something out before I make a decision."

Elijah studied her face, employing every skill he'd used in his years as a Dom to read her.

She was telling the truth. And he knew then that she had come here to see if she was truly interested in this kind of lifestyle before the deadline he had set for her. She'd seen through his offer of the commission, then.

He did want a sculpture of hers—he would never lie about that. But he was more interested in the fact that it would put the two of them in each other's space for a prolonged length of time.

"I want you again, Samantha." Ignoring the other man, Elijah focused entirely on the woman he desired, catching and holding her gaze. "You want me. Let me do this scene with you."

Elijah expected a knee-jerk *no* from the fiery woman. Instead, she caught her breath, her eyes widening as she took him in.

"Is this what you want, Samantha? You can say no. You don't have to listen to him." Angelo cast an agitated glance Elijah's way before returning his attention to the beautiful sub that was chained in front of them.

Samantha inhaled deeply, causing her breasts to rise and fall enticingly. It was a full minute before she replied.

"Yes." Her voice was husky, her stare focused on Elijah. "Yes, I want this."

Pleasure washed over him in a surge of desire. She had said yes. She wanted him as badly as he wanted her.

No matter what many believed, in a D/s relationship it was the sub who had all of the control.

Easing back now that Samantha had made her choice, the man she'd called Angelo pulled a sheaf of papers from his back pocket. He handed them to Elijah, nodding curtly.

"I'll leave you to it, then." Turning, the man cast one more look at Samantha. "You're sure? You can use your safe word."

Samantha's eyes never left Elijah's face, and in that moment he felt bigger than the entire world.

"I'm sure." She spoke softly. And then Angelo was gone, and Elijah was faced with the goddess who had somehow managed to capture his every thought for the past two days.

"I'm going to cuff your legs." He felt the incredible need to see her in *his* bonds, to put his mark on them. "What is your safe word?"

"Glass." Her face was turned against him as she spoke the word. He savored her shiver as he knelt before her, clasping her left ankle, then circling it with hard steel.

He repeated the process with her right ankle. Unable to resist, he pressed a kiss to the inside of her thigh before again rising to his feet.

She shuddered, and he drank in her response.

Elijah took a quick moment to scan the papers that Samantha had filled out. His mind whirled with all the things he wanted to do to her, but he pushed them aside.

This first time had to be all about her.

"No sex?" This had been marked as a hard limit. It often was on a sub's first visit, until they felt more sure of themselves and their partner. He already knew what it felt like inside her, but he still couldn't presume, no matter how much he was already aching to return to her wet heat.

Samantha hesitated, then nodded. "No sex."

"All right, then." He tilted her chin up so that she looked directly at him. Those glass green eyes were full of defiance and heat.

"I need to say something," she announced.

He paused, his hands inches from her shoulders. His fingers itched to touch.

"What do you need to say, little cat?" Though there was still a thin ribbon of space between them, Elijah swore he could already feel the warmth of her skin pulsing in that empty space.

"Just because we've already had sex, and just because I've agreed to do this . . . this scene or whatever it's called with you . . . it doesn't mean that I've agreed to your deal." Though she didn't clarify, Elijah understood what she was referring to.

She wasn't just talking about her resistance to accept his commission—and he knew that there was more to that resistance than she was letting on.

She was referring to the *other* thing that lay between them. The sexual connection that drew hot and tight between them.

If she had been any other submissive, Elijah would have used this opportunity to introduce some discipline. Her tone was one that many other Doms wouldn't tolerate.

He wasn't most Doms, and he found that he had no desire to quell her attitude. Not yet.

She was acting out, certainly, but it wasn't to get him to pay attention to her. It was a part of who she was, and a very large part of what had attracted him to her.

When concocting the idea of the commission, he had intended to seduce her slowly into an affair, to savor what he still wasn't convinced would be any more than vanilla sex. Amazing vanilla sex, but vanilla all the same.

But chance had put her in his arms right now. He was going to take the opportunity and run with it.

"Close your eyes." Since he hadn't intended on going to a club when he'd left the resort that evening, he didn't have his bag of toys with him. He would have to make do with nothing more than his hands.

He intended to push her a bit tonight, to see if she really was interested in what she thought she was. He was already in deep enough with Samantha that, if it turned out she wanted nothing more than sugar kink, he needed to protect his heart.

"Hold on to those chains, and no matter what I say, what I do, don't let go."

No *matter what I say, don't let go.*

Samantha's heart began to pound double time in her chest. She'd closed her eyes when he'd commanded her to, but at these last words, she popped them open again.

Her disobedience earned her a sharp swat on the hip.

"Ow!" Eyes fully open now, she looked over her shoulder and glared at Elijah. "What was that for?"

Cupping his palm, he spanked her again, this time fully on one of her ass cheeks. She felt the skin beneath his blow spark to life, heating and tingling.

"You opened your eyes. I told you not to."

She'd read about spanking when she'd done some research. The mere thought of it had turned her on. But she'd expected—somehow she'd imagined—that it would be discussed beforehand, and that there would be some kind of... warm-up, maybe, before it happened.

She'd never dreamed that he would simply spank without asking. Would simply lay his palm across her flesh while she was restrained and could do nothing about it.

His palm again met her ass, and she jolted, swaying in the chains.

"Close your eyes." Elijah's commanding voice held nothing but confidence, as if he expected no other outcome than that she would obey.

It was really freaking hot. The blows had brought her skin to life, had focused her attention fully on Elijah. But they hadn't excited her, not the way that being restrained had.

As if he sensed that, he stopped the spanking. Her eyes were closed tightly, but she could still sense his movements as he circled her, disturbing the air as he walked.

"My options tonight are limited, Samantha. I don't have my toy bag with me."

She turned her face in the direction his voice came from, letting it wash over her.

His voice was warm and powerful, and she would never have admitted it to him, but it made her a little bit weak in the knees.

"I could spank you some more. I could release you from the

chains, could turn you over my knee and lay my hand flat on that pretty pale skin."

Samantha inhaled sharply at the words, sensing he was searching for something.

She couldn't give it to him, because she had no idea what it was.

"I could borrow a crop from someone. Or a paddle. Maybe a whip." His voice was calm, as if he was discussing what they would have for dinner. Samantha's body tightened, partly with anticipation and partly with dread.

The pictures she'd found during her research had been titillating, and she'd found the idea of being whipped . . . intriguing. But in the moment, right then and right there, the thought didn't sit well.

"Not yet, hmm? Well, what else can I do to you?" Samantha sensed him stop in front of her, guessed that he was looking down at her face. She understood then what he was doing.

He didn't have the toys to play with, to discover what she liked and what she didn't. So he was using words, watching to see how she responded to the ideas he brought up.

She wanted nothing more than to have him grab her, to do what he would to her.

She couldn't find the words to ask, and didn't think she was supposed to, at any rate.

"I think I know." These words were whispered directly into her ear, followed by a light nip on her earlobe with his teeth. A small moan escaped her lips.

Elijah chuckled, and she frowned.

"Frowning at a Dom can be risky business, Samantha." A hand swept over her shoulder, and she felt the strings holding up her short nightie fall down.

A sharp cry escaped her when, with both straps sliding down her shoulders, the bodice of the nightie dropped, revealing her breasts and her stomach. His hands cupped the mounds of flesh with just the lightest of touches, but it brought every nerve in her body sizzling to life.

She started to pant when his thumbs brushed over her nipples, which contracted tightly, almost painfully. She felt the touch all the way down to her pussy. It lit a fire that made her ache.

"How can I possibly be frowning at you when I can't see you?" She made sure her voice was light and sweet, not testing him, even though his hands on her breasts were driving her wild.

There was a long moment of silence. A knot in her stomach grew as she wondered what on earth she'd done that was so wrong.

She dared to open her eyes just enough to peek at him, and instead was confronted with the sight of Elijah trying to suppress laughter.

Repressing a smile herself, she closed her eyes all the way again.

"I saw that." Elijah's voice was mild but stern, and Samantha cursed under her breath. How the hell had he seen? She'd opened her eyes only the tiniest crack. "For disobeying yet again you'll receive one more punishment."

"Are you going to spank me again?" She hoped not. She felt on the edge of something—something big—and another tap on the ass wasn't going to help her find it.

"No, I have something else in mind this time," he said. Samantha heard mischief in his voice. "You can open your eyes."

Her eyes flew open to find Elijah kneeling before her. He looked up at her with a grin so wicked it transformed his angelic countenance into something dark and dangerous.

"I'm going to taste you, Samantha. I'm going to use my tongue on you."

Samantha's entire body jerked at the very idea. "That, uh . . . that doesn't really sound like a punishment."

Elijah looked up at her with something enticing in his eyes.

"That's not your punishment. Your punishment is that you're not allowed to come until I say you can."

Samantha's mouth fell open with incredulity. She watched as, with sure fingers, Elijah pulled her lacy bikini panties to one side and bared the triangle of russet curls that lay beneath.

"Very pretty." His murmur was so close to her flesh that she could feel his breath misting warmly over her lower lips.

She barely had time to register what he was about to do, and then his thumbs were parting her flesh and his tongue was sweeping into the crevice in between.

"Oh my God," she choked out as her entire body rocked, pulling on the chains that held her legs apart, her arms above her head. The clanking of the metal reminded her that she couldn't do anything but accept what he was doing to her, not unless she wanted to use her safe word.

As his tongue swirled over the hard nub of her clit, Samantha discovered that she *really, really* didn't want to use her safe word.

"That's right," Elijah murmured against her, his tongue flicking over her with a teasing touch. "You don't have the control here. All you can do is accept what I give you. It's not your choice. Your body is not yours right now. It's mine."

His words worked at something inside her. They released the feelings that she had been storing away, the ones she hadn't allowed herself to fully explore. They exploded free, combining in a dizzying arousal that washed over her and made her shake.

"So responsive." Elijah swept his tongue through her cleft again. "You like that. You like the idea of not being in control."

Samantha liked it so much that she felt the tensions that signaled climax already coiling inside her. She was amazed—he'd brought her to climax quickly the day before, but she'd thought it was a onetime occurrence. But once again she found herself so aroused by the touch of his hand that she knew she could come again, and soon.

Except . . . oh, he'd said . . .

She wasn't allowed to come until he told her she could. For reasons she didn't quite understand, she didn't want to disappoint him.

"Eli . . ." Samantha tried to tense her body, to hold off the rising wave of pleasure. "Oh, please stop . . . I'm going to . . ."

Elijah withdrew his mouth just for a moment, then slid his tongue all the way inside her, and it was all Samantha could do not to scream.

"Do you want me to stop?" Elijah caught her clit between his two thumbs, dragged the rough edge of calluses over the tender flesh, and Samantha shuddered. "Tell me the truth."

"No . . . God, no." She was a live wire, a bomb about to explode. "But . . . you said . . . you said I can't . . ."

"Come for me, Samantha." Removing his mouth from her lower lips, he stood, his body pressing against hers all the way up. He wrapped a fist in the length of her braid and tugged her head back until the line of her neck was exposed. "Come for me now."

He closed his teeth over the tender spot where her pulse beat, just below her jawline. Samantha's muscles sagged, then snapped tight like a rubber band. Pleasure whipped through her, blinding her, stealing her hearing, her breath.

She loved it. She hated it.

Elijah was there holding her as she rode out the unexpected storm. She cried out, pulled on her chains until it hurt, but the bliss went on and on.

When it finally faded, Samantha was left wide-eyed and stunned, staring incredulous at Elijah.

"What the fuck was that?" she asked when she was finally able to speak. This time he couldn't hold back his amusement, and he shook with laughter as he undid the cuffs holding up her arms and massaged the skin that had chafed against the metal.

"*That* was good," he said, his hand stroking lightly over her back. She could feel the rock-hard length of his erection as he held her to him, and she arched her hips in invitation, wanting to give back some of the pleasure that he'd just given her.

To her confusion, he pulled away.

"Did you like it?" His face was serious, those intense blue eyes searching her face, trying to read her.

Samantha furrowed her brow as something dark worked its way into the light. She didn't like that question. Why didn't she like that question?

"I—" The words caught in her mouth as the darkness rolled over her again.

Did you like that, little girl?

The words from her past slammed into her with enough force that her knees buckled. Elijah caught her in his arms before she could fall.

"Let me go. Let me out." She shoved at Elijah's chest, her breath beginning to rasp in her throat.

No. *No.* She wouldn't let these memories ruin this for her. She was stronger than that.

She struggled to inhale, then worked to release the breath again as Elijah dropped to his knees in front of her and released the cuffs that bound her ankles. She was trembling enough that once her feet were free she stumbled.

This time when Elijah caught her up in his arms, she didn't shove him away.

"Thank you," Samantha whispered through numb lips. Elijah scowled in response, snapping at a young man in a collar who stood nearby to bring them a blanket and a bottle of water.

He settled into an overstuffed armchair, Samantha on his

lap. She curled into him, her breathing slowing as she registered whose arms she was in.

She was with Elijah. She was in his arms, at the club, and she was safe.

"Drink." A fuzzy blanket was wrapped around her, and Elijah held a bottle of water up to her lips. Obediently she sipped at the liquid, felt its coolness ease some of her throat's swelling from panic.

She shook her head when Elijah held the bottle up again. She felt him shift beneath her as he set the bottle aside.

Then he caught her chin in his hand and turned her head so that she looked right at him.

"What happened there?" Elijah pinned her with the intensity of his stare, and Samantha squirmed.

"Nothing. Just momentary panic." She kept her voice light. She had spent a very long time trying to put the past behind her, and she wasn't about to drag it out now.

"I told you not to lie." Elijah spoke sternly, as if bestowing an important lesson, and prickles of guilt rode out over Samantha's skin.

She didn't know quite why, but she really didn't like the thought of disappointing him.

She didn't know what to say, so she pressed her lips together tightly, sealing the words inside.

"You liked being bound." It was clear that Elijah wasn't asking her a question. Still, she nodded in agreement, though the movement was stiff and jerky.

The sensation of being locked into the cuffs, the chains— it had been more than sexual for her. It had made her feel free.

"You enjoyed my touch on your breasts. And you liked it when I used my mouth on you." Again, Elijah spoke surely. Samantha felt as though she should be embarrassed to be dissecting their encounter like this, but Elijah was so matter-of-fact about it that it didn't make sense for her to feel mortified.

"I did," Samantha agreed softly. There was no use denying it, not when he'd made her come the way he had—in public, no less.

"So it must have been something after. Either when I released you from the cuffs or when I spoke to you." Bingo. Samantha schooled her face into what she hoped was an expressionless mask.

This was not open for discussion. Not now, not ever.

"Samantha." There was a command in his voice, and Samantha found that she couldn't look away. There was deep concern in his eyes, and the depth of it startled her.

Why should he care about any of this? Why would he bother to find out anything about her? It was clear that she was interested in him physically. Why would he want any more?

"I can't." Samantha tried to rid herself of the tremble in her voice. She'd never been the type to enjoy feeling like a damsel in distress.

"Can't or won't?" Elijah asked.

Samantha didn't hear any judgment in his tone, but she reacted as if she had.

"I won't." Struggling to free herself from his arms, Samantha looked away, feeling the tears well up in her eyes before she gathered up her self-control and faced him again. "It's not something I'm going to be talking about. Not ever again."

Elijah pressed his lips together tightly, finally letting go so she could free herself. She stood up and tensed, preparing herself for an argument.

Instead she found herself blinking in surprise as he unwound the fuzzy blanket from her legs, then smoothed the skirt of her nightie around her hips. He hooked sure fingers in the straps of the bodice, pulling them up until they were again settled on her shoulders.

Elijah stood as well, and Samantha noted that, even though he'd been on his knees in front of her, even though he'd had her crushed in his arms, he didn't appear wrinkled or mussed in the least.

He held out a hand for her, and after a long moment she finally took it, enjoying the warmth of his palm pressed into her own.

"Come on. Let's get you something to eat."

Elijah watched with eagle eyes as Samantha tugged uncomfortably at the short skirt of her nightgown. He knew she was uncomfortable dressed as she was in public, though he'd assured her that the diner that sat next door to the club catered to clientele in all states of dress—or undress.

He'd been there once before, when he'd checked out the other BDSM club in the area prior to opening Devorar and, to his relief, nothing had changed. People dressed in rubber, dog collars, and hobble skirts sat at booths with cracked leather seats, drinking sodas and eating nacho chips with no more self-consciousness than if they'd been wearing blue jeans.

He felt Samantha relax a bit as they pushed through the glass door and walked into the steam-and-spice-infused air of the diner. She didn't relax as completely as he knew she was capable of, though, and he was glad.

He wanted her off balance. In his experience, people tended to be more honest when they were.

"What would you like to drink?" he asked as he settled her into a booth, regretting the embarrassment that was on her face. So many people worried after letting go in a scene, after spilling a secret that they'd held close to them.

But the entire point of the BDSM lifestyle was exactly that: to let go.

"Diet cola, please." Samantha kept her eyes down and Elijah frowned. It wasn't that she was feeling submissive, he knew, but that she felt embarrassed.

He needed to give her something else to think about.

Leaning over, he placed his hands on her shoulders, wishing it was her soft skin he was touching rather than the thin weave of the cardigan that she'd insisted on putting on over her nightie. She looked up at the touch, startled.

Though he wanted to take a moment to inhale that floral scent that was so uniquely hers, he kept her needs in the front of his mind. Without any warning, Elijah slanted his lips over Samantha's in a kiss that was hot and hard, demanding more.

He heard her swift intake of breath—felt his own breath catch—and savored the feeling of her trembling beneath his fingers. He deepened the kiss, swiping his tongue over the seam of her lips, demanding entrance.

He'd started the kiss as a distraction for her, but felt the heat flash all the way through his body.

She didn't become limp and pliant beneath his caress; instead, she answered with her own fire. He hadn't expected it, but he thrilled to it just the same.

A wolf whistle pierced the lust-fueled haze that surrounded them, reminding Elijah of where they were, of why he had kissed Samantha in the first place.

Slowly he pulled back, feeling the heat of her lips imprinted on his own.

As she blinked up at him with those mesmerizing green eyes, her fingers strayed to her lips to trace the path that his mouth had just traveled.

"I'll go get you some food. Why don't you stay here?" Truthfully, Elijah was relieved to have a moment to clear his thoughts.

Shit. That kiss had made his head spin . . . and it was simply a *kiss*. It made him wonder what would happen when he was deep inside her again, her wrists bound, her body beneath his.

His cock liked that image and threatened to stand at attention. He inhaled deeply to calm himself down. A raging erection might have been perfectly normal at a BDSM club, but in other public places, even a diner that catered to the same crowd, it wasn't exactly the norm.

He ordered a meal for the two of them and carried it back to the table. Samantha immediately grabbed the soda he offered her and sucked deeply on the straw, her cheeks hollowing as she did and bringing all kinds of other naughty images to his mind.

She frowned and looked at him over the plastic lid of the cup. "This isn't diet." Unlike many women he'd met, who would have sulked or made a fuss, she simply raised an eyebrow in question.

"You don't need diet," he replied, offering her a crooked smile.

What she needed was the sugar and caffeine of the regular version after the intensity of their scene at Pecado.

"I haven't made a decision yet." Samantha didn't wait for him to start the conversation.

"You have until tonight." Elijah pulled the tray of food to him, picked out a fish taco with salsa and sour cream, and handed it to Samantha.

She took it, but looked disgruntled.

"I have until tomorrow," she reminded him, then sniffed at the taco. "And I don't like fish."

"I think you'll like this," Elijah promised, picking up one of his own and biting into it. The flavors exploded across his tongue, and he found that he even resented the potency, because it chased away the taste of Samantha.

"And, no, you have until the end of today. It's after midnight."

Craning her neck, Samantha looked around until her gaze faced a large clock mounted on the diner's wall. She muttered something under her breath, then glared at the taco.

"I've never found a fish I like." She sniffed again, and Elijah swallowed a chuckle when he heard her stomach growl.

He made a show of shrugging carelessly. "That's all I ordered."

She eyed the taco again, clearly considering it. She raised it, then lowered it again, watching curiously as Elijah finished his first taco and picked up a second.

"Yes?" he asked her, reaching for her soda to steal a sip.

"I didn't take you for the kind of man to enjoy cheap tacos at an all-night diner," she said, then finally nibbled at the corner of the tortilla. Elijah watched with satisfaction as pleasure spread over her face—pleasure that she visibly tried to repress.

She was so damn cute when she was contrary . . . which was all the time. She intrigued him enough that he was willing to indulge her contrary streak a while longer.

He knew that when she finally did submit to him, it would be well worth the wait.

He watched as she took a second bite of the taco, pursing her lips when she caught him watching.

"How is it?" he asked seriously, holding back another grin when Samantha raised her nose in the air.

"It's better than it should be, given that it's fish." She met his eyes and the corners of her lips turned up warily, seeming to know she'd been caught.

"I'm not sure I should tell you this, but I will. You confuse me." Elijah cocked his head at her to observe her reaction, studying the way the low light of the diner's interior shone on her cherry red curls.

Samantha swallowed a bite of taco. Man, he could watch

her mouth all day. Her tongue flicked out over her lips and he stifled a groan.

"Why do I confuse you?" Her voice was hesitant. She reached for a napkin to wipe her fingers, then crumpled it up in a suddenly tight fist.

"I don't think I believe you want to be fully submissive," he said finally, and he made sure to make his tone arrogant. He wanted to rile her up, wanted to see what her reaction would be.

She didn't disappoint. Her cheeks flushed with temper and she tossed the crumpled napkin down on the tray as her shoulders stiffened.

"Don't tell me what I want." Her eyes were like green arrows pinning him where he sat.

Elijah calmly picked up the shared soda for another sip.

"If I was your Dom, that's exactly what I would do."

"What do you mean?" Her brow furrowed, and he saw that he had taken her aback.

Good. Just as intended.

"If we were together, you would give care of yourself to me. You would do what I said because you would trust me to fulfill your needs, and often your wants as well." He watched as she inhaled sharply, her cheeks flushing beneath his intense scrutiny. "That includes telling me things that might be uncomfortable. I will never abuse any of the knowledge or trust that you give to me, but in order for me to take care of you properly, you need to be open."

He continued after a pause. "You would need to give yourself to me entirely. And I don't know that you're entirely capable of doing that." The more time he spent around her, the more Elijah wondered about it.

She was like a flame: beautiful, ever changing, dangerous.

He wasn't sure he could stay away.

"I . . . I don't know what to say." Samantha pushed the tray across the table, having clearly lost her appetite. Her color was better than it had been in the club, thanks to the food and drink, and he was satisfied that she'd be able to make it home without passing out.

"You've seen a lot tonight." Elijah stood and offered his hand to Samantha. She stared at it for a long moment, as if no one had ever offered her help before. Slowly she took it, and stood as well.

The naked length of her legs, capped by those siren red shoes, and the memory of what lay between them tested his patience sorely. He wanted to pick her up, to have her wrap those long legs around his waist while he pressed her against the diner wall, shoved her panties aside, and drove himself inside her, audience or not. In fact, the idea of having spectators turned him on even more.

The lifestyle had taught him, however, that the longer gratification was delayed, the bigger the reward. So he pushed down his base urges and did no more than rub a thumb over her hand.

"You'll contact me tonight." It would be a long, long wait until then, but he had no choice but to ride the wave of anticipation.

When she came to tell him that she would accept the commission—and he was sure she would—he would take it one step further. He would ask her for a night together at Devorar, his club, where he could take her further into her explorations.

"Here—" Reaching into the pocket of her cardigan, Samantha withdrew a handful of peso notes, which she tried to give to him. Elijah gently folded her hand back around them and pushed it away.

She opened her mouth, and he knew she was going to argue. He frowned.

"I like to take care of the woman I'm with. You would need

to get used to that." He enjoyed the way her lips parted in surprise. Silently she tucked the money back into the pocket of her sweater.

He could all but hear the gears turning in her brain. She'd been introduced to a lot over the last few hours, and Elijah knew that now it was time to give her some space to process.

"Come on. I'll walk you to your car." He just hoped that she would come to the right conclusion, because he was certain of one thing.

He wanted her more than he'd ever wanted anyone or anything in his life.

He was a planner, a strategist, and he had more than enough money to help him with his ideas. He would do whatever it took to persuade her that she wanted him too.

CHAPTER SIX

nstead of feeling tired when she arrived home from Pecado, Samantha had been filled with nearly manic energy. By two in the morning she'd had to go out to her studio, to try to capture her feelings in a glass piece that she planned to color the palest shade of pink to represent the evening's encounter with Elijah.

She hadn't had any success—hadn't been able to concentrate on the work.

The bubble of glass on the end of her pipe began to hang lopsided. She cursed; she hadn't been paying enough attention, hadn't turned the pipe evenly. The result was thicker glass on one side than the other.

Sometimes this was a happy accident, something that worked into the piece she ultimately had in mind. Yet since what she was trying to create showed balance, a yin and a yang, this looked all kinds of wrong.

"Bloody hell." Exhaling harshly, Samantha rose to take the pipe back to the furnace. There, she scraped the creation back into the melt, where it would become something else some other time.

Closing her eyes, she placed her hands behind her head and arched her back, stretching out the muscles that had cramped during her hours of work. She was sore, but it wasn't anything she wasn't used to.

The tender flesh between her legs, though—that was a new sensation. She pictured Elijah's golden head as it had been that night, nuzzled at the apex of her thighs, and felt heat flash all over her body.

"Submissive." Samantha whispered the word, then repeated it to herself more loudly.

Was that really what she wanted?

She thought back to her night at the club. She'd been startled by a lot of the things she'd seen—even appalled by some of the activities mentioned on the questionnaire that Angelo had had her fill out.

When Angelo had given her commands, she had felt herself respond, but it had been a mild sensation. Like when someone walked by with an ice-cream cone after she'd just finished dinner—there was interest, but not a deep desire.

Yet when Elijah told her what to do, it had been like a tsunami descending upon her entire being. She'd found that she had no choice but to respond. And more, she wanted to follow his commands.

She still wasn't entirely sure how she felt about being spanked. Wasn't certain she liked the idea of crops, or whips, or canes—even if the lashes were delivered by Elijah.

But being restrained—that had been a major turn-on. More than that, the manner in which Elijah had taken her in his arms after she'd had her momentary panic attack had filled something deep inside her. The way he'd wrapped her in a blanket, held her close, fed her—it had been strange and some kind of wonderful to be taken care of.

That was what she wanted, more than anything she'd seen in the BDSM club. She wanted a strong man, a man who would take care of her without questioning her endlessly about it. A man who wasn't put off by the fact that she could be argumentative and stubborn.

Elijah was that man. She was absolutely sure of it.

"I can do this." Suddenly too warm, Samantha strode across

the small studio and wrenched open the door. The early-morning air was cool, refreshing her and filling her with new purpose.

The man seemed to have gotten it into his head that she couldn't—wouldn't—submit. He was so stuck on it that Samantha figured it must be really important to him.

She needed to prove to him that she could do it. Her evening at the club had simply been to test the waters before she dove in.

She now felt ready—as ready as she would ever be.

She would accept his offer of the commission, because she needed the money for her sister and it could pay off the remainder of Beth's student loans, as well as buy her diabetic supplies for a full year.

But along with the money, she had a request to make of him. She wanted to learn how to be a submissive, and the month it would take her to finish the piece of glasswork seemed like a perfect opportunity to ask the man she wanted to be with to teach her.

The idea of an entire month in Elijah's care made her skin flush, made her ache in that empty place between her thighs.

She wanted a strong man. She was sure that Elijah was the one she'd been looking for, and she wasn't about to let him get away.

"Señorita Collins is here to see you." Elijah's administrative assistant at the resort office, Lupe, knocked on the door even though it was cracked open. Her eyes were wide as she regarded him. "She's very pretty."

"She certainly is." Elijah felt his spirits lift. He'd been filled with anticipation ever since he'd left Samantha at her car the night before. He'd managed to catch a couple of hours of sleep, but it hadn't lessened the sensation.

He'd promised that she could have until the end of the day,

and he'd built his business reputation by honoring his word. But he found that he couldn't focus on his work, as images of Samantha in that lacy little nightie, legs and arms spread and in chains, kept running through his mind.

He hadn't expected to hear from her until early evening at the very soonest. He certainly hadn't expected her to show up at his office, but his body came alert at the very mention of her name.

"Bring her in, please, Lupe." His assistant disappeared around the door again, and Elijah felt his nerves humming in pleasant anticipation.

Samantha appeared in the doorway, her face a study in nervousness.

"I didn't think I'd hear from you so soon." He wanted to rise, to pull her to him and reenact the kiss that had haunted his mind since the night before.

But for this to work, she needed to come to him. Though his muscles twitched, he forced himself to remain seated.

"I'm going to create your sculpture." Though Samantha's face revealed her tension, her voice was strong. Elijah savored the sound.

It took a very strong woman to submit. And he hoped she would prove strong enough.

"I'm accepting the commission, and I'm hoping you'll do something for me at the same time." She stepped closer to him. He cursed inwardly when he saw that she was wearing those red fuck-me sandals again, paired with a lacy white sundress that made her seem sweet and innocent.

He wondered if she was wearing anything underneath the sundress.

Her contrasts were driving him crazy.

"What is it you want?" Elijah watched the way her breasts quivered as she exhaled.

She stepped closer and planted her hands on his desk.

Samantha flipped her long braid back over her shoulder, and he caught a hint of her wildflower scent. His body was already conditioned to respond to the smell of her, the taste, and he felt his cock begin to thicken.

Elijah looked into those vivid green eyes, felt the pull of attraction.

Samantha hesitated for a moment, moistening her lips with the tip of her tongue, and his eyes tracked the movement.

"I want to explore my . . . my submissive side."

Elijah felt his entire body clench with anticipation.

"And I would like your help."

"I need you to say the words." Of all the things she might have asked for, this had never crossed his mind.

"I want to know what it's like to be someone's submissive." Her words were soft but sure. "*Your* submissive. At least for the time it takes me to complete the sculpture. And then I can decide whether it's really right for me."

He watched as she inhaled deeply, then sank her teeth into her lower lip. Next, in one swift movement she bent, fisted her hands in the hem of her sundress, and lifted it up and over her head.

She was gloriously naked beneath it. Elijah prided himself on always being in control, but when Samantha's body was bared to him entirely, he felt his jaw hit the floor.

He stared, rising partially in his chair, his hands fisting with the need to touch. He was aware that she had spoken, but had to tear his eyes from the rose-colored nipples that had peaked under his stare while she repeated herself.

"I want to explore submission. And I want to explore it with you."

Elijah felt his breath leave him in a heated rush.

"Why are you asking for this?" He stood, getting a better

view of Samantha, naked except for those red sandals, and his cock hardened to the point of pain.

It was what he wanted: Samantha, in his care. A month to explore whatever this was between them.

"You know why." Her voice was soft, but she still looked him right in the eye. It was a reminder of why he had reservations over her submission to him, a reminder of the reason he couldn't simply bend her over his desk and plunge into what he knew would be an inferno of slick heat.

If she wanted to learn what it was like to submit, then he needed to take the power away from her.

"Come here," Elijah commanded, his voice pitched low. He saw something spark in the depths of her eyes, but there was no hesitation; she rounded his desk quickly until she stood before him.

"Bend over the desk until you can put your cheek on it. Put your hands behind your back." Lifting his shirt, Elijah undid his belt buckle, then slid it out through the belt loops.

He knew that she heard and identified the sound, because she tensed. But rather than lashing that creamy skin with the leather of the belt, he looped it around her wrists and fastened the buckle, sliding a finger between the leather and her wrist to make sure the binding wasn't too tight.

The night before had told him that pain wasn't what got her excited. No, Samantha liked being bound—liked having control taken away and being told what she could and couldn't do.

This was why he needed to teach her this lesson before he could accept her submission. He ached to have her as his sub, but he wouldn't be doing either of them any favors if he didn't see this last thing through.

Silently, he undid the zipper of his shorts, let them and his briefs fall to the floor. He stroked a hand up and down the length of his erect cock, then moved closer, letting his hips cup her naked ass, and his cock nestle into the cleft that divided it.

She moaned, the sound vibrating throughout her body.

"Do you like being caged in like this?" Deliberately Elijah arched his hips, pressing against her heated flesh. He swallowed a curse as his cock rubbed against her ass.

He wanted to slide it *into* her ass, and prayed that this lesson went the way he wanted it to.

She nodded her head yes, and Elijah bent over her, pinning her down.

"Do you like having control taken away from you?" Again she nodded, and without warning he worked his hand between their bodies and slid his fingers between her legs. Her hips bucked back against him and she cried out, but he didn't do any more than hold his fingers still inside her.

"Say it," he commanded her. He nearly moaned himself when her cunt clenched around his hand.

"I like having control taken away from me."

Elijah crooked his fingers inside her tight passage then, pressing against the spot that would drive her to orgasm. He reveled in her response, the way she writhed against him, the way she stiffened in his arms right before she came.

Though it nearly killed him to do it, he pulled his fingers from her heat before she could come. She cried out at the loss, then groaned with disappointment when he stepped back and moved away from her.

She started to rise as he circled the desk.

"Don't move!" he snapped, coming around to the front of the desk. Placing his palm flat on her cheek, he pushed her head back down.

She whimpered, but let him move her.

"Why?" she whispered. "Isn't this what you want?"

Elijah held back a sigh of frustration. He wanted this more than anything.

But she had to understand.

"You organized this entire scenario, Samantha." Elijah remembered so many similar circumstances with Tara, where she had topped from the bottom.

He listened to her sharp inhalation, saw her part her lips, likely to protest.

He pressed his finger to her mouth, hushing her so he could finish.

"You dressed to seduce me. You blindsided me with your request. You stripped. You had an entire scene planned out, controlled to your liking, and that isn't how this works."

Elijah watched Samantha's face closely. She opened her mouth to speak, defiance blazing in her eyes, but he could see her mind reeling. Before she spoke a word, realization seemed to wash over her.

"Oh my God."

Elijah exhaled with more than a hint of relief. She understood.

Now it was up to her to decide where to go from here.

Rounding the desk again, he undid the buckle of the belt, then unwound it from her wrists. Tossing it to the side, he massaged the skin that had been abraded by the leather, then helped her to a standing position, turning her at the same time.

She looked mortified. It pained him to see it, but he knew that it was what she needed in order to understand how things would really work in a D/s relationship.

"I'm sorry," she whispered, and even when he placed a finger beneath her chin, she looked down. "I . . . I didn't . . ."

"You didn't what?" he asked softly, and increased the pressure beneath her chin. "Look at me, Samantha."

Her eyes flicked up and met his stare.

"I didn't realize that was what I was doing," she said. Elijah saw genuine remorse in her gaze. He winced inwardly.

Humiliation was not one of his favorite activities. And yet a

Dom had to do things that he didn't particularly savor when it was what his sub needed.

"What is it that you want, Samantha?" God, he wanted this woman. "Do you want to call the shots, to play at bondage in the bedroom and nowhere else? Or do you want to give up control, and in return be cherished as the treasure that you are?"

Samantha swallowed audibly, and when she pushed him back, Elijah felt his heart sink.

He received the shock of his life when she clasped her fingers together and looked up at him with pleading eyes.

"I want you," she said, her voice strong and sure. A surge of emotion that he hadn't expected to feel lanced through him, combining with the arousal and giving his heart a painful tug. "I want you and no one else."

Samantha held her breath as she waited for Elijah to respond. She wanted—desperately wanted—him to take the decision out of her hands.

"You want me, and you want the things that I want?" Elijah asked.

Samantha understood that this was her last chance.

She was sure. He was the key to everything she wanted and couldn't attain for herself.

"Yes . . . *Sir.*" Her entire body tensed.

She watched as the disbelief on his face melted into pleasure. Giddiness washed over her when she saw that she'd made him happy.

"How long will it take you to finish this sculpture?" He pinned her with his eyes, and she froze in place, as immobile as if he'd physically bound her.

"Four weeks. Give or take." Samantha's heart was pounding.

"All right. Let's say four weeks. Four weeks to create the

sculpture. And let's say four weeks as well for you to explore your submissive side."

An entire month to explore the things she wanted with the man she wanted. It seemed too good to be true.

Catching both her hands in his, Elijah pulled her with him as he moved to the desk. He positioned her as she had been before, the edge of the desk pressing into the soft flesh of her belly, but didn't bind her hands or bend her over.

She yelped when he smacked an open palm over the globe of her ass.

"Answer me."

She forced herself to swallow the retort that was on the tip of her tongue—she would have responded if he'd phrased it as a question. "Yes, Sir." She tried to keep the irritation out of her voice.

"That's a good little cat." Elijah stroked a hand over her spine, and Samantha shivered.

"In this month you will be my submissive in all areas. Is this understood?"

"Is that what you want?" she asked softly. "A full-time submissive?" The research she'd done had told her that some Doms did indeed want someone to be submissive to them twenty-four/seven.

The idea terrified her. She wanted to give up control, but she didn't know if she could do it that fully.

"For the next month, I expect you to be a full-time submissive." Elijah paused, as if measuring his words. "If we decide to continue the relationship beyond that . . ."

Samantha felt her heart skip a beat. He was thinking beyond the next month. Was it possible that this gorgeous, intriguing man wanted her for more than sex?

"If we continue it beyond that . . . then we can discuss new terms. But I expect that the woman I'm with allows me to call the shots and trusts me not to push her further than I know she can go."

Relief was a wave that battered her skin.

"I want a man who will take control, not ask for it," she whispered, and felt his body stiffen behind her. "I've had to be in control for so much of my life. I don't want to do it anymore."

"Samantha." Elijah whispered her name into her hair, stroking a hand over the long braid at the same time. She felt like the little cat that he'd called her beneath the touch.

She gasped when, without warning, he wrapped her braid around his hand and tugged. His other hand pushed roughly between her legs and pressed inside her again, the way he had been only minutes before.

Samantha hissed as he entered her—the rough entry stung. But then he began to crook his fingers inside her once more, pressing against that exact spot in her womb that made the pleasure intensify.

"You are going to come for me *now*," Elijah commanded. Samantha gasped, a high-pitched sound, as the banked sensation returned in an instant, bringing her to the brink again. She realized that she had no choice but to follow his order, her body betraying any semblance of free will that she might have held on to.

The orgasm came hot and hard, a slap in the face that left her weak and wrecked and, impossibly, wanting more.

She whimpered when he pulled his fingers out of her. He drew a soothing hand down her back, then reached for the sundress that she had tossed onto the desk. She watched, dazed, as he bunched the material in his large hands, then pulled it over her head with surprising gentleness.

As if she were nothing more than his doll, he moved her arms through the thin dress straps, pulled her back against him as he smoothed the skirt over her hips.

"Are you okay?" He spoke into her hair, inhaling deeply.

Was he *smelling* her? Was Elijah Masterson, hotel tycoon, actually sniffing her hair after bestowing a massive orgasm on her like magic?

She didn't have the energy to even ask.

A quick squeeze on the hips reminded her that he'd asked a question.

"Yes . . . Sir. Thank you." Samantha drew in a shaky breath as Elijah released her. She watched through suddenly heavy eyes as he opened one of the drawers in his desk and retrieved a slender leather folder.

He opened it, and she saw that it was a checkbook. The sight brought reality crashing down, reminding her of their complicated situation, and she squirmed uncomfortably.

If he noticed, he didn't comment—and Samantha took that to mean that he was giving her a moment to compose herself, since she realized by now that the man missed nothing.

He scribbled on the check, then signed it with a flourish. He passed it in front of her eyes before folding it in half and tucking it into her cleavage.

"I thought the agreement was for half down payment, half on delivery." Samantha eyed him narrowly, wondering what he had up his sleeve.

He smiled benignly, his fingers lingering on the plump swells of her breasts. She shivered beneath the dance of his fingertips.

"Here's another lesson for you. Dominance and submission are about trust," he reminded her, allowing his hands to dip into her dress and play over her nipples. Samantha moaned and pressed into his touch. "That trust goes both ways. Your commission and our other agreement have nothing to do with each other, but I'm using this as an opportunity to demonstrate that trust."

Samantha shivered as he slid his hands out of her dress, over her torso, and around her waist. He leaned forward and nipped at the tender flesh of her earlobe.

"I'm going to enjoy the next month more than you know."

CHAPTER SEVEN

"Las Vegas?"

Samantha shifted on the leather bench seat and tried not to let her disbelief show in her expression. Only a few hours had passed since Elijah had bound her hands with his belt and pleasured her against his desk, but it seemed like a lifetime.

Elijah smiled but said nothing, and she shook her head to clear it, certain that the movement would wake her from the incredible dream that she'd been swimming in for the past hour.

"I'm confused." Samantha eyed him from the corner of her eye. She wasn't entirely sure of what her "complete submission" entailed. Was she allowed to ask him questions?

He didn't frown at her, so she took it as a sign it was okay to continue.

"We are in a limo. This plane is *your* plane. We're going to Las Vegas, to your club and your home. And all I have is the dress I'm wearing."

"Watch your tone," Elijah replied, "or you won't even have that dress."

Samantha gulped. She wasn't sure if he was joking or not.

"I'm sorry, Sir." She had to repress the urge to smile cheekily every time she called him by the title. Somehow she didn't think he would see that as acceptable submissive behavior. "It's all just a little surreal."

His expression softened, and he held out a hand for her. "Come here."

Elijah pulled her into his lap, shifting so that she straddled him. Her skirt hiked up around her hips, and she hissed as her bare pussy pressed against his torso.

"Yes, we're going to Vegas. It's my home, and I find that I very much want to show it to you. I'll have a temporary studio built for you so that you can work. If you're missing anything, all you'll have to do is ask."

I find that I very much want to show it to you. Samantha felt her heartbeat stutter, then speed up. She'd known Elijah for only a few days, but knew she was falling head over heels for him.

If he decided to walk away once the month was over, she'd move on, because that's what she did. But she knew that her heart would break, at least a little.

"You don't have to worry about needing anything. That's my job." Elijah bent his head and pressed a soft kiss to her lips. It was only a whisper of a touch, but it stole her breath.

"Okay." She frowned when a thought occurred to her. "I do need to deposit this check. I need to wire some money to my sister."

"You have a sister?"

She froze as she realized that she'd revealed something about her past. She'd agreed to complete submission, and she intended to honor it—she would answer whatever he asked. But she'd really rather avoid the past altogether.

She felt that it wouldn't break her agreement with Elijah if she concealed some details of her past. As far as she was concerned, some memories were best forgotten entirely.

She had to think that way in order to live some semblance of a normal life.

Elijah was waiting patiently for an answer. Samantha bit her tongue until she tasted blood, then nodded reluctantly.

"Yes. Her name is Beth." She waited for Elijah to ask more questions, but he was silent for a long moment, seemingly content with what she had given him.

She tried to hold back a frown. She couldn't keep up with the man.

A sharp knock sounded on the door to the limo.

"The plane is ready," Elijah said, lifting her gently off his lap. She could see the muscles of his arms rippling even beneath the sleeves of his shirt, and she fully appreciated the view.

Elijah opened the door to the limo, then urged her forward. Samantha felt spectacularly ungraceful as she clasped the proffered hand of the driver standing outside, then tried to clamp her legs together as she exited the limo.

The last thing she wanted was to give the entire tarmac a peep show.

"Roberto—" Elijah nodded to the driver, then pressed a paper bill into his hand. "*Gracias.*"

"Your chariot awaits," he whispered into Samantha's ear as he bent toward her. One hand pressed into the small of her back, urging her forward.

Samantha took a last, somewhat desperate look around at Cabo San Lucas. Mexico had been her refuge for nearly two years, and she hadn't been back to the States since. She had mixed feelings about venturing there now.

Casting a sidelong glance at Elijah, she pondered that. She supposed it was symbolic that she was returning now, as she was stepping into something new.

As if sensing her anxiety, the hand at the small of her back slid to her hip and squeezed. She looked up and caught Elijah smiling down at her, with a look so full of possession that it made her pulse skip.

She couldn't help but smile back.

She didn't have to worry, because Elijah was in control.

Elijah grinned at Samantha's exclamation of surprise when they stepped through the entrance of his private plane.

"Holy smokes." Her voice was full of wonder. "This is yours?"

Over the years as he amassed his fortune, Elijah had acquired a taste for the finer things, and he wasn't ashamed to admit it. But nothing before this had given him as much pleasure as Samantha's expression of surprise over the luxurious surroundings.

They had known each other for only a couple of days, but he found that he cared what she thought. The intensity of his reaction to her was making his head spin.

Mattias, his pilot, stepped from the cockpit of the plane into the spacious sitting room, where he and Samantha stood.

"Samantha, this is Captain Mattias Wright, my private pilot. He'll be flying us to Vegas tonight." The captain saluted, and Elijah watched as Samantha mouthed the words "private pilot."

"It's a pleasure to fly such a beautiful woman." Mattias took Samantha's hand and bent to press a kiss to it. Her mouth parted slightly in surprise, and Elijah knew that she had taken note of the fact that the captain, while at least fifteen years older than her, was a good-looking man.

"Can I get you anything before we take off, Mr. Masterson?" Mattias closed and latched the door with the smooth competence that had impressed Elijah when he'd hired the man. Seeing that Samantha was busy looking around the plane, Mattias turned to his boss and winked with approval.

Elijah felt a flash of jealousy, but not the searing burn he'd experienced when he'd come across Samantha at the club with Angelo. He'd hired Mattias both because of his impeccable flight record and because the man hadn't batted an eyelash when Elijah had told him of some of the things he might see on private flights when Elijah brought a woman on board.

Mattias didn't mean any disrespect. It was an innocent wink. And the man couldn't be blamed for appreciating Samantha's incredible beauty.

"If you wouldn't mind opening some wine, Mattias." A beam of the setting sun outside the plane fell across Samantha's face as Elijah spoke, and he felt that strange twisting around his heart again.

This woman was special. He had to take care with her.

"Anything in particular, Mr. Masterson?" Mattias asked.

Elijah shook his head, his eyes still on Samantha. "Feel free to choose. Thank you, Mattias." The only wines on board would be ones that Elijah appreciated, so he wasn't concerned. The pilot returned to the galley, and Samantha grinned up at Elijah, looking for all the world like a kid in a candy store.

"I can't even believe this." She did a giddy pirouette on the plush carpet, her eyes wide. "I've only ever flown coach. And then only once."

Elijah studied her as he planned out his next move. He knew she was no gold digger—she'd initially refused the amount of money he'd tried to pay her for the sculpture, something no self-respecting social climber would ever have done.

So he was eager to spoil her. When Mattias returned, he took both glasses from the man's hands and handed one to Samantha himself.

"Taste this." He lifted his own glass at the same time that she did, sipping at the ruby liquid in the glass, recognizing the smoke and dark plum and cherry flavors that hit his tongue.

"Harlan Estate Cabernet Sauvignon. Excellent choice." He nodded with approval at his pilot, who nodded back.

"Will there be anything else before we take off, Mr. Masterson?"

"As a matter of fact—" Elijah sipped again, looking at Samantha over the rim of his glass as she sipped. "How is it?" he asked her. She ran her tongue delicately over her lips, and he felt his cock begin to pay attention.

"It's the best wine I've ever tasted," she answered simply, staring at the glass as if it held the secrets of the universe. "I— I'm not sure I can get used to this kind of thing."

Elijah knew that she was referring to his wealth, but the moment was as good as any for transitioning to what he had planned next. He cast a quick glance at his pilot, and couldn't miss the gleam in the man's eyes.

"I'd better distract you, then." Nipping her glass from her fingers, Elijah set it on one of the mahogany coffee tables that dotted the massive cabin.

"Take off your dress."

Samantha looked at him sharply, as if she hadn't heard him properly.

"What?" Her voice was incredulous.

"Did you not understand me?" Elijah felt the rush of blood that came when he started breaking in a new submissive. It was a mix of pleasure, of anticipation, a hint of that heady, almost indescribable rush that came when he and a submissive entered their own little world.

Samantha didn't question him again and he was proud of her for that. It was very bad manners to question your Dom in front of others. But she looked at him, looked at Mattias, then looked back at him.

She was wavering; he could see it in her eyes. Again Elijah

wondered just how far she would take her submission, because no matter what she claimed she wanted, she hadn't experienced enough of the lifestyle to show a true commitment to it.

Pride was a rush to his head when she clasped the hem of her sundress in her hands. He watched those same hands tremble a bit as she slowly raised the dress up, revealing her long, shapely legs, the swell of her hips, the curve of her belly.

Her breasts came into view, and then her dress was off. She clutched it in front of herself, a shield, then tossed the dress down in front of him.

"Are you happy now?" she asked. More than anger, Elijah heard the tremble of fear in her words. Unlike his ex-wife, she wasn't acting up simply for the attention—he could see that she was genuinely unnerved. As a Dom he enjoyed pushing a sub's boundaries, because that was what was most needed. But it was his duty to show them why he did as he did.

"Take your hair out of your braid. I want to see it loose. And I will be happy when you obey my orders with my pleasure in mind." Samantha frowned but pulled the elastic from her braid, combing her fingers through the long plait until it hung loose in thick waves.

Stepping forward, Elijah gave her body a leisurely perusal, then cupped her breasts in his palms.

"Elijah," Samantha squeaked, and though he thought the sound was about the cutest thing he'd ever heard, he refrained from smiling. He needed to teach her how she should behave with him for this to work between them.

He silenced her with a stern look.

"You offered me a month of complete submission. Are you reneging?"

There, he thought. There was her Achilles' heel—her pride. Her honor.

She would do what she had said she would, or would at least try her very best.

"No," she replied as boldly as she could. "I'm not reneging."

They would have to work on her tone, but right at the moment Elijah found that he was enjoying her fire.

"Good." He rubbed his thumbs over her nipples, watched her eyes blur even as she struggled to look over his shoulder at Mattias, to see if the other man was watching.

Elijah knew that Mattias's eyes would be fixed on Samantha, just as his own were. She was absolutely stunning.

"I'm pleased that you obeyed my order. But I'm not happy about the way in which you did it." He pinched her nipples, watched her jerk from the touch, noted that her breath didn't seem to come any faster.

It confirmed his suspicions that pain wasn't big on her list of kinks. That was fine. He could take it or leave it himself.

"You need to be disciplined. And since you displayed attitude in front of the captain here, I think I will allow him to administer your punishment."

Samantha's eyes widened as she sucked in a great mouthful of air and looked up at him with wide eyes. She again looked at Mattias, then at Elijah, and he could see her nervousness in the visible tension in her muscles.

He also noted the way that her nipples puckered. Her mind may have rejected the notion, but her body did not.

"Mattias, you have five minutes. In those five minutes you have full access to Samantha's breasts. You may do whatever you wish to them." He stepped back and gestured the other man forward. "And I intend to watch."

"Elijah!" Samantha cried out. "You can't be serious!"

In two steps he was in front of her, one hand held tightly at her waist. The other he plunged between her legs, rubbing through folds that he found slick and ready, just as he had expected they would be.

He plunged his fingers in and out of her slick chasm several times, causing her knees to buckle and a small cry to leave her lips. Then, once he had her attention completely, he withdrew his hand, holding it in front of her face.

Her slickness shone on the tips, and he could smell her, the scent inviting him to bend her over one of the couches scattered throughout the sitting area and to plunge between her ready thighs.

She wasn't ready for that. Not yet.

"I'm going to go easy on you for now, because you're very, very new to this." He kept his voice quiet, but knew that his confidence and dominant nature rang out in his voice. "But if you continue to speak to me in this manner—if you continue to question me—you will be punished."

He watched as her defiance wavered.

"Punished how?" she asked warily. Though he pushed the thought to the back of his mind, he wondered again why her questioning wasn't angering him. Rather, he just wanted to delve deeper, suspecting that if she submitted in the end it would be the most beautiful thing he'd ever experienced. "Like . . . a spanking?"

Elijah felt his lips twitch, but he swallowed his smile.

"No, I don't think I'll use a spanking." He studied Samantha, letting his stare linger on the glistening curls between her legs. She might have been acting out with nerves, but she was thoroughly aroused.

He decided on her punishment. "If you question me again, you will give Mattias a blow job."

Samantha's entire body tensed and her mouth fell open. It was a reminder to him of *exactly* how new she was to the kind of life he lived, but if he backed down it would be a disservice to them both.

He saw her swallow hard, her eyes sparkling. He waited for what he thought was her inevitable protest.

He was very surprised, and very pleased, when she snapped her jaw shut and nodded stiffly, casting her eyes down to the ground.

Maybe this was what drew him so much. She was inexperienced, and she had a temper that made it hard for her to submit, but she was determined. She knew what she wanted, and she was going after it.

"You will enjoy what Mattias does to you as if I was the one touching you." Releasing Samantha completely, Elijah stepped back and allowed the other man to take his place. "You do not have a say in whether this happens or not, not unless you use your safe word. Your body is pleased by the idea, and I will be pleased by your acquiescence."

He didn't spell it out any further, knowing that she was quite capable of making that last connection on her own.

You can feel free to enjoy this, because I have given you permission, he thought.

Samantha opened her mouth as if to speak, then closed it, and Elijah felt a surge of triumph. Seating himself on one of the sofas, he shifted until his erection was as comfortable as it could be while trapped in his pants and watched as Mattias raised his hands to Samantha's naked breasts.

"Don't feel the need to keep quiet on my account," his pilot said, grinning as he stroked his fingers over Samantha's pale skin. "If you want to protest, I sure don't mind delaying our flight for your punishment."

"Oh!" An unintelligible sound escaped Samantha's lips when the older man's hands began to massage her flesh. She stood completely still, though Elijah could see her muscles trembling with the effort of doing so.

"Beautiful," Mattias said reverently. Elijah knew that the man wasn't at all dominant, didn't participate in the lifestyle at all, but he clearly enjoyed having a willing woman in front of him to play with.

Samantha cast a nervous look at Elijah as her nipples hardened and contracted. He understood that she was asking for reassurance that she was allowed to enjoy this, and he was happy that she thought to look to him already.

"It's a heady thing for a man to see another man wanting what is his," Elijah spoke quietly, watching as Mattias lowered his mouth to one of Samantha's nipples and her hips rocked forward just the tiniest bit. "And you are mine. Your body is mine. I can do whatever I want with it. All you can do is enjoy it . . . or not."

As if his words threw open a floodgate, Samantha threw her head back with a moan, then threaded her fingers through Mattias's hair. Elijah had to stifle a laugh as she pulled a bit too vigorously and the other man hissed at the sting.

"Sorry." Samantha eased her touch, but arched her back to allow Mattias better access to her breasts. The man chuckled around a mouthful of her flesh, kneading the breast that wasn't suckled into his mouth with long fingers.

"Don't apologize." Mattias sounded breathless. Elijah knew how he felt. "This is the best job perk I can imagine."

Samantha nodded, then closed her eyes. Elijah watched, entranced, as the pleasure played over her face. Her hips shifted restlessly, and he knew that she felt empty, wanted to be filled.

He wanted to be the one to fill her, and soon. Yes, very soon . . . but not quite yet.

"Time's up."

Both Samantha and Mattias moaned as the captain pulled his mouth away from her nipple with a wet sound of suction.

The captain wiped his mouth with the back of his hand, then looked over at Elijah. "Thanks," he said. Unembarrassed, the man reached into the waist of his slacks and adjusted his obvious erection. He groaned ruefully. "It's going to be a long flight."

"Thank you, Mattias." Elijah nodded at the other man with sincere thanks. He was more than aware of how hard it was to walk away from this woman.

"Anytime. I mean it." With a nod Mattias disappeared through the cockpit door. "Get seated and fasten your seat belts, please. We're preparing for takeoff."

"Noted." Elijah waited until Mattias had closed the door behind him before turning to Samantha. Her skin was flushed a beautiful shade of pink, her nipples swollen and damp from Mattias's attentions.

He wanted her so badly he had to fist his hands to keep from touching her. But he needed her to see that her submission was not ultimately about his carnal satisfaction.

At least not always.

"Come here." He seated himself again on the couch, pulling out and fastening the hidden seat belt.

Warily Samantha approached him. The closer she came, the more potent her smell of musky arousal became.

Elijah's mouth watered with the need to taste.

"Sit down." He patted the seat cushion behind him, loosening the seat belt. Samantha cast him a forlorn look.

"May I put my dress back on?" She looked so cute that he was tempted to allow her to do just that.

But he wanted her naked and accessible to him. And more than that, he wanted her to be aware that all he had to do in order to have her was to reach out next to him.

"No." He waited, patiently, as she huffed out a breath and seated herself beside him. Her fists clenched, then released, as if she wasn't quite sure what to do with them.

"Hold still." Elijah fastened the seat belt over her naked flesh, then reached for the blanket that hung over the back of the sofa. He tucked it over her body.

He mourned the fact that he could no longer see her naked skin, but if she caught a chill it would be his fault.

Once she was tucked in, Elijah reached for his laptop, then settled back in his seat. He powered on the computer and prepared to get some work done, though he was hyperaware of Samantha pressed against his side.

"Um . . . now what? Sir," she added hastily when she caught his raised eyebrow.

"Now I simply want you next to me as I work." What he really wanted . . . no. He couldn't think about what he really wanted, or he wouldn't be able to hold out for even another minute. She'd given herself to him, true enough, but he sensed she needed some time to think about what had just happened. "You will drink your wine and relax."

He stroked a hand over a lock of her curly hair, then pressed a kiss to her temple. He caught her puzzled glance as he turned back to his computer, and hid his own answering smile.

That she didn't truly expect to be cherished made doing it all the more pleasurable. And though she couldn't know it, they had only just begun.

CHAPTER EIGHT

S amantha awoke in the dark, sleep clinging to her thoughts like delicate cobwebs, and a wave of pleasure driving deep between her thighs like a tornado.

"Oh my God!" She struggled to sit up, to gather her thoughts, and found that she couldn't.

Her arms were handcuffed to something above her head. And the sensation between her legs overwhelmed everything else.

"Have a good sleep, little cat?" She recognized Elijah's voice instantly, though she couldn't see him in the black of the room.

"Oh . . . oh!" The vibrations between her legs increased, driving her higher still. Her hips bucked and she pulled at the handcuffs, reaching for something, something she needed more than her next breath.

"Don't fight it. You're going to come for me. It's not your choice." Elijah's voice was to one side of her, and she surmised that he was sitting or standing next to the bed she was lying on—and it was a bed, because she could feel the softness of a pillow caressing her face, the mattress bending beneath her movements.

She felt a hand slide between her legs, driving the vibrator deeper. Elijah pushed the device in, then pulled it out nearly all the way, causing Samantha to dig her heels into the bed and thrust up with her hips.

"Now!" Elijah pushed the vibrator in to the hilt, and the sensations vibrated throughout Samantha's womb. The tidal wave started in the tips of her toes, rolling over in a crescendo that she was powerless to stop. She thought she might have screamed, but couldn't have been sure, she was so lost in the sensations.

When the tremors finally subsided, Samantha found that the vibrator had been removed from between her legs, and she felt strangely bereft without it. A light began to glow in the room, increasing in brightness. She turned her head, blinking, to find Elijah with his hand on a dimmer switch.

He was entirely naked, his cock swollen to what looked like the point of pain, and Samantha felt her mouth go dry at the sight.

"You come so prettily, little cat." He stood still, seeming to understand that she wanted to look at him—at all of him. "I think you need to do so again."

Though she was still trembling from the orgasm that had started before she'd even been fully awake, Samantha felt her hunger grow as she looked at the magnificence that was Elijah Masterson naked.

"You're beautiful." She cringed as soon as she said it, because she didn't know any men who would appreciate being called beautiful.

Elijah, though—Elijah just smiled and stood still, letting her look.

The soft golden light made his gilded hair gleam. The hair, combined with those cobalt eyes and lush lips, lent him the image of an angel. But she knew by now that he was capable of all kinds of dark, devilish things.

His body backed up that claim. Surely an angel wouldn't have a body that was made for sin. Her eyes raked over his strong, wide shoulders, the rock-solid chest, the arms that looked like he could lift her without even a hitch in his stride. One of those arms was ringed with a tattoo, dark ink etched in some sort of tribal design, and Samantha wanted nothing more in that instant than to run her tongue over the lines.

His stomach was flat, the slant of his hip bones the sexiest thing she had ever seen. His legs were solidly muscled and dusted with golden hair.

In the middle of it all, his cock rose up, long and thick and impossibly hard. Her eyes widened a bit even as she sucked in a breath of anticipation.

He was huge, something that hadn't fully registered with her when they'd had sex before—it had all happened too fast.

"Holy hell." Her stare flicked up to his face, where his lips had twisted into a hint of a smile, then back down to his cock.

Elijah laughed then, startling her with the great roar of sound. She looked up at him with wide eyes as he moved toward the bed, his intent clear on his face.

Instead of simply parting her thighs and entering her, the way she expected him to, Elijah bent and trailed a series of quick kisses up the inside of Samantha's thigh. The press of his lips felt like the flutter of butterfly wings, and she shifted restlessly, wanting more.

"I can't hold back any longer." He slid his lips from her thigh to her belly, swiping across the skin with his tongue. "I have to be inside you. I have to have you."

Samantha nodded her head with breathless assent as he trailed those frustratingly light kisses over the soft skin of her belly. She was wet and ready, and felt so empty that she ached.

Again, when she expected him to plunge inside her, he did the unexpected. Ranging his long body over hers, he settled his elbows on either side of her face and looked down at her.

"The papers you filled out at Pecado said you aren't on any form of birth control. Is that the case?"

Samantha arched her hips, felt the coarse rub of his pubic hair against her damp lower lips, and whimpered.

"Yes. I mean no—no, I'm not on anything." Oh, she couldn't *think* when he was on top of her like this, when his hot skin was pressed to hers, when all he had to do was shift his hips to take her, and she wouldn't be able to do anything about it.

"We'll use a condom." With one hand he stroked down the side of her face, and with the other he reached over to the small bedside table, returning with a condom in hand.

"Bite down." He pressed the edge of it against her lips. Samantha took the edge of the wrapper in her teeth and he tugged against the force with his fingers. The foil wrapper ripped, and Samantha smelled latex as he removed the condom carefully.

"Next time you'll put this on me," Elijah promised, and Samantha flushed at the thought of such an intimate act. "I wish I could be inside you raw. I want to mark you as mine."

The image was so primal, so erotic, that Samantha felt yet another surge of moisture wet her lower lips. She arched up against him, tugging at the cuffs that bound her to the bed.

"Please." She licked her tongue over suddenly dry lips. "I need . . . more of you."

Elijah settled back on his heels, and she watched through heavily lidded eyes as he rolled the sheath of latex over his erection. Watching his fingers on his own cock was the hottest thing she'd ever seen.

"Open for me," he said as he lay back down on top of her. Strong fingers parted her thighs, and then his hardness was pressed against the entrance to her slick heat.

Samantha cried out when the head of his cock breached her entrance.

"You're so fucking tight." Elijah groaned as Samantha thrashed beneath him. "God, I can already feel your pussy milking me and I'm barely in."

"More!" His dirty words had sent Samantha's need into

overdrive. She bucked her hips, widened her legs, invited him to seat himself, hard.

Instead he chuckled and slid in another leisurely fraction of an inch.

"You're going to come for me one more time," Elijah promised, stretching her just a little bit more. Beneath him Samantha panted, trembling with her desire.

Elijah groaned as he slid in farther, then farther still. Samantha felt a deep ache when he was nearly all the way in, her tight flesh protesting against the massive intrusion, and she cried out as her hips pulled back from the discomfort.

"Open for me, little cat." Elijah nudged forward, then pulled back. Forward, then back. Finally her muscles relaxed, opening the rest of the way, and he slid home, sheathed to the root in her pussy.

"Oh my God," Samantha whispered. She felt more than full. She felt like he had claimed her entirely, and she could do nothing but absorb the pleasure that he gave her.

"So. Fucking. Tight." Elijah pulled back, then again thrust forward until his hip bones pressed into her stomach.

Samantha closed her eyes to keep them from rolling back in her head.

"So. Hot." Each of his thrusts was so incredibly controlled that Samantha felt ready to scream. She wanted him to pound into her, to make the pace match the insanity that was swirling inside her.

He continued in that manner, that slow, thorough possession, until Samantha was a limp, quivering mass beneath him.

When he paused, she opened her eyes, seeing the world through the blurry haze of pleasure.

"Come for me, Samantha." Reaching between their bodies, Elijah caught her clit between his thumb and forefinger. Her eyes flew open and she screamed as all of the banked pleasure rushed to that one square inch of flesh at his touch, pulling back then rising up in a tidal wave that slapped her in the face.

"Keep your eyes on me," Elijah commanded as she shuddered. Finally, *finally*, he began to move faster, driving into her with strong, heated strokes, prolonging her orgasm until he finally seated himself one final time, sinking so deeply into her that she cried out, the force as he emptied himself inside her tinged with pleasure/pain.

As their tremors began to subside and Samantha tried desperately to catch her breath, Elijah reached above her head and undid the bracelets of her handcuffs. He caught one of her hands in each of his, his fingers rubbing over flesh that had gone slightly numb as he trapped her between his muscled thighs and rolled, settling on his back with her on top of him.

She knew she should say something, and yet her mind was blank, emptied of everything but bliss and comfort.

"Sleep now, little cat." Elijah wrapped her in his arms as he tugged the covers over their bodies. His hands stroked over her disheveled braid, down the curve of her spine, and she did indeed feel deliciously feline as he petted her, soothing the nerves that were still firing.

"Sleep." His voice was like a snifter of rum, she thought, warming and delicious.

It was her last thought before she succumbed to sleep, just as he had commanded.

"Wake up, sleepyhead." Elijah's voice cut through Samantha's luxurious dream. She cracked open her eyes, squinted as he flicked on the light in the plane's bedroom.

"Wha—?" Samantha grunted, trying to close her eyes again. She yelped when chilly air hit her skin.

She rolled over, glaring up at Elijah, who grinned down at her, the bedcovers in his hands.

"We'll be landing soon." His gaze raked unashamedly over her naked frame. Though his stare very much reminded her that she was bare to his eyes, she found, strangely, that she didn't want to cover up.

He had claimed her body, both with words and in the most primal way. It was strangely . . . freeing.

"I've laid out clothing for you." Elijah gestured to the bureau that sat across the room. "You will wear these items and nothing else. You are welcome to shower, and will find everything you need in the bathroom."

"How come you're so perky?" Blearily Samantha rubbed her eyes. She was exhausted, despite having just had a nap.

Elijah's genial expression faded, and he scowled down at her.

"Because I get a decent night's sleep every night. I also eat properly. And exercise." Again his stare raked over her, but this time there was no heat in his gaze. "While we are together, you will make sure you sleep and eat in a sensible fashion. Understood?"

"Will you make me exercise, too?" She kept her voice sweet, but mentally she was calculating how long it would take him to recover if she kneed him in the testicles.

Said testicles were now fully covered, sadly. She didn't think she'd ever find another sight as amazing as Elijah in the buff.

Though the black leather pants and plain white T-shirt that he'd pulled on over that glorious skin . . . *yum*.

"Oh, you'll exercise." Elijah pinned her with a sexy stare and then, without warning, fisted his hands in her hair and pulled her to him for a kiss. This wasn't any soft brush of the lips, but a scorching melding that branded her skin and left her panting.

"But the exercise will be of the carnal variety." Elijah's lips curled up in a cocky grin as he released her. Samantha swallowed hard, her fingers straying to lips that now felt swollen.

"I'm going to fix you something to eat. You will be showered, dressed, and in the sitting room to eat what I have made you in twenty minutes." Catching Samantha's wrists in one hand, he tugged her to her feet, then leaned in close to whisper in her ear. "Don't be late. I'm not sure Captain Mattias could handle another punishment."

And then he was gone, leaving Samantha staring after him, openmouthed.

I'm not sure Captain Mattias could handle another punishment.

"I'm not sure I could, either," Samantha said to herself, then hurried into the bathroom, her skin flushing at the memory.

The feel of another man's hands on her body had been deliciously taboo. She'd been scared at first that it had been some kind of test—that Elijah wanted her to hold her desire in check for anyone but himself.

But he'd given her permission to enjoy it. And with those words, it was as if it had been *his* hands on her body, stroking her skin, suckling her nipples.

Though she'd already come twice that afternoon, Samantha felt another surge of heat to the tender space between her legs.

"Good grief." Hastily she ran a brush through the hair that had tangled as she slept. She braided it tightly, then splashed cold water on her face, hoping it would snap her out of the lust-filled haze in which she was currently floating.

It didn't really help, but it did make her feel a bit more awake.

Next were the clothes that Elijah had laid out for her.

"Oh, hell no." Samantha cringed as she picked up the first

item. She was pretty sure it was called a bustier, a confection of crisscrossing straps and lace.

It was also almost the exact same shade of green as the sculpture that had brought her into Elijah's life. Considering how observant he was, she knew that that wasn't an accident.

"That's kind of sweet," she murmured under her breath as she tried to figure out how to get into the contraption.

Intensive searching revealed a zipper hidden down the side. She sighed with relief, then slid into the garment.

Samantha dared a glance in the mirror once she had added the short, tight skirt in a matching shade of green and the black boots that covered her all the way up to midthigh.

She was startled by what she saw. She'd never been the kind of woman to pay much attention to how she looked—in fact, for many years she'd done her very best to downplay any of her physical assets.

But right in that moment, in the clothing that Elijah had chosen for her, she felt attractive. Sexy, even.

In the past she had avoided dressing to look that way, afraid of feeling as though she had deserved what had happened to her.

But she hadn't chosen to dress this way—she had donned these clothes to please Elijah.

It was satisfying in a way that she had never before considered.

Look out, Elijah. It was with a decided sway to her hips that she left the bedroom and entered the sitting room. The swagger disappeared the moment she saw the golden-haired man, the moment those blue eyes fixed on her.

Devoured her.

"You look lovely," he said warmly. She was startled when he rose from his seat and held his hands out for her. His gaze made her acutely aware that he'd now seen every last bit of her ... and that she wasn't wearing any underwear.

"Thank you." She took his hands, trying not to squirm as he looked her up and down.

"You didn't shower." His voice was inquisitive, not angry, but Samantha still found herself squirming.

"Uh, no. I didn't." Hoping to change the subject, she looked over his shoulder to the coffee table, where he had set a plate with two lopsided sandwiches and a bottle of water. "You made me a sandwich. Thank you."

"Samantha." Clasping her chin in his fingers, Elijah pulled until she had no choice but to look right at him. She sighed internally, just beginning to understand that this man had an attention span like nothing she'd ever encountered before.

"Why didn't you shower, Samantha?" She cringed inwardly as she tried to find a way to escape the question. Elijah waited, still as a statue, her chin clasped in his fingers.

Finally she huffed out an impatient sigh.

"I didn't ... I didn't want to wash you off of me." She winced as the words hit her own ears. *Oh, that sounds so incredibly needy and lame.*

"You didn't want to wash me off of you?" Elijah repeated her words, disbelief coloring his voice.

She nodded, casting her stare to the floor.

Before she could even inhale her next breath, he had gathered her up in his arms and she found herself with her legs around his waist. His hands were cupped beneath her ass, pressing her naked, tender pussy into the front of his leather pants as he consumed her in another of those hot, hard kisses that stole her breath away.

When he pulled back, she stared at him in confusion.

"What was that for?" she asked, hearing the tremble in her own voice.

"You please me." Elijah smiled down at her, but she saw something more in the depths of his eyes—something he didn't seem willing to share with her.

Though curiosity clawed at her, she didn't press. She had secrets of her own.

Then Mattias's voice sounded over the intercom, interrupting the intimacy of the moment. "Mr. Masterson, Miss Collins, we're beginning our descent into Las Vegas. If you would please have a seat and fasten your seat belts, it would be greatly appreciated."

The man's voice was a reminder to Samantha of how his mouth had felt on her breasts.

Of the look on Elijah's face as he watched.

"What happens now?" Samantha turned to Elijah as they sat on the couch. As before, he buckled her in himself, as if he needed to make sure that she was safe.

Her short skirt rode up as she curled her legs beneath her, and Elijah's eyes immediately found the pale skin that was revealed.

He turned to her and grinned, then ran a finger over the newly naked skin with a touch so light yet so sensual that she shuddered.

"Now you're going to eat your sandwich. Then we're going to In Vino Veritas."

CHAPTER NINE

The Vegas club was nothing like Samantha had expected. Rather than the neon lights and pulsing music she'd seen outside Pecado, In Vino Veritas looked more like a large, sedate house. The only clue that it was anything more than a personal residence was the long, curving drive in front of it and the dreadlocked man who took keys and greeted those arriving.

Elijah had told Samantha a bit about the club once they were cozily ensconced in the limo that had driven all the way onto the tarmac to collect them at the airport. But she was having trouble getting her mind around the fact that he owned a chain of resorts in Mexico and another club here.

She said so, and Elijah cast her a sidelong glance.

"I own a lot of things, Samantha." His thumb stroked over the sensitive skin behind her knee, and she had to struggle to stay focused.

"You own a lot of things, or you own a lot of places?" She suspected it was a little of both. The man owned his own luxurious private jet after all.

"Well . . . both." Elijah turned fully then, catching one of Samantha's hands in his own. "What is it about wealth that makes you so twitchy?"

Samantha felt her body stiffen. She shouldn't have been surprised that he'd noticed, because the man had eyes in the back of his head, but it still made her nervous.

Elijah wasn't the type to appreciate secrets; she knew that

about him already. He wouldn't be impressed by the fact that she'd embarked on this kind of relationship with him while keeping part of her past hidden inside.

She'd just have to make sure he never knew.

"Oh, I'm just not used to it, that's all." Though it wasn't the entire truth, Samantha wasn't lying. Her mother had had plenty of wealthy lovers, but those lovers had never felt the need to take care of her children. In fact, most of them had seemed to prefer pretending that Gemma Collins didn't *have* two young daughters who needed clothing, food, and, more than anything, their mother's attention.

Samantha shook her head as if to clear it. She was not her mother, chasing after fantastically wealthy men who were already married and would never take her as more than a mistress. And Elijah was not one of those men, immune to her needs and desires.

The comparison still made her twitchy, but she pushed it out of her mind. She wasn't going to deny herself something that she wanted so badly simply because her mother had made poor choices.

"You're not telling me everything, little cat." Elijah pinned her with that stare again, and Samantha felt his eyes stripping away the defenses she'd blocked up around herself over the years.

She opened her mouth to deny it, then snapped her jaw shut again. She wasn't going to lie to the man—that wasn't fair.

But she wasn't going to share more than she figured he needed to know.

"I'll let it go for now, Samantha." His voice was steady, but his tone sent a frisson of anxiety through her. "But only for now. We have a lot of work to do together, you and I, and I know that I can't expect your complete trust yet. But I will earn it. Don't imagine that you're off the hook forever, because you're not.

Part of the complete submission that we agreed on means that when I ask you a question, you answer honestly . . . and you give me the entire answer."

Samantha found that her desire was making her defensive. "I asked you if you own a lot of things or places, and you certainly didn't give me a list." She was indignant—it wasn't fair for her to be judged by one set of rules and Elijah by another.

To her relief, Elijah threw back his head and laughed, which lifted some of her tension. His question was deflected . . . for now.

"All right, then. I own a chain of resorts. I own a few shopping malls and some hotels. I have stakes in various other businesses, buying and selling them as they interest me. These include but aren't limited to a line of natural soaps, a video game company in Japan, and a company that produces cloth diapers."

Samantha's mouth fell open as the list continued. She barely noticed when the door to the limo opened and the dreadlocked man outside held out a hand for her.

"There's also In Vino Veritas, of course, which, as I've told you, is the business closest to my heart. Right, Julien?" Pinching her on her ass under the miniskirt, Elijah urged her forward and out of the car. She stumbled from the low-slung vehicle rather than making the graceful exit she'd been hoping for, thanks to the extremely short skirt and the sky-high boots.

The man Elijah had called Julien pretended not to notice, righting Samantha with one smooth movement and grinning at Elijah as he did so.

"Damn glad you're back, you lazy-ass," Julien said.

Samantha blinked, sure that Elijah was going to throw a punch, or at the very least verbally slap down the other man. On the surface Elijah was easygoing, but Samantha had learned quite quickly that beneath the amiable top layer was a core of steel.

"Alex and Luca running the place to the ground already, are they?" Elijah snickered as he exited the limo behind Samantha. "Figured. I'm clearly the alpha dog here."

Julien quirked his lips, stuffing his hands into his pockets as he did so. "I'm not touching that one with another Dom's dick," he started, rocking back on his heels and eyeing Samantha with interest. "Pretty new sub, E. Where'd you find her?"

"Mexico." Elijah clasped his hands around her waist, the touch light but decidedly territorial. Samantha eyed the other man curiously, noting that he carried himself with the same bearing that she'd noted in Elijah and Angelo.

"If you dared to look at me so boldly inside the club, sub, I'd ask Elijah for permission to lock you into the stocks." Julien spoke mildly, but his words sent shock waves through Samantha. She looked at the floor so quickly that she felt her neck muscles protest.

Elijah chuckled softly, but she felt his hands squeeze her around the waist with reassurance. No one was going to be locking her in the stocks, which was good, in case they turned out to be exactly what they sounded like.

"Did you get the studio built?" Elijah asked. Samantha heard another car approach, tires crunching on the ground, and had to fight the impulse to look up.

"I did." Samantha watched Julien's feet, clad in slick black leather shoes, as he accepted the keys from the people who were noisily exiting the next vehicle. "And Luca is dying to tell you how pussywhipped he thinks you are for doing it."

"Shut up, Julien. Hello, Angie, Charlotte," Elijah said, greeting the new arrivals, who, based on the sky-high high heels that came into view, were clearly female, and likely subs. "Good to see you."

Samantha felt a surge of jealousy, which she knew was irrational, given that Elijah was here with her, his hands banded around her waist.

She didn't like the feminine giggles that followed.

"Master Elijah," one of the voices cooed in a sugar-sweet tone that made Samantha grind her teeth. Growing up, she'd given Beth hell during the one occasion that her sister had decided to try out the role of silly girl.

"Oh, you have a sub with you tonight. I was hoping you might let me serve you this evening," one of the women said. A sleek blonde with legs that seemed to go on forever dropped to her knees at Elijah's feet, putting her in Samantha's view. "If you bore of this submissive, I hope that you will seek me out."

The woman took the time to send a nasty glance Samantha's way, hiding it from Elijah behind the curtain of her perfect hair. She then looked down at the ground, her expression nothing but sweetness and light, the picture of a perfect submissive.

Samantha saw red. The woman had spoken about her as if she didn't matter. Even the Doms she had met, while bossy, treated her with more respect.

"He doesn't need you, you bleached bottle blond bitch. He has me," she murmured.

To hell with the rules. Samantha fisted her hands on her hips and glared down at the other woman. *The nerve!* she fumed. She couldn't blame the woman for trying—Elijah was, well, Elijah. But she was right *here*!

She looked over her shoulder and caught Elijah's stunned expression, then registered Julien's howl of laughter. The other submissive looked up at her, anger painted all over her face.

"Got yourself a guard dog, do you, E?" Wrinkling his nose at the woman on the ground, Julien caught one of Samantha's hands in his and pressed a kiss to her palm. "We haven't been properly introduced, little sub. I'm Julien Knight. I'm the manager of In Vino Veritas, and Elijah's right-hand man. And if you come to your senses and leave him, make sure you come straight to me."

Flustered, embarrassed, Samantha took a quick glance around before letting her eyes fall to the floor. The blond woman was still glaring at her, and the woman's friend, a gorgeous creature with a long fall of dark curls, looked mortified.

Elijah's expression was inscrutable, and it was fixed on Samantha.

"Charlotte, you are dismissed," he said to the nasty blonde, keeping his eyes on Samantha the whole time, which lifted Samantha's spirits. "I want you to find Master Luca once you go inside. Tell him that you have been very rude to my sub, and ask him to punish you however he sees fit."

Charlotte's eyes widened and she shook her head, her mouth open, to protest.

Elijah lifted a hand in warning. "Don't make it worse," he said quietly. "Now go."

Charlotte rose and turned toward her friend, but not before she managed to send another glare at Samantha. Samantha found herself shaken, though not because of anything Charlotte had done.

She'd faced worse.

No, she was startled by the depth of her own reaction. She'd acted before thinking, something entirely out of character for her.

It was something to ponder later. Right now she would worry about how Elijah would respond to her boldness.

"You make me very happy, little cat." Relief washed over her as Elijah enfolded her in his arms and nuzzled the side of her neck. "Not a dog, though, I don't think. No, I have my own personal guard pussycat. I like it."

Sliding his hands down until their fingers were entwined, he pressed a kiss to the side of Samantha's head. She looked up at him with astonishment, and he winked at her.

"Julien, if you could arrange for our bags to be taken up,

please. And stay away from my woman. If I'm 'pussywhipped,' as you say, then I should at least get her all to myself."

Julien chuckled as Elijah tugged Samantha toward the front door of the club.

"Come, Sammie Cat. I find that I want to play."

Samantha followed Elijah through a heavy but fairly innocuous-looking door and into a Gothic wonderland.

The entryway was dim, lit by sconces that glowed warmly down the length of the walls. The furniture was masculine in its colors and lines, but still invited a person to sit down—to lie down—and enjoy.

"You need something here." The artist in Samantha would have placed a large sculpture right in the entryway, a sinuous twist of glass that only hinted at the pleasure that could be found in the depths of the club. "Art of some kind."

"Is that your professional opinion?" She caught the eyebrow that Elijah raised in her direction and blushed. First she'd initiated that embarrassing display outside, and now she was telling him how to decorate his club. What would come out of her mouth next?

"I'm sorry . . . Sir," Samantha mumbled, looking at her feet. Her words, though, had reminded her of the sculpture that Elijah had already written her a check for. The one that she didn't feel quite right cashing, because, as separate as they had decided their agreements were, she found that she had more feelings for this man than she had ever intended. "Sir, where am I supposed to work when I'm here?"

She was slightly embarrassed that she hadn't thought about that yet. But Elijah seemed to delight in keeping her decidedly off balance, and she hadn't thought of much besides him since he'd swept her onto his plane in Cabo.

Elijah stopped abruptly, turning and facing her. He placed his hands under her elbows and lifted her right off her feet, startling a squeak from her.

"Samantha, you don't have to apologize for stating an opinion. Unless I've told you otherwise, I want to hear what you have to say. You fascinate me. I'm not interested in a submissive who is little more than a mannequin."

Samantha trembled. She wasn't about to admit it, because she was pretty sure that feminists everywhere would groan, but the fact that Elijah had just literally swept her off her feet was making her want him . . . *bad*.

"I had a hard enough time getting you to agree to this one commission." He leaned forward, swept his lips over hers in a soft kiss. She was glad he was holding her up, because the gentleness of the touch made her weak in the knees.

"Making a piece for In Vino Veritas would be *my* choice." Samantha planted her feet once Elijah put her down, having already resolved to do it.

"We'll see." Bending, Elijah pressed a kiss to her temple, then urged her ahead of him. "Come on. Let's go get a drink."

Unsure how to take his words, Samantha allowed herself to be nudged forward. *We'll see?* What did that mean exactly? Did he not actually like her work? Was this commission really just an elaborate ploy to . . . Well, she wasn't quite sure.

They passed through an open, arched doorway, and Samantha forgot all about it.

"Welcome to In Vino Veritas, the wine bar." There was a layer of pride to Elijah's words, and Samantha could easily see why. This was clearly not the area of the club where most of the play happened, but it took her breath away in another way entirely.

The room was . . . *opulent*. That was the word that immediately came to mind. Fantastic.

Rich.

None of the tables and chairs matched, though each was some form of black and gold, and as a whole they formed a cohesive picture. They were arranged in a way that looked accidental but Samantha knew had likely required a great deal of planning.

Long strings of golden lights tangled on the ceiling like vines, their light absorbed by the midnight black of the cloths that covered the tables.

The bar, formed from a slab of dark wood, stretched the entire length of the room. It had been polished to a shine and reflected the rows of golden wineglasses that hung upside down above it.

But the most stunning thing about the room was the wine. Semihidden behind walls of pale gray glass, it turned function into art.

"It's gorgeous, Elijah." She started forward, fingers outstretched, entranced by the sight of all the bottles in various shapes and colors behind the glass. Her mind began to whirl, thinking of what she could do with the concept. Wine bottles, whole or partially melted. Combined with her own colorless glass.

The possibilities were endless, and her fingers itched to go to her melting furnace.

Elijah chuckled, breaking her out of her trance.

"You can come back here tomorrow and study this all you want." He reached out and traced the tips of his fingers over the swells of her breasts, and she felt her nipples peak against the silky fabric of her bustier. "But tonight I want all of your attention. We're going to play, Sammie Cat, and I guarantee you're going to like it."

She didn't doubt it, and her excitement grew as Elijah waved across the room to four people sitting at one of the larger black-draped tables. Elijah was the only thing, the only person, who fascinated her more than the possibilities of hot glass. Swallowing hard at the thought, she followed him across the large room, where the group of four seemed to be waiting for them.

"Am I—? Is this—?" she started, the words sticking in her throat.

"Is this what, little cat?" Elijah held up a finger to the group, indicating that he would be a moment. The two stopped just out of earshot of the group.

Samantha felt ridiculous, but forced the words out anyway.

"I don't know how to act around other . . . other Doms." Her eyes widened as she realized that, at some point that night, they were going to enter an entire club full of them. She'd been so nervous when she'd met Angelo at Pecado that she hadn't given the notion much thought.

But now . . . well, now she wanted to make Elijah proud.

She seemed to have done just that by asking the question, to judge by the expression on his face. He tucked a stray red curl behind her ear, his fingers lingering on the lobe.

"Here, in the wine bar, act however you wish. There is no protocol here besides that within your own personal D/s relationship. I will enjoy calling the shots, but you won't need to interact with other Doms in a D/s manner."

Samantha's heart began to beat faster, as it always did when she realized how very similar her desires lined up with Elijah's. She so badly wanted to make this work, and was terrified that it wouldn't.

"In the club, however . . ." Untucking the strand that he'd just placed behind her ear, Elijah stroked it through his fingers, watching as the curl bounced back toward Samantha. "Some Doms are more strict than I am. Address them as Sir or Ma'am or, if you wish, Master or Mistress. But if you do that, you have to add their name, or you're implying that you belong to them."

Samantha frowned, thoroughly lost.

Elijah clarified. Samantha felt her stomach do a slow roll.

"For instance . . . I'm about to introduce you to my friend Alex. Alex is also a Dom. It would be correct to address him as Sir or Master Alex, but not simply Master." Samantha caught the blaze of heat that flared in Elijah's eyes a moment before he wrapped his fist in her braid and tugged her toward him.

"That title belongs to me."

Samantha's insides were liquid when they finally approached the table where Elijah's friends were waiting. The man turned her inside out.

"Samantha, this is Alex Fraser. He's one of the two other owners of Veritas." A tall man with raven black hair and startlingly blue eyes stood, surprising her.

She hadn't thought a Dom would stand to greet a sub.

"Samantha." The man's bright eyes twinkled with mischief. "It's lovely to meet you. Elijah hasn't brought a woman here in years."

Elijah cast a warning look at his friend, and Samantha looked at Elijah in turn. "Oh, really?" She bit her tongue as soon as she'd spoken, sure she'd broken some sort of submissive rule with her questioning stare.

But he didn't scold her. Rather, for the first time since she'd met him, Elijah looked discomfited. He slid his hands into his pockets and rocked back on his heels.

"Stop harassing him." A woman—one of the most beautiful women Samantha had ever seen, with a figure to match and dressed in a sheer dark blue dress—tugged on Alex's slacks. The massive diamond on her ring finger caught the light as she pushed a long fall of chestnut hair out of her face. "Can't you see you've embarrassed him?"

"That's entirely the point." Alex turned and looked down at

the woman with the look that Samantha thought she might label "Dangerous Dom." "And did you really just lecture your Dom?"

The woman rolled her eyes across the table at the second woman, a petite redhead wearing clothing that looked more suited to a flower child than a submissive. The redhead smirked and rolled her eyes back.

"No, I lectured my fiancé, who is being rude." Leaning across the table, the woman offered Samantha a hand. "I'm Maddy Stone. I'm engaged to the rude one."

Maddy gestured to the petite redhead, who was now glowering at the other man, who was large and had a head shaved to the skin.

"This is Kylie Anderson—she's Alex's personal assistant. And Declan St. Adams is his head of security."

Declan nodded at her, then returned to stoically ignoring Kylie.

Samantha was beginning to feel entirely out of place among what were obviously some very close friends. She looked at Elijah, uncertain, only to find that he still seemed put off by Alex's comment.

"Why don't you menfolk run along and devise ways to torture us while we have a drink with Samantha? I'm dying to meet the woman who's important enough that Elijah would build her a studio on the grounds." The way Maddy spoke said that this wasn't really a suggestion. She picked up her glass and drained the remaining inch of golden liquid.

Alex winced.

"That's the Château Cheval Blanc you're chugging, babe." He raised his hands in mock surrender when she turned and raised an eyebrow at him. "Okay, we're going."

Samantha sat in the chair that Maddy gestured to after a quick glance at Elijah to see that it was okay with him. He nodded curtly, then left with Alex and Declan, leaving Samantha with an unpleasant tangle of nerves in her stomach.

"Is he mad at me?" She winced as soon as the words came out of her mouth. She sounded so needy. But Elijah was, if anything, gregarious, outgoing, charming.

Seeing him in a foul mood was a new thing for her.

Kylie snorted and reached for a full bottle of wine that was resting in a metal bucket of ice. She poured a full glass for Samantha, then topped up Maddy's and her own.

"Actually, the fact that he's grumpy about that comment, and the fact that he brought you here, bodes pretty well for you." She cast an arch look Samantha's way. "So, are you into the kinky games too, then?"

Samantha had just lifted her glass to her lips, and the wine went down the wrong tube when Kylie's comment forced her to suck in air.

"Uh . . ." She looked at Maddy, who smirked and held out her wrists, which were braceleted with . . . were those *cuffs*?

"Kylie's been feeling experimental lately," Maddy said. "And she's hoping to tempt the man who could be voted 'least likely to administer a spanking' into some of that kink."

"Least likely to administer a spanking . . . Declan?" Samantha asked.

Maddy hooted with laughter and Kylie glowered.

"Gee, how'd you guess?" Kylie stared down into her wine-glass, suddenly morose. "I'm doomed to vanilla sex for the rest of my life."

Samantha thought of Elijah, of the way he'd taken her in the bedroom of his plane, and she flushed all over.

"There's something to be said for vanilla."

Maddy grinned at her and raised her glass to clink it against Samantha's. Samantha felt the ice caused by Elijah's rapid mood swing begin to thaw.

"Drink up. We're going to need it to face whatever those men are devising for us right now."

Samantha thought of the checklist she'd filled out at Pecado, the items she'd indicated she might be interested in, and felt heat suffuse her body.

"Do you . . . do we all . . . play . . . at the same time?" She felt ridiculous even asking the question, but beautiful as she found Maddy and cute as Kylie was in her long flowered skirt, Samantha was pretty sure she wasn't interested in getting it on with other women.

There had been an item on that checklist, though—one that had mentioned watching two men together . . .

That was an intriguing thought. And it was one that she pushed right out of her mind, certain that a man as clearly into women as Elijah wasn't going to even entertain the possibility of that one.

The other two women looked at each other with stunned expressions, then burst into laughter. The ice returned, a giant shard of it slicing right through her core as Samantha quickly began to feel like an outsider again.

"I'm going to go find Elijah," Samantha began, rising stiffly from the table. She tensed when Maddy placed a hand on her wrist, keeping her from leaving.

"I'm so sorry. We're not laughing at you." Maddy swallowed most of her laughter, though an undignified snort escaped. Kylie still giggled, though her hand was pressed tightly over her mouth, as though trying to bottle her laughter inside.

"No. It's the idea of Alex playing . . . like that . . . anywhere near where I am." Kylie chuckled as she refilled her glass with wine the color of wheat. "We're cousins. And not the kissing kind. I'm like his little sister. He'd be freaked out at the very idea."

"It might be kind of fun to see," Maddy mused. "Almost as much fun as seeing you tame Declan."

The women grinned at each other, and this time Samantha didn't feel left out. They still hadn't answered her question exactly, though, and she said so.

"Alex and I will be in the club, but it's hard to say if we'll be playing or not." Maddy pouted a little. "He's not usually a fan of public scenes, though sometimes he gets in the mood."

"Declan's not a Dom. He's only around if Alex needs him for security. And I only ever come for a drink," Kylie adding, scowling. "But one night when Alex isn't here, I'm going to come see what all the fuss is about."

Though Samantha knew she shouldn't have cared, the giant knot in her stomach began to loosen. She knew she shouldn't have been jealous, but the idea of Elijah touching either of these women drove her insane.

Maddy tipped the last of the wine into Samantha's glass. "Finish that. Then we'll go see what mischief the boys are up to." Maddy swallowed the rest of her wine and sighed happily.

"Best seven-hundred-dollar bottle of wine ever."

"S-seven hundred?" Samantha choked and gaped at Maddy, incredulous. The other woman patted her on the hand and grinned.

"If you can't get them to stop blowing scads of cash on bottles of wine, you might as well join them."

"Do you need anything else from me, Mr. Fraser?" Elijah watched as Declan shifted his weight from one foot to the other. Though this movement might have been nothing more than a twitch on anyone else, on Declan it signaled that something major was going on.

The man had been doing his best to avoid entering the play part of the club for the better part of a month now. Knowing him as he did—Declan had been with Alex for nearly as long as

Alex and Elijah had been friends—Elijah knew he had a reason, but he couldn't for the life of him imagine what it was.

"Go ahead and go home, Declan." Elijah saw Alex cast a sidelong glance at him, likely to see if he had noticed Declan's odd behavior as well.

He didn't comment, instead stuffing his hands into his pockets. He was irritated with Alex, though he knew it was irrational.

When his friend had told Samantha that she was one of the first women Elijah had brought to the club in years, he'd insinuated that she was different. Special. And Elijah was the first to admit that she was unique.

But—even though the thought of her with anyone else made him see red—the thought of having more than an affair, however intense, made him restless.

"See you tomorrow." Declan nodded as he left. The moment the bald man was gone, Alex opened the door to the play area, holding it open for Elijah as he frowned himself.

"What's eating you, man?" Alex asked.

Elijah kept his face carefully blank as they made their way to the bar, where Luca was polishing wineglasses.

The giant of a man grinned when he saw them approaching.

"Heard you've got yourself a pretty little strawberry sub tonight, E." Luca nodded toward where Charlotte was locked into the stocks just out of earshot. Her ass was a fetching shade of pink, and her behind was the only side of her that was visible. "She the one you tore up the backyard for?"

Elijah ignored the question—after all, he would hardly call building a discreet glass studio tearing up the backyard. But when he'd informed his partners of his plans for Samantha's temporary studio, they hadn't been able to resist poking at him mercilessly about it.

"Your handiwork?" Alex asked as the three men watched

Charlotte, his voice bemused. Charlotte was known for acting up—no one would be sorry that she was paying penance in this way, least of all Luca, who loved nothing more than leaving his mark on a beautiful ass.

"You know it." Luca laid a small flogger on the top of the bar, then nodded at Elijah. "Thanks for sending her my way."

"Did she tell you what she did?" Elijah felt his small frown turn into a full-fledged scowl.

"She said she had been disrespectful to you." Luca smiled wickedly.

"She propositioned me in front of my sub." Elijah growled. Here was the root of his discomfort—he was already more attached to Samantha, more possessive of her, than he'd ever intended to be with anyone ever again.

Beside him Alex whistled through his teeth. Elijah knew what he was thinking—it was a serious breach of protocol for a sub to proposition a Dom at all, let alone in front of the sub he was with. To insult the sub was to insult the Dom.

All three men looked at the bratty sub, considering, and Elijah knew that none of them had the curves of her ass on their minds.

"You're the one who was wronged, E. You want to use the flogger?" Luca offered it, though his friend had to know that Elijah would refuse even before he shook his head.

"No, man." Elijah didn't mind dispensing a bit of pain when it added to a sub's pleasure, but he'd never been fond of corporal punishment. Just another reason that Samantha seemed like such a good match for him—she wasn't overly interested in pain, either. "You go ahead."

"I'll take care of that right now, then." Whistling a jaunty tune, Luca flipped the flogger in the air, caught it, then strode over to the woman whose ass was about to get even pinker.

The two old friends watched as Luca circled the stocks, said something to the woman, and smiled grimly.

He might have put on a good show, Elijah knew, but none of them liked doling out discipline when fun wasn't involved.

"I don't think Charlotte's brattiness is what's bothering you." Elijah watched as Alex rounded the counter, then searched the wooden wine rack that was reserved for the three owners. It wasn't a surprise that he selected a bottle of Mouton Rothschild—Maddy's favorite—and held it up for Elijah's inspection.

Elijah nodded, and slid two glasses down the polished surface of the bar to Alex.

Once his glass had been filled, Elijah leaned over the bar, resting on his elbows, his face pensive.

"You remember Tara."

Alex nodded, joining Elijah in sipping at the dark red liquid in their glasses. Elijah knew his ex-wife was hard to forget. Exceptionally beautiful, incredibly kinky, she'd fascinated them all, but it was Elijah's heart she'd captured. He'd thought he was the luckiest man in the world, a Dom new to the scene who had found a beautiful sub willing to fully explore the dark side of BDSM.

But Tara hadn't been submissive at all, not really. She'd enjoyed sugar kink, true enough, but hadn't been interested in submission outside the bedroom. And though he'd never admitted it to his friend, he'd also come to suspect that Tara had been more interested in his money than in building a life with him. When he had used financial domination as a way to try to get her to submit, she had turned into the biggest brat any of them had ever seen, making Elijah discipline her when she knew he'd never enjoyed it—*because* he'd never enjoyed it, even.

By the time the dust of the divorce had settled, they were

both miserable. Elijah had even doubted himself and thought for a time that he was a failure as a Dom.

"Samantha's not . . . She's not your typical submissive." Elijah was pensive, staring down into his wineglass as though it held the secrets to the universe. "I'm still not convinced the lifestyle will be right for her. She responds to my commands, but they don't seem to subdue her, not in the way a sub is normally dominated."

"Is she acting out? Do you have to discipline her?" Alex asked.

Elijah frowned at his friend's words.

"Not really, not more than a little nudge here and there. I'm just . . ." Elijah trailed off and stared across the bar, watching Luca flick the flogger across Charlotte's backside.

"I'm falling hard, Alex. And I need someone who is truly submissive. I can't help worrying that if this goes south, it will damage both of us."

Alex seemed to weigh his response carefully.

"A true submissive doesn't necessarily mean she's going to look away whenever you glower at her, E." Elijah knew that Alex was thinking of his fiancée as he spoke. "Take Maddy. She's absolutely submissive, beautifully so, but she speaks her mind to me whenever she feels the need. I respect her submission all the more because of it."

But ever since Tara, Elijah knew he'd had a hard time separating the lines between spunk and bratty behavior. He still questioned his ability to be a Dom when a scene didn't turn out as planned.

It was one of the reasons he was surprised that he enjoyed Samantha's outspokenness as much as he did. But with Samantha, it seemed to be a true part of her, not an act put on for his benefit.

"It could be that she has something in her past that caused her to become so strong willed. To stand up for herself. It's not necessarily a bad thing."

Elijah wondered what Alex was thinking, a slight frown marring the space between his brows. His fingers tightened on the stem of the wineglass until he thought it might snap.

"That's the other thing, Alex. She's hiding something from me. She thinks I don't know, and she's not ready for me to push her yet. But at the end of this month, if I can't get her to open up, I'm going to have to walk away. You know I will."

"Another one bites the dust, huh?" His friend's voice was wry, and Elijah opened his mouth to protest. But over Alex's shoulder Elijah saw the doors that led into the play area swing open, and watched Maddy and Samantha come through.

Elijah locked eyes with the woman who was his for at least the next month, and felt a surge of possession unlike anything he'd ever experienced.

He slugged back the rest of his seventy-year-old wine, his attention focused solely on his submissive. "I just hope like hell that I don't fuck this one up."

Samantha's eyes found Elijah as soon as she entered the room. He was standing by a bar that was a lot smaller and more casual than the one in the wine bar, his hair standing on end as though he had raked his fingers through it more than once.

His eyes were impossibly blue, even in the dim light, and they were focused entirely on her.

She forgot all about Maddy as he moved toward her in the darkened room. Metallica played on speakers discreetly hidden overhead, giving the entire room a Gothic, darkly sexual feel.

Samantha felt desire pooling low in her belly, just from the way he was looking at her. She watched as he reached into his pocket and pulled out two unattached yellow cuffs.

"Give me your hands." His touch burned her skin as he snapped first one cuff, then the other, around her wrists.

"These mean that you have a Dom. No one else will touch you unless I give them permission to." Grabbing her by the elbows, he lifted her again, just as he had in the entryway to Veritas.

"Do you understand? You are mine. Mine."

CHAPTER TEN

"What is— Is this a dog toy?" Samantha stared down at her hand, in which she clasped a red rubber toy shaped like a bone. Some of the heat that had flared when Elijah had clamped the cuffs around her wrists and carried her across the play area floor seemed to cool. "Is this another guard dog joke?"

Elijah snorted in the most undignified sound she'd ever heard come out of such a suave man. He paused in the act of sifting through the large leather satchel he'd referred to as his "toy bag" and, leaning over, squeezed the toy in question.

It squeaked. She looked from the toy to Elijah, and back to the toy again.

"You won't be able to speak for what I have planned for you." Elijah smiled at her in a way she loved, that decidedly sinful curve of the lips that caused the space between her legs to ache with desire for him. Wariness combined with the heat, waking the nerve endings all over her body.

"I won't be able to speak?" She craned her neck, trying to see what he was taking out of the bag. A tub of what she assumed was some kind of lotion, a leather strap with a circular ring in the middle of it, a pair of—were those tweezers? Two silky pink scarves followed, causing her to raise an eyebrow.

"Pink?" she asked. Samantha was reminded of the polo shirt Elijah had worn that first time he had come to her house, the time she had shown him how to breathe life into glass.

On him, pink wasn't a color for a girl. It was sexy.

"I like the color." His expression was unapologetic as he crooked his finger at her, beckoning her forward. "Especially when it's against the soft skin of a woman."

Wrapping his hand in her braid, he pushed gently on her head, urging her downward. "On your knees, kitty cat."

Samantha did as she was ordered, her pulse beginning to race.

"Hands behind your back."

Slowly, Samantha rolled her shoulders, then clasped her hands together at the small of her back. The squeaky toy was still clutched tightly in her fingers, and when Elijah knelt behind her, he adjusted her fingers so that she had a better grip on it.

"I'm tying your hands with one of the scarves."

Samantha felt the silk wind around her wrists, felt it pull snugly as he fastened it. As she'd learned to expect, Elijah slid a finger between the restraint and her skin, ensuring that it wasn't too tight.

"I'm going to do the same thing to your ankles."

Samantha shivered when she felt the brush of silk over her calves and the soles of her feet in a teasing caress, awakening each spot that it touched.

She heard a hum of satisfaction, and then felt him stand again, circling back in front of her. She watched warily as he picked up the black strap with the ring, holding it out for her to see.

"This is called an O-ring gag."

A small sound escaped Samantha's lips as the words sank in.

"A gag?" She felt her body tense, but she couldn't go anywhere with her arms and legs bound. "I don't know if I like that."

"You like bondage," Elijah said, his voice matter-of-fact. "This is another layer of that. My job as your Dom is to push you, so I would like you to try this once. If you don't like it, we won't do it again."

"But..." Samantha's voice trailed off. Having her hands and wrists bound was one thing, but losing the ability to speak...

It seemed like giving up so very much more control.

"How do I use my safe word if I need to?" She glanced up at Elijah nervously. She trusted him not to push her too far—at least, she was pretty sure she did—but she wanted to have an escape route open to her anyway.

"That's what the squeaky toy is for." Elijah ran the supple leather of the gag through his fingers, and Samantha had to admit that it looked pretty in the dim light. "Squeeze it once to tell me no, and twice for yes. If I can't tell how many squeezes you've done, I'll stop. If you drop it, I'll stop. Okay?"

Samantha's fingers clenched involuntarily, and the toy emitted its high-pitched sound, making her jump. She giggled nervously.

"Okay."

Elijah took a step toward her, the gag held loosely in his fingers. "I'm going to put this on you now. Then I'm going to ask you some questions before we start to play."

Samantha inhaled a deep, shaky breath and nodded.

"Open your mouth." Swiping her tongue over her lips first, Samantha did as she was told, parting her lips and stretching her jaw. Elijah gently worked the leather-wrapped metal ring into her open mouth, adjusting it so that her lips wrapped around it.

He pulled the sides of the leather strap around the back of her head and secured them snugly, then rested his hand on Samantha's cheek for a moment, watching her closely.

She fought through a small wave of panic. There was something almost... claustrophobic... about not being able to close her mouth.

You can do this. One look at Elijah reminded her of why she was putting herself in this situation. *This is for him.*

"Good girl," Elijah murmured as he watched her begin to relax. Reaching for the small plastic tub, he unscrewed the lid to reveal a thick white cream.

Samantha, focusing on trying to keep her breathing steady with the ring in her mouth, wasn't prepared when Elijah swiped his fingers through the cream and then slid them between her legs.

Her breath whooshed out in a startled gasp when, with a sure touch, he pulled her teeny skirt up around her hips, parted the folds of her lower lips, and rubbed the cream over the hard nub of her clit.

Elijah held the fingers that still showed traces of the cream up to her nose. The thick white substance smelled of fresh mint, and she furrowed her brow as she tried to discern what its purpose was.

"Give it a minute." Elijah chuckled as he screwed the lid back onto the tub, then placed it back into his bag. Samantha followed him with her eyes as he picked up the two small tweezer things, then turned back to her.

"Feel anything yet?" Elijah asked, grinning down at her. She shook her head, still eyeing the tweezers, shifting instinctively away from them.

The movement caused her thighs to rub together, warming the flesh, and then she felt it. Her clit, covered in the cream, began to tingle, reacting to the heat.

She hummed through her parted lips, looking up at Elijah with wide eyes.

"I thought you might like that." Again without warning, he pulled the top of her bustier down, cupped her breasts in his hands, and rubbed his thumbs over her nipples.

The dual points of pleasure had her shifting her hips and

moaning. Elijah looked down into her eyes, and she saw banked heat reflected there.

"This is going to sting for a moment." Releasing one breast, he continued to cup the other, and with his free hand opened the tweezer.

Surely he's not about to put that where I think he's about to put it.

She whimpered as he placed the tweezer over the pointed tip of her nipple, then quickly repeated the process with the other.

"Nipple clamps. They'll feel good soon, I promise." Elijah trailed gentle fingers over the sides of her breasts, then underneath, and the contrast of the soft touch with the pinch on the sensitive tips was enough to drive her mad.

"Good." With a last gentle squeeze of the soft flesh of her breasts, Elijah let her go. As if her gaze was pulled by a string, she followed his movements, not wanting to lose sight of him for even a second while she was bound the way she was.

"Remember, one squeeze for no, two for yes." Elijah's hands strayed to his waistband, undid the button of his slacks, and Samantha felt her very core melt.

"Your name is Samantha," Elijah said. He stared down at her, and Samantha furrowed her brow, not sure what he was getting at.

He mimicked squeezing something with his hand, and she understood, quickly squeezing the toy twice.

"You think I'm sexy." Elijah's lips twitched as he spoke. Samantha couldn't smile around the gag, but rolled her eyes as she squeezed the toy twice. She understood what he was doing—training her, in a way, so that if she panicked and needed to use the toy, she wouldn't forget what she was doing.

"On the checklist you filled out at Pecado, there were several items you left blank. I'd like to see if you have answers for them now." Elijah's eyes darkened as he ran through a short list.

Samantha remembered leaving almost all of the items blank, mostly because she hadn't known what they were. Now she answered either yes or no with the toy as he ran through the list, not answering for the ones she still didn't understand.

There had been one item on the list, however . . . one item she'd left blank because she'd been embarrassed by her answer. This item, of course, was the one that Elijah left for last.

"When the checklist asked if you were interested in a scene involving more than one man, you didn't answer. I'm asking again, yes or no?"

Samantha blanched, embarrassed.

"I'm not going to judge you, Sammie Cat. There's no shame in feeling what you feel." Elijah's voice was serious, his eyes hot but full of understanding. "I'll only be upset if you lie." He paused.

"Now, I'll ask again. Are you interested in participating in a scene with me and another male?"

Slowly, Samantha squeezed the toy once . . . then stopped.

Elijah fastened his stare to her face, nodding as if processing the information.

"Are you interested in watching me with another male?"

Samantha felt the flush start at the roots of her hair. She'd learned early on in life to control that blush, the curse of so many redheads, but once in a while it came on regardless.

She knew the pink hue to her skin would give her away no matter what she did with the toy. Inhaling sharply through her nose, she squeezed the toy twice.

She'd thought that it would be a big revelation, but Elijah simply nodded thoughtfully, the way he had with all of her answers.

"Very good." With swift, sure movements, he unzipped the fly of his slacks and pushed them down until they rested on his hips. His semierect cock escaped the elastic of his gray boxer briefs.

His cock hardened fully under her stare, and she shifted, suddenly hot all over.

"We haven't been together long, Samantha, but I've already learned that you find freedom in bondage."

She raised her eyebrows, and would have argued if she hadn't been gagged. But as he waited, ever patient, she felt a jolt straight through her body.

It was true.

"Right now I want you to imagine that you are fully bound. There are walls on every side of you, and you can't move an inch." Samantha closed her eyes, felt the sweep of her eyelashes tickle the heated skin of her cheeks.

He was right. When she was bound, when she pictured being constrained even further, she ceased to be herself—the big sister, the one in charge. She had only to do what Elijah told her to do, and to feel.

"I'm going to fuck your mouth now, Samantha." The crude words excited her, and she shivered. "And you can't do anything about it."

Impossibly, his words made her nipples in their clamps ache even more, and blood surged to her clit. If her mouth hadn't been held open, she would have parted her lips for him, eager to do as he'd commanded.

"Don't move," Elijah warned her as he clasped the base of his cock in his hand. He tangled the fingers of his free hand in her hair, urging her forward even as he pressed his hips toward her.

The end of his cock slid through the ring and rested on her tongue. She moaned around the gag and pressed the tip of her tongue against the head of his erection, tasting salt and man.

"Don't do that." His fingers tugged on her hair, and she hissed around the sting. "Don't do anything. Do you understand?"

She would have pouted if she could, but she settled for two squeaks of the toy.

"I have to have control here, Samantha." As he spoke Elijah surged forward slowly, his thick length filling her mouth. "If you do something and I come before I'm ready, I could choke you. Do you understand?"

Two squeaks.

"Good." His voice was filled with tension as he continued to press forward, filling her mouth further. Samantha's eyes widened as she tried to relax her throat, tried to take his entire length.

For one long moment she felt herself gag, felt her eyes widen and her nose threaten to run. Then the muscles of her throat relaxed and Elijah surged the rest of the way, hitting the back of her throat.

It took every ounce of willpower that she had not to swirl her tongue over the heated length of him, not to swallow down the musk and salt that played over her tongue.

But the fact that she'd been given strict orders, that she knew exactly what she was and was not to do, allowed her to empty her mind of everything beyond the sensations currently taking over her body.

The satin-over-steel sensation of Elijah in her mouth. The tight burn of the clamps on her nipples. The intense arousal between her legs.

The only time she'd ever felt truly alive in her life was when she'd discovered the power of glass and flame. This, she realized suddenly, was just as consuming.

"Samantha . . ." Above her, Elijah sighed out her name. Though his fingers were threaded through her hair and his muscles were tense with constrained need, his eyes were fastened on her, and only her. He watched every nuance of expression on her face, every shift of her muscles.

To be the sole object of his attention was absolute bliss.

"Fuck," Elijah muttered as he surged deeper still, shuddered, then pulled himself free of her mouth entirely. She felt a strange sense of loss as he stood above her, his hand fisted around the base of his cock, looking down at her through heavy-lidded eyes, his breath coming in pants.

"I wish I could do that all day. You have the most amazing mouth," Elijah said, his voice both regretful and wicked. "I'll just have to find a new game."

Samantha shuddered as the possibilities rolled through her mind. The look in his eyes was so wild, she half expected him to push her to the floor and take her then and there.

Instead, he reached behind her head to undo the fastenings of the gag. Tossing it aside, he gently massaged the stiff muscles of her jaw, then pressed a tender kiss to her forehead.

"Amazing," he muttered to her as he signaled a passing sub, who then scurried back with a bottle of water. Opening it with those sure hands, he held it up to Samantha's mouth for a sip.

"Thank you," she said. The act of drinking very narrowly saved her from the confused tears that welled up at the backs of her eyes.

She hadn't yet appreciated the tender side of Elijah, had been focused entirely on the dominant aspects of his personality.

She willed her heart not to tremble as she came to understand how caring he could be as well.

"You're looking a bit too content there, sub."

Startled from her reverie, Samantha looked up to find Elijah's eyes glittering with amusement and . . . Was there something else, some hint of what she was feeling herself?

His hands found her breasts, and she lost track of the thought.

"This should bring your mind back to matters at hand." Elijah's voice was smug. He cupped her breasts in his palms, weighed them, then jiggled them up and down. The heavy beads at the ends of the tweezer clamps bounced, causing sensation to flow through the blood-deprived nipples.

"Brace yourself." Elijah removed both clamps at the same time, his movements easy and sure.

Liquid fire rushed to the tips of Samantha's breasts, and she couldn't hold back a scream.

"Fuck. I can't wait anymore," Elijah said. Clasping her around the waist, he lifted her easily and carried her the few steps to a padded waist-high bench. He laid her across it so that the width of the padded leather cradled her from sternum to hip, her bound arms coming to rest on the small of her back.

Her sensitized nipples pressed into the cool leather and her entire body shuddered at the shock waves of sensation radiating out from those dual points.

"Have to have you. Right now."

Samantha rested her cheek on the cool leather, closed her eyes, and listened to the tearing of a foil wrapper. Her legs were still bound, her toes barely touching the floor, and she felt weightless, a puppet to be maneuvered.

Elijah slid his fingers between her legs, making Samantha shift restlessly and groan.

"So wet. So ready. Such a good little cat." The smell of latex filled the air, and then Samantha felt the hard tip of Elijah's cock position itself at her hot, ready entrance.

Anticipation and panic twined together inside her. He was going to take her, right here, right now. They were going to have sex—in public. It seemed so much more intense than everything else they'd already done.

Though her mind struggled to accept that this was okay, her body trembled with anticipation and heat.

"Brace yourself," he warned her, and she barely had a moment to inhale before he seated himself fully, pulled back, and slammed home again. His fingers dug into her hips, holding her steady as he set a fast, furious pace.

Samantha could do nothing but close her eyes and let the sensations overtake her. Her nipples chafed against the surface of the bench, and with every thrust Elijah rocked her clit against the edge of the table, making her shake. When his pace increased and she sensed desperation in his movements, he slid a hand between her pelvis and the bench, his fingers seeking and finding the swollen nub of her clit.

"Oh, fuck!" Samantha couldn't hold back her scream—the first touch of his fingers on her clit set off an explosion. He continued to manipulate the engorged flesh, drawing out the pleasure as he seated himself one final time, his hip bones jutting into the soft flesh of her rear as he came with a shout.

All Samantha could hear when the shudders subsided was their breath—his and hers, fast yet soft. He stayed inside her, covering her, protecting her, and she felt like a bottle emptied of liquid and refilled with bliss.

Every thought floated from her grasp like a leaf in the water. She simply breathed.

CHAPTER ELEVEN

"You live upstairs from a BDSM club?" Elijah heard the incredulity in Samantha's voice as he carried her out of the club and around to the back of the building. She had been so completely relaxed—boneless, even—when he'd untied the pink silk scarves and helped her down from the bench that he hadn't trusted her to walk.

Not that he was much better. Her response to his commands had milked a release from him that he thought might take days to recover from.

He chuckled at her sleepy question.

"Of the three of us—Luca, Alex, and myself—I've always handled most of the day-to-day operations of Veritas. It makes sense for me to live here."

What he didn't add was that he had moved in after his divorce from Tara . . . and that he'd never brought a woman here before. It had been easier to play down in the club, then to excuse himself and go home.

No entanglements that way. No mistakes. And while he carried his toy bag back and forth, he didn't have a dungeon in his place.

With the playroom of Veritas downstairs, he didn't see the point.

"I think you'll find that you have everything you need here. If you don't, just ask." Elijah swiped his key card through the lock on the door, which led directly into an elevator. Originally an old Victorian home, the house was only three stories high, but he liked the speed and convenience of the private lift, which serviced only his place.

"Pretty slick," Samantha murmured as the elevator reached the top floor and a second set of doors opened on the opposite side of the elevator. He watched her eyes widen as she took in the entrance to his home.

Letting the elevator doors close behind them, Elijah carried Samantha into the arched entryway. Without pausing, he moved down the wide, softly lit hallway to the very end.

"Getting right to it, are we?" Samantha arched an eyebrow at him as he slowly slid her down the length of his body, setting her softly on the massive bed in his bedroom.

Catching her chin in his hand, he squeezed once, gently. He enjoyed watching her eyes widen as his touch reminded her that, though they were outside the club now, playtime wasn't yet over and she had rules to follow.

He began to shed his clothing and watched as she looked around, her eyes curious and eager. He liked her curiosity, enjoyed the fact that she wasn't passive about life.

"Does it pass inspection?" he asked wryly as he stepped out of his pants. Then, naked, he took her hands and lifted her from the bed. He found the hidden zipper at the side of her bustier and unfastened it, letting it and the micro-miniskirt fall to the floor.

His cock stiffened as all of that creamy skin came into view.

She gasped as he picked up her naked form and, slinging her over his shoulder, carried her to the massive en suite bathroom.

"Elijah!" Samantha was wiggling enough to make him contemplate pinning her against a wall and taking her again. "I can walk! You don't have to go all Neanderthal."

He grinned and nuzzled his cheek against the curve of her hip.

"This is called aftercare, kitten. It's my responsibility to take care of you after a scene."

He could all but hear her roll her eyes as she stopped struggling, which was a pity in his opinion.

"And just what does this aftercare consist of?" Samantha purred, arching her body into his.

Elijah cursed inwardly, ignoring the heady desire that she was wringing from him yet again. Grabbing two plush, oversized bath sheets from the towel warmer, he placed one on the bamboo bench that sat beside his bathtub.

"Down you get." Wrapping his arms around her waist, he placed Samantha on top of the heated towel. He wrapped the second hug of warmth around her shoulders.

"Oh, that's lovely." Samantha closed her eyes and savored the warmth. He took the opportunity to start the water in the lake-sized bathtub.

Females liked bubble bath, didn't they? Frowning, he looked around. He and his partners had originally fashioned the upper floor of Veritas into a series of apartments for their personal use, and for staff members like Julien. After his divorce, when he'd decided to live above the club full-time, he'd renovated the space, turning the six apartments into one massive penthouse.

He had everything he wanted . . . except bubble bath. Inspired, he moved into the shower stall and grabbed a bottle of shampoo, oblivious to the expensive Italian tiles or the multiple rainfall showerheads.

Samantha, however, was not blind to those details. Elijah saw curiosity warring with something else in her eyes as he returned to the bath and squeezed a liberal amount of shampoo into the water.

"I never would have expected all of this from outside." Her voice was quiet, as it tended to be when she was confronted with his wealth. "Sometimes you're just so normal that I forget how very rich you are."

"You're a puzzle, little cat." Satisfied with the froth of bubbles, Elijah removed the towels he'd wrapped around her and, lifting her one more time, carried her to the stone steps that led down into the beckoning water.

"How am I a puzzle?" She looked at him with those direct eyes—eyes he would never have guessed held a secret if he wasn't so adept at reading people. Holding the gaze, looking back over her shoulder, she waded into the bath, steam curling around her and reminding him of Botticelli's *Birth of Venus*, one of his favorite paintings.

"Most women I meet know what businesses I'm involved in, my estimated net worth, the restaurants I frequent." Reaching for her shoulders and pulling her back until she was floating against his shoulder, he let his hands skim over her breasts without lingering.

He hadn't been lying when he'd told her that he wanted a woman who would let him care for her. To his way of thinking, the need came hand in hand with dominance, which was, at its root, about the needs of the sub. Though he felt satisfaction when he saw the cherry color of her nipples, still tender from the clamps, and though his cock had fully hardened when he'd watched her walk into the steam, this moment was about her.

"And though we have a rigorous screening process at Veritas, once in a while one of these gold diggers gets through. They don't seem to much care whether they get the attention of Alex, Luca, or myself, but they're usually more interested in securing a wealthy lover than in submission." Elijah felt Samantha's shoulders tense, then quickly unclench as he poured cupped handfuls of water over her hair, wetting it.

The silence stretched out for a long moment, but when he positioned himself so that he could reach over to get the shampoo, she turned and pinned him with that inquisitive stare again.

"I know I'm new to this, and I don't always know what I'm doing," she started, moving toward him in the waist-high water. "But you have to believe . . . this is what I want."

Elijah was uncharacteristically taken aback by her directness.

"I don't know if you and I will work out any more than any relationship ever does," she continued, and Elijah felt a tight clenching begin in his gut, accompanied by a surge of stubborn male pride.

He found that he didn't want to think about Samantha moving on, not at all. And though it was contrary to some of his own concerns, the idea that she might leave made him want to chain her up in his bedroom until she came to her senses.

"But our days together have already shown me that this is what I've been searching for," she concluded.

Suddenly uncertain, she widened her eyes and laced her fingers together. Elijah continued to study her. Confusion was rare for him—he liked to live a life that was as straightforward as possible.

But this woman, with her combination of sweet submission and boldness, wasn't like anyone he'd ever met before.

"I've come to feel more for you in these few days than I've felt in a long time," he said carefully, twisting the shampoo bottle in his hands. "But to fully submit to me, you have to share everything with me, Samantha. *Everything.*"

Her eyes widened slightly, and he knew that she understood what he was referring to. He had to give her credit for not denying it, for not pretending she didn't know what he was talking about.

But from the stubborn set of her jaw, he saw that if he pushed in that moment, all she would do was dig in her heels.

Damn. Her refusal to bend was the single most frustrating thing he'd ever encountered.

He wouldn't tell her it was all right to take the easy way out, because she needed to learn to obey his commands. She was new to this, yes, but she had to try.

He also needed honesty from her if this was going to work.

Needing a moment to think about how exactly to handle her, he took her by the shoulders, turning her so that he could work shampoo through her hair.

"Oh!" Samantha started as he turned her to face the window. Elijah smiled as he squirted the liquid into his hand. It smelled spicy, he supposed, and wasn't at all suited to her. He'd have to get her something more appropriate.

She sighed as he worked his fingers against her scalp, but didn't relax. She leaned forward to better see out the window, and he let her have her first spectacular view of Vegas.

"It's not Baja, but it has its own appeal." Elijah continued to work the shampoo through the heavy ropes of wet hair as Samantha inched them both toward the window. Planting her hands on the sill, she leaned forward until her nose touched the glass.

"I've never seen anything like it." She cast a quick look of delight over her shoulder at him, then returned, craning her neck to see more of the neon lights.

"You can see it better from most of the other buildings." He resolved to take her on a tour of the city, so that she could see it in all its neon glory. "Veritas was meant to be unobtrusive."

"It's amazing." Samantha finally tore her eyes away from the brightly lit night and relaxed against him. "I've never been to a big city before."

Elijah's fingers paused for the briefest of moments before resuming their methodical work. Though she'd seemed closed off only moments before, the unexpected view seemed to have pulled an almost childlike enthusiasm from her, opening her up to him.

Whatever her issues were, he suspected they lay with her family, her home. He was certain that by moving to Mexico she'd deliberately distanced herself from whatever it was she wanted to forget.

He had decided—he was going to push her. But there was more than one way to do that.

"I hadn't seen a city like this before I moved here, either." Elijah urged her to lean back against him as he began to rinse the shampoo from her hair. "I grew up in a small town in Arkansas, got my start there, and was dazzled by Vegas."

"*You* are from Arkansas?" Finally tearing herself away from the window, Samantha turned. Elijah's fingers slipped from her hair, and he took the opportunity to tilt her backward. She released a startled noise as, with one hand steady beneath her back, he held her in the water and gently rinsed the remaining suds from her hair.

This gave him a second to think. Elijah had made the very deliberate decision to not tell many people about his past, because he didn't care for the idea of nosy paparazzi converging on Harley, Arkansas. Alex, Luca, Tara—they were the only ones he'd ever told. And he was surprised that Tara hadn't shared his secret in revenge, acrimonious as their divorce had been.

It felt strange to make the decision to trust her with this. But he was certain that Samantha would rather give up her glass studio than betray a trust. And though with a more experienced sub he would insist on revelations from his sub first, telling his secrets second as a reward, he knew already that that strategy wasn't going to work with Samantha.

She needed to feel safe. He was secure enough with his dominance to give her this before he challenged and pushed her. But he would push—hard and soon.

Elijah placed her gently back on her feet. Pulling the plug in the tub, he reached for another heated towel, wrapping it around her when the water dipped to their hips.

"My first ever business was a convenience store back in Harley." Elijah scooped Samantha into his arms and carried her up the steps that led out of the tub, then out of the bathroom and to the bedroom. When he slid her down his body to stand, he felt his erection begin to stir anew, awakened by the feel of her soft, naked skin sliding over his.

But this wasn't the time for that. This was the time to urge her forward, to try to gently move her past whatever she was holding back.

"You owned a convenience store?" The look on her face was disbelieving, and Elijah hid a chuckle as he dropped his own towel and strode naked to his bureau. After putting on a pair of lounge pants and a T-shirt, he pulled another T-shirt from a drawerful of neatly folded cotton, then returned and helped Samantha put it on.

"A convenience store doesn't really fit the tycoon stereotype," Samantha mused as she relaxed and let him work her arms through the sleeves of the shirt. Satisfaction washed over him. She enjoyed being dressed, as if she were his doll, which was fortunate, because he enjoyed doing it.

"What does fit the stereotype, then?" Elijah skimmed his hands over her hips as he pulled the shirt down over her torso. Though he imagined she thought she was being sneaky about it, he saw her nuzzle her nose into the ribbed collar and inhale.

The simple gesture made dominance of the most primitive kind roar through him. And though he fully intended to obtain her full submission, it worried him that he was allowing himself to grow attached to her.

Then the nymph with the sea goddess eyes turned to him

and flashed that mile-wide grin, and he knew he would risk it. He had no choice.

"You know. Fancy cars, expensive wine. Bathtubs so big you could swim in them." Her saucy grin had him aching to lay her over his knee for some "punishment."

He'd save it for later. He could see by the set of her muscles that she was relaxing a bit, and he didn't want to disrupt it.

He needed to focus, not something he'd ever had trouble doing until meeting Samantha. His instincts told him that he needed to reveal just a little bit more of himself, and she would give him something back.

"When I was a teenager, I got involved with the wrong group of friends." Elijah turned Samantha so that her back nestled against his chest. He didn't want to hide from her, but he wasn't sure he'd be able to speak about this with those probing eyes on him.

"I started experimenting with drugs, with alcohol . . . with girls." He felt his own body stiffen, remembering how easily he could have done something so simple and so careless as getting a young, small-town girl pregnant.

It had happened to so many of his high school friends. And many of them had made it work.

But it hadn't been what he'd wanted. Even back then, before he'd known any better, he'd had a hunger for more.

"Doesn't sound so different from a lot of kids," she said.

He read the quick tension in her body and wondered whether she had done the same, or whether she'd gone the opposite way and shunned every vice.

"No, but the difference was that I had parents who cared." Elijah stroked his hands through her tangles of damp hair, finger combing it. "They approached one of their longtime friends, asked if he would give me a job to keep me out of trouble. Chief could barely afford to pay himself a salary, but he did it."

"Chief?" Samantha tried to turn around, but he held her still. His memories of the old man still hurt, and just as his submissive wasn't ready to share with her Dom, neither was it always easy for the Dom to spill his guts. "That's not a name you hear every day."

"He was part Cheyenne. He moved to Harley from the middle of a cornfield in Kansas on a whim. Ran his little store for almost thirty years. When he died, I managed to scrape together enough to buy it from the bank. That was my first business." One that had cost him more sleepless nights than he'd been able to count, as he sweated not just to pay back the loan from one of the other men in town, but to make the store prosper.

Adding to the pressure he'd felt to make the store succeed just to pay back his debts, he'd felt that he owed it to Chief. The man had become his surrogate father when his own parents died in a boating accident when he was barely an adult. When Chief died, it had been like losing another parent.

He would keep the convenience store alive as a memorial to all three, even if it never made another cent.

"From Arkansas to Vegas, huh?" Samantha sounded engaged, but didn't volunteer any other information. She was proving even more resistant to opening up to him than he'd anticipated.

There might be some punishment coming for her after all, then. And damned if the thought didn't make his cock swell.

"The only other people I've told that story to are Luca and Alex." This time he let her turn in his arms when she wiggled. He sucked in a breath when her curious fingers danced over the tattoo that decorated his biceps, the one he and his friends had chosen together when they'd opened In Vino Veritas.

He waited, reading the internal struggle in the lines of her body. She huffed out a breath, looked evasively from side to side, and then finally laid her cheek against his chest.

The simple gesture quickened his pulse.

"The sister I told you about . . . she has type 1 diabetes," Samantha said quietly.

Elijah already knew this, from the digging he'd done on her, but she hadn't told him herself.

"Her medical needs are expensive, and she doesn't have insurance."

Elijah didn't have to be a Dom to hear the shame in her voice. *Shame?* Frustration he could understand. Even anger, to some extent. But he wondered where the shame was coming from.

He was dying to push her further, to persuade her to tell him everything. But he'd learned from long experience that he needed to be patient.

It was time to encourage that positive behavior with a reward. He had to bite the inside of his cheek to keep from grinning when he thought of what Samantha's reaction would be if she knew he intended to train her like a puppy.

"Do me a favor," he started, placing his hands on her shoulders and turning her to face the door. Then he led her down the hall and to the elevator.

She eyed him warily when he pressed the button to open the door.

"Where are we going? I'm not dressed." A gasp escaped Samantha's lips when Elijah, having reached his limit with her sassiness, spun her and pressed her against the cool plaster of the wall beside the elevator.

"What—?" Her words caught in her throat as Elijah pulled her wrists behind her back with one hand and hooked the hem of the oversized shirt over their entwined fingers with the other.

Her ass was pale and jiggled just the slightest bit as her breath heaved in and out. Elijah smoothed his hand over the soft curves and savored the sensation when she pushed back into the touch.

Elijah cupped his hand slightly, pulled back, then let it land on her ass. Samantha's cry mingled with the sharp crack that sounded in the otherwise silent air, and he watched as the flush of pink spread over that perfect skin.

"Wh-why?" She tried to look back over her shoulder at him, but he tangled his fingers in her hair and turned her back to press her cheek against the wall.

"Keep talking," he taunted as, releasing her hair, he laid his palm on her ass again. She jolted, and he traced gentle fingertips over skin that he was sure was on fire.

He watched as she glared from the corner of her eye, opened her mouth—probably to yell at him—then swallowed whatever it was she'd intended to say.

"Good girl." Leaning in close, pressing his erection into the small of her back, he pushed his hips forward, letting her feel how aroused he was.

"I've gone easy on you, because you're so new to this." He flexed his hips again and enjoyed the small whimper that escaped her lips. "But if you keep on questioning me, it makes me think you need a little incentive to learn to behave."

He pulled away from her abruptly, flexing his fingers, watching as her body drew tight with anticipation. Pain play was never his favorite, and Samantha wasn't any kind of pain slut, either.

But a little spanking as discipline—and the chance to watch that gorgeous creamy skin ignite by his hand—was undeniably hot.

"I think we'll do five more." He grinned at Samantha's choked cry, then let his palm fly again.

By the time the last blow had landed, she was trembling, her skin the color of rosé wine. She was still glaring over her shoulder at him, but the way she was moving her hips and panting told him that she'd enjoyed it as much as he had.

"Gotta be sure." Elijah slid his hand between her naked legs, pushed two fingers inside her, felt her buck against the intrusion.

He released her and held his fingers up to eye level. They were coated with her wetness.

"That's my girl." Bending to plant a kiss to the nape of her neck, Elijah pulled her away from the wall and wrapped her in his arms for a hug. She hissed when his crotch pressed against the tender skin of her bottom.

"You're going to be a bit sore for a while. That's going to help remind you of what will happen if you get too sassy."

She hissed. He chuckled, releasing her.

Samantha spun to face him, her hands clutching the hem of the T-shirt, her eyes sparking.

"So you're going to spank me every time I question you?" Her voice was incredulous.

Elijah smiled, a slow, dangerous curve of the lips.

"Some Doms would." Her face paled beneath his stare. "But for reasons I don't quite understand, I like that you're spunky. You can express your opinion, but you must do it respectfully."

Elijah turned and stepped through the yawning elevator door, then held out a hand, inviting her to join him. She planted her hands on her hips, a stance far more aggressive than the look on her face.

"You can't punish me for asking a question." Her voice was bewildered. "That doesn't make any sense."

Reaching out, Elijah tugged her into the elevator. He stroked a finger down her cheek, smiling when she shivered at the touch.

"I won't punish you for some questions, so long as they are polite. I will spank you, or give you whatever other torture I dream up, if you push at me in a way that says you don't trust me to lead you." Sliding his hand past her breasts and down her torso to squeeze her tender butt, he pulled back and grinned down into her disconcerted face.

He waved the fingers that he'd plunged inside her in front of Samantha's face. Though the moisture had dried, the scent of her arousal was still a perfume in the air.

"Besides . . . I have proof that you like it."

Samantha was silent as the elevator descended, and all while Elijah led her out of the building and across the large span of grass that was the backyard of In Vino Veritas. He waited for the small shed in the back corner to fall in her sight line. If she didn't notice it soon, the noise was sure to draw her attention.

For now, Samantha was entranced by the small paradise that was the landscaped beauty of the backyard of Veritas. "This is lovely," she said.

Elijah felt a surge of pride at her appreciation. He'd done a lot of it himself, enjoying the planning, the sweating, even the dirt as he made the view from his windows beautiful.

It made him feel less like he was living above one of his businesses. Made it feel more like home.

Elijah led Samantha to the door of the shed. It wasn't particularly elegant, building a hot glass studio in his backyard, but it had been the obvious solution.

He would give her privacy while she was working . . . but he still wanted her close.

Elijah was nothing if not practical.

He wasn't sure what he would do with the shed and the equipment inside it . . . after they had parted ways. Donate it, maybe. But that was a worry for another time.

"I left something in this shed. I would like you to go get it for me."

Samantha looked back over her shoulder, narrowing her eyes at him. "What is it?"

"You looking for another spanking?" He held back a grin when she blanched, schooling his features into a stern expression.

He saw her hesitate, then start across the yard. He waited until she had opened the door that still smelled of fresh paint, waited for her startled inhalation of breath before he crossed to stand behind her.

He was looking forward to her reaction.

CHAPTER TWELVE

"Holy shit," Samantha yelped. After a stunned pause she charged into the shed. She circled the room once, not sure what to look at first.

"How did you know what to get?" With a stunned glance back at Elijah, Samantha's eyes followed the flue that extended down from the ceiling and landed on a Kokomo pot furnace.

A freaking Kokomo pot furnace. Those things were hellishly expensive. Add to that the top-of-the-line tools—the steel blowpipes, the pontils, the shaping tools. And the sacks of glass melt. And the colorants.

And the soundproofing, she thought as she registered the intense heat in the room and the roar of the furnaces. She hadn't heard even a hint of the deafening sound of the furnaces from outside.

He had spent a fortune on a top-notch art studio for her. She just couldn't believe it was because he wanted one of her sculptures that badly.

"I did some research. Looking at you naked distracts the hell out of me, but I still want a sculpture from your hands." Elijah's voice was husky, and Samantha felt heat pool low in her belly when she looked over her shoulder and found him coming toward her.

For once Samantha had no words, her mouth becoming dry as cotton as he approached. She could have told herself that it was because of the heat in the room, but she knew that was a lie.

He blew her mind. And she knew that if she wanted to keep him, she would have to give him everything.

"If you find that you need anything, let me know," Elijah murmured as he dipped his head down to hover a frustrating whisper away from her lips.

"I can think of something that I need right now," Samantha said, casting her stare down the solid length of Elijah's body. Even though he was clothed from neck to toe, the light from the furnace made his exposed skin seem like it was lit from within.

In contrast, still dressed in nothing but his T-shirt, she felt more naked than ever.

He brushed his lips over hers, just one light ghost of a kiss.

Samantha closed her eyes, waited for the rest of the kiss that she was sure would follow. Her eyes flew open when she heard the door quietly close.

"Argh!" She let out a muffled scream of pure frustration when she realized that, instead of moving his hands to her breasts, her behind, all the places she'd expected him to touch, Elijah had left her alone to play with her new toys.

For a long moment she considered going after him, running her fingers over lips that were tight with need for the kiss that hadn't come. She was still keyed up from their encounter by the elevator, desperate for some kind of release.

But somehow she didn't think Elijah would approve of her touching herself, not unless he had given her permission to. And the press of her own fingers between her legs would pale even in comparison to that light kiss.

Then—*there* it was. That little spark, the little seed of an idea in her mind that suddenly sprouted into more.

The need to create.

Samantha turned to survey the room that would be her studio for the next month. It lacked the personal touches that she liked in a work space—the small fridge to hold bottles of water and cans of cola, the scarred table with her current favorite creations on it.

But she could hardly complain about working with a Kokomo glass furnace.

Trying to push Elijah to the back of her mind, Samantha was almost tentative in her approach, crossing until she stood in front of the beautiful instrument. She sighed with pleasure when she opened its door and saw the inferno within.

"Hello, gorgeous." Picking up a virgin blowpipe, Samantha inserted it into the furnace, delighted with the angel white gather of molten glass that she twirled onto the end of the pipe.

Turning it carefully, both to keep the glass even and to learn the feel of the new pipe in her hands, Samantha carried it to the small bench, where she would breathe life into the thick liquid.

She wanted to try to capture that whisper of a kiss in glass—the promise, the heat.

The familiar thrill that always rocketed through her when she began to create was like fire in her blood. She took a moment to inhale, breathing in the smoky scent of the furnace, the familiar scent of hot glass.

There was also one note in the fragrance that was pure Elijah, even in here, the place he'd intended to be her domain.

"All right, here goes." Though it was difficult, she tried to push thoughts of that man—who had so firmly lodged himself inside her—to the back of her mind.

"Let's make some magic."

"What the hell is that?"

Samantha tore her eyes away from the inside of the new kiln to find Elijah lounging in the doorframe. She hadn't heard him enter, and she was slightly disappointed to discover that he was still fully dressed, his lean, muscular frame hidden from her yearning stare.

Knowing exactly what he was referring to, she closed the kiln door and smiled sweetly at him.

He fixed her with a *look*, then crossed the room and laid his hand on top of hers on the kiln door. He gently lifted her fingers away from the handle. The touch made her acutely aware that he had showered and changed, while she was still wearing nothing but his baggy T-shirt.

The heat of the room, though vented, had made her hair curl in wild strands around her face.

She raked her fingers through those strands as Elijah opened the door to the kiln and looked at the sculpture she'd just set to cool.

"You've been in here for hours," he said, turning to look at her, resignation plain on his face.

Samantha bit the inside of her cheek to keep from laughing.

"A sculpture with this amount of . . . detail . . . takes time." The corners of her lips quirked up with amusement.

Elijah closed his eyes, looking almost as if he was praying. He squinted one eye open again, eyeing Samantha with exasperation.

"It's not exactly what I had in mind when I commissioned you." Elijah studied the sculpture that sat on the shelf in the kiln, and to Samantha's entertainment, the faintest hint of a blush stained his cheeks.

"I worked on your sculpture for a long time, but it's not quite coming together at the moment." Samantha crossed the room to where the other sculpture—the one she'd *wanted* to make—sat. Similar in shape to the graduated green one still on display back in Mexico, it had a central column, a flowing fall of glass extending from the top. But it hadn't captured the magic she'd been hoping for, so she'd set it aside. She would look at it with fresh eyes in a day or two.

But she hadn't been done playing with her new furnace or her new tools. So she'd gathered glass on her pontil, her only thought to make Elijah smile.

"Samantha, did you make a nude sculpture of me?" Elijah turned away from the sculpture she'd made instead, raking his fingers through his hair, turning to stare at her with barely suppressible amusement—which had been her goal.

Samantha moved back to the kiln and studied the clear glass statue with a sober expression. She hadn't added color to it, so it could be scraped back into the melt to be reused, though she was actually quite pleased with it. Maybe she'd keep it as a memento of her time here—the glass melt in its raw form was cheap, and Elijah surely wouldn't begrudge her the materials.

Headless, legless, and armless, it nonetheless showed great attention to detail in the torso and pelvis areas. She snuck a sidelong glance at Elijah, saw that he hadn't been able to hide his grin, and beamed with contentment.

"Why would you assume it's you?" she asked, tongue in cheek.

Within moments, her mirth had been burned away in a great burst of passion as, with one smooth motion, Elijah had her hands pinned behind her back, her body pressed against the work table that stood in the middle of the room.

"If it isn't me, I'm going to be very jealous," Elijah murmured, lowering his head and fastening his teeth directly over the pulse that beat beneath the line of her jaw.

Samantha felt her knees liquefy.

"Maybe I should check." She worked her hands free, then slid her palm over the hard planes of Elijah's chest, feathering her fingers down over his flat belly. "Make sure I got everything right."

"Far be it from me to stop you."

Samantha savored the hint of breathlessness that she heard in Elijah's voice. When he laved a path down her neck with his tongue, she slid a finger into the waistband of his slacks, pulling him closer to her.

"You're so hot." Elijah cupped his hands under her ass and lifted until she perched on the edge of the table. Fisting his hands in the neckline of her T-shirt, he pulled hard.

"Elijah!" Samantha let out a screech as the cotton shirt ripped down the middle. She clamped down on his shoulders as he peeled the fabric down her shoulders until her arms came together behind her back.

He twined the torn shirt around her wrists, secured it snugly, then pressed a kiss to her temple as he pulled her hips to the edge of the table.

"So hot, Samantha," he said again, nipping his teeth into the cord of her neck.

"Yeah." Samantha panted against his neck, squirming as she struggled to find purchase on the slick metal table. With her hands tied behind her back, she could do nothing but trust that he wouldn't let her fall. "Hot. It's a sauna in here."

Sweat beaded on her forehead, slid down the curve of her spine. Beneath her lips, Elijah's chest was damp, and she could smell the salt and musk of his sweat.

Parting her thighs with a rough hand, Elijah moved between them, then tugged one-handed at the zipper of his slacks. Samantha caught a quick glimpse of plain black boxer briefs, and then he had pushed them down around his lean hips.

As always, she sucked in a breath at the sight of his erect cock. She had never paid all that much attention to the male member before, but Elijah's appealed to the artist in her—part of the reason she'd been led to create the silly nude of him.

It was thick, and long, and the most delicious tawny color, springing up from its nest of dark golden curls. And when he took his erection in his hand and slid it through her slick folds, her sex spasmed and she arched her hips toward him.

"Please." The glass furnace roared in the background, and Samantha knew she would never again be able to hear its familiar roar without thinking of Elijah. "Please. Now!"

"I think you need another punishment, little cat. Making a nude sculpture of your Dom is bratty behavior if I've ever seen it." He slid the head of his cock back and forth between her lower lips, and Samantha's breath shuddered out of her lungs.

"Making it isn't bratty—if I put it up for display at Veritas, that would be bratty." Samantha gasped as Elijah's fingers dug into her hip. Before she could catch her breath, he'd spun her around and pressed her down, bent over the table.

"Don't move." Her head turned to the side, her cheek against the slick metal of the tabletop, she tracked Elijah's movements, watched as he perused the tools he'd purchased for her to mold her glass, settling on a wide wooden paddle that she hadn't yet had a chance to use.

"I never much enjoyed dispensing punishment before I met you." She could hear in his words that he wasn't truly upset.

She knew she was going to get the paddle pressed against her ass regardless. And crazy as it seemed to her, she wanted it.

She wasn't all that interested in exploring the sexual side of pain. But when Elijah was administering it, a bit of punishment added a delicious bite to her pleasure.

"Yes. Please, Sir. Please punish me."

From the corner of her eye she saw a flicker of disbelief trickle through Elijah's dominant stance. Then he grinned, the cold smile of a predator.

"As the lady wishes," he said smugly. She heard the wooden paddle whistle through the air before it slammed into the right side of her ass. A sound of choked pleasure escaped her lips.

"Yes!" she cried out, feeling even more wetness surge between her legs. "Like that."

"This isn't for your benefit, sub." Elijah ran his hand over her burning skin before again swinging the paddle. This blow hit on the opposite ass cheek, spreading the heat and making her arousal nearly unbearable.

She thought about sassing him back, caught up in the delightful exchange that was surging between them, but when the third blow landed on her skin she instead closed her eyes and sank into the sensation.

Three more blows, one on each of her cheeks and one in the middle, and then Samantha heard the paddle land on the floor, tossed aside.

"This is going to sting," Elijah warned before spinning her, lifting her until she lay back on the table, her ass perched on the edge.

"Holy shit!" Samantha couldn't hold back the yelp as the slick metal of the tabletop pressed against the inferno of her skin that she knew would be crimson from the kiss of his paddle. The edge of the table dug into the tender flesh, its touch a sharp bite, and she squirmed as a hint of discomfort threaded its way through the pleasure. The discomfort faded away in the onslaught of sensations as Elijah spread her legs roughly with one hand and positioned his erection at her entrance. The thick head of his cock slowly pushed past her folds, sinking into her just one delicious inch.

"Fuck!" Elijah cursed and pulled out. Samantha groaned and dug her fingernails into her slick palms.

"No. No, don't stop." Samantha panted, trying to close the distance between them as Elijah fumbled in his pocket.

"Condom. Almost forgot. Shit." Triumphantly Elijah removed a square foil packet. Securing it in his teeth, he ripped off an edge and withdrew the tube of latex.

"Don't move." Elijah set Samantha upright, then quickly smoothed the condom over his erect cock. Once it was securely in place, he grabbed her hip with one hand, splayed the other between her shoulder blades, and thrust himself inside her.

"Oh my God!" Samantha had been wet since Elijah had pushed her against the table, but she still wasn't quite prepared for the hardness as he seated himself inside her. She hissed at the sting of pleasure/pain as her flesh stretched to accommodate him.

"I can't be gentle. Not this time, Samantha." Elijah placed a hand on her cheek, turned her with a gentle touch until she was looking at him. She saw the same hunger, the same need to possess that she felt, reflected there in the navy depths.

"I don't want you to be." Her words were a breathy moan as he slid his hands down her body to grip her hips. His fingers dug into her flesh, and sparks of excitement radiated out from the bites of pain.

Then he pressed forward, the head of his cock nudging against her womb, and Samantha felt everything on her mind begin to fade.

Everything besides Elijah.

With short, hard thrusts, Elijah had them both panting within moments, quivering with the need for release. Samantha's legs trembled as her muscles tensed, coiling tight with pleasure.

"Open for me." Elijah cupped the cheeks of her ass as he pressed all the way inside, locking their flesh tightly together. She felt the fingers of one of his hands dip into the crevice between her buttocks, tracing the hidden pucker, and she arched at the touch, trying to move into it and escape it at the same time.

"Come *now*." He pressed against the tight muscle, working a finger in, setting virgin nerves firing. Sweat trickled sinuously down Samantha's spine as the tight rubber band of her need snapped.

She cried out as Elijah pulled back, then slammed forward one final time with a hoarse shout. The fire licked along her skin, heating her both inside and out.

Elijah pulled her close as they finally stilled, muscles lax, breathing hard. Something about the embrace was more intense than Samantha had anticipated, and she wasn't entirely sure what to do about it.

But for the moment, she had everything she needed.

CHAPTER THIRTEEN

" I think whoever designed this might have been compensating for something." Samantha eyed the impossibly tall marble-colored tower in front of them, an elegant column that stretched up to the sky.

Shielding her eyes against the neon sunlight of midday, she found that she couldn't see the top of it. She eyed it with both wariness and excitement as Elijah dismissed their driver, then came to stand beside her.

"You'll notice I don't have a tower." Elijah's words were smug as he laced his fingers through her own. Samantha bit back a laugh as he pulled her to the door.

Confidence was one thing, but Elijah . . . she'd never met anyone so sure of himself.

"Is it a Dom thing?" she asked, curious, as he nodded to a security guard and led her into a small lobby. "And why are we the only ones here?"

"Is what a Dom thing?" Elijah led Samantha across the small lobby to a waiting elevator. Their footsteps were the only ones echoing on the empty floor. "And we're the only ones here because I reserved the entire tower."

Samantha closed her eyes in exasperation and discomfort. She shuddered to think how much it must have cost to rent out an entire tourist landmark in a city like Vegas.

"Have you always been like this?" Samantha continued, letting herself be tugged into the spacious elevator. "Everything you do—you never hesitate. You always seem to know just what you want."

She bit back the rest of the words that were on the tip of her tongue. She couldn't—wouldn't—tell him that she was envious of that confidence. That she thrilled to the taste of it when she submitted to him.

Samantha stilled when she felt Elijah's hands closing around her waist. He turned her so that she was looking out the glass wall of the elevator, down at the city of Las Vegas, rapidly shrinking beneath them. Hands resting at her waist, he pressed a kiss into her hair, still damp from the shower.

The tenderness of the gesture made her heart race, pressing against her rib cage as if trying to escape.

"I wouldn't say it's a Dom thing, no," Elijah said as Samantha drew in a shaky breath as the elevator rocketed higher, taking them closer to the top of the immensely tall building.

His hands at her waist squeezed gently to steady her.

"I've seen people who are not dominant who are even more confident than myself, or more than Alex or Luca," Elijah continued.

The elevator drew to a smooth stop, the bell chiming as the doors opened.

They stepped into bright sunlight. Samantha winced and squinted, covering her eyes just as Elijah pressed something into her hands.

It was a pair of sleek tortoiseshell sunglasses. The label on the side was designer, and Samantha bit her lip at the thought of how much they had likely cost.

"I'd have been happy with a pair from Walmart, you know." By this point, she knew that resistance was futile. She slid them on, adjusted them, found they fit perfectly. She was strangely touched that he'd chosen a pair that she would have picked for herself—well, if she ever spent more than twenty dollars on a pair of sunnies.

She looked up to find Elijah glowering down at her.

"What now?" It was windy on the top of the building, and she pulled the elastic from her hair, smoothed the windblown strands back, and secured it again.

"Cheap sunglasses can do more harm than good." Pulling his own from his pocket, he slid them on. Samantha felt her mouth water as she looked at him. Though she didn't sketch much, preferring to work with hot glass as her sole medium, she felt the urge to capture him as he was, the wind pressing against his hair, the sun slanting over his skin. *Billionaire at Play*—that's what she would call it.

She was too shy to ask him to pose for her. She'd sculpted a nude of his torso, true enough, but it had been a joke.

The urge she had was to lay him bare on canvas. And if she got to the heart of him, she was afraid that she would reveal more of herself than she wanted to.

"Come." Elijah took her hand and led her across the slate tiles that covered the roof of the building. She'd been too caught up in him to notice it before, and he'd ushered her inside the building so quickly she hadn't had a chance to look up. But though they were on the roof, they still hadn't reached their destination.

There was another part of the building even higher, resembling a turret on a castle. It speared the brilliant blue sky . . . and launched a roller coaster, one that, though small, was still terrifying, being as it was seemingly miles off the ground.

"No way. Elijah, I can't do this." Samantha planted her feet on the ground. She wasn't afraid of heights, but surely only an idiot would think that riding that thing was a good idea. "I'll stay right here."

Elijah raised his eyebrows at her in a manner that had rapidly become endearing and familiar, and Samantha knew that she was about to have her mind changed for her.

"As I was saying," he started, and Samantha narrowed her eyes at him, not sure what he was up to. "Having extreme confidence doesn't necessarily mean that a person is dominant. But every Dominant that I know has nearly unbreakable confidence."

"Talk in circles much?" Samantha muttered, stuffing her hands into the pockets of her jeans. She sucked in a deep breath when Elijah strode forward, caught her chin in the palm of his hand, and looked down into her eyes.

"A Dom must have confidence in him- or herself, or else it's unthinkable to ask a submissive to place their trust in them."

Samantha found herself caught in the pull of that brilliant blue stare. Her mouth went dry.

"So you're saying that I can borrow your confidence for a while?" Her voice was light, her tone joking, but she found that there was a note of seriousness in her question.

The hand holding her chin squeezed gently, then released. Elijah stepped back, looking down at her with a neutral expression. Did she imagine that she saw a glimpse of tenderness there?

"Only until you find your own."

Elijah watched as Samantha's expression shuttered. What was she hiding? he wondered. The need to find out was clawing at him.

And yet he wasn't ready to risk sending them back to square one, or, worse, to a place beyond repair. He found that he still possessed a measure of patience, to wait for Samantha to feel ready to confide in him.

Lacing his fingers through hers, he tugged her in the direction of the tower. Pushing limits was what a Dom did, both in the bedroom and out, and he was hoping that the roller-coaster ride would loosen her tongue so that they could find a new level of pleasure together.

"Elijah, please, no." His stubborn little redhead planted her feet and looked up at him beseechingly. She looked so damn cute it was all he could do not to grab her and kiss her.

He suspected that she would breathe flames if he told her what he was thinking, so he kept his mouth shut.

"Samantha, are you afraid of heights?" The way she'd looked out his bathroom window at the soaring lights of Vegas told him that she wasn't, but he wanted to hear it from her lips.

Her brow furrowed, and he knew she was trying to think of a way around his question.

"No," she finally admitted, pinching her lips together. "But that's not the point."

He simply waited, looking at her with the calm that had come from years of practicing self-discipline.

She looked away from him, looked back, and finally just sighed.

"I'm not the kind of person who just does stuff like this." He could tell that she was trying to compose herself, and Elijah felt a surge of triumph. He could see from the suddenly glassy sheen in her eyes that the roller coaster was bringing some sort of emotions forward. Though he hadn't intended for the emotional purge to come *before* they'd gone on the ride, he was satisfied nonetheless.

"And what kind of person does do stuff like this?" Elijah fastened his stare on Samantha's face, not wanting to miss a nuance of her expression.

She scowled, but beneath the scowl was . . . longing?

"Samantha?" he prompted, thoroughly intrigued. The little cat was just full of twists and turns. She fascinated him as no other woman ever had, not even Tara.

"People who have fun, okay? People who have fun do things like this!"

Elijah was certain she wasn't aware that she'd shouted. Her hands were balled into fists, and she bounced on the tips of her toes with agitation.

"And why aren't you a person who has fun?" He leaned in close, until their faces were only a whisper away from each other. He watched as she tried to look to the side, to break eye contact, but at such close range she couldn't.

She squirmed, then pressed her lips together stubbornly. Elijah rocked back on his heels, considering how to punish her.

"All right." Inhaling deeply, he reached for the dominance inside him. It was almost like an actor reaching for character, he'd once thought, except that he knew dominance was more a part of him than a character could ever be part of an actor.

"You have two choices. You can explain that comment further—and I expect a full answer. Or we can get on the roller coaster. The owner ensured that the most skilled operator would be waiting for us and we'll have a spectacular view of the city." He winked at her, making sure that his grin was over the top, designed to make her smile. "Plus the sex after an adrenaline rush like that is out of this world."

He watched as Samantha's cheeks flushed. She shuffled her feet, then finally squeezed her eyes shut and held her free hand out to him.

"Let's go before I lose my nerve."

Riding an impulse, Elijah bent and scooped Samantha over his shoulder. She shrieked and slapped her hands against the backs of his thighs as he carried her across the roof to the tower.

"You have got to stop doing that!" Samantha was breathless and gorgeous when he set her down, making sure to slide her along his body as he did. His cock was hard from the feel of her womanly curves against him—not, admittedly, an uncommon occurrence.

But now was not the time to jump her. He'd have to make up for it later. But he couldn't resist laying his hand over the curve of her ass.

"Samantha, I'd like you to meet Ted." Elijah gestured to the man who stood just inside the door to the tower. Samantha whirled, startled to find someone else there.

Blushing, she tried to bat at Elijah's hand. He kept it where it was. Ted had been employed at this hotel for years. He'd surely seen worse.

"It's my pleasure, miss." Ted took Samantha's hand and, dipping his head, kissed it. The flush on her cheeks deepened, and Elijah smiled to himself.

He would have bet his sizable fortune that she was remembering the moment in his plane when he'd introduced her to Mattias. When he'd ordered her to strip naked and had commanded Mattias to play with her breasts.

It was tempting to revisit the scenario—and he was sure that Ted wouldn't mind at all—but there would be time for play later.

"Nice to meet you, too." Samantha looked from Ted to Elijah hesitantly, looking suddenly uncertain. Though she followed them into the second elevator, Elijah could read the tension coming off of her in waves.

It troubled him. As her Dom, at least for the month, he considered it his responsibility to push her out of her comfort zone. But the last thing he wanted was to scare her to death.

"Are you sure you're okay with heights?" Maybe he'd read her wrong, though he didn't think so.

"No. I mean yes—heights are fine," she said as she nibbled on her lower lip. When the elevator reached the top, Elijah cast a look at Ted, communicating that he wanted a moment alone. Once Ted had stepped out, he turned back toward her.

"What's bothering you? And don't try to get out of it." He scowled, though he was really feeling more concern than anger.

Her mouth fell open and her eyes narrowed. "You said if I went on the ride with you I wouldn't have to tell you."

Interestingly, her distress seemed to increase as she was faced with the notion of spilling her problems.

"So far you haven't gotten on that ride with me. And the way you're acting is telling me that you might not after all." Elijah raised an eyebrow and waited.

Samantha twisted her fingers together, looking down. Elijah had topped a lot of submissives, but never before had he seen such avoidance.

"I just— Growing up, I had to be the responsible one." Her lips pressed together in a firm line, and he knew that it must have taken a lot for her to say even that much. "Having fun was not an option. And when I finally left home, I wasn't looking for fun so much as peace. It just feels wrong to have this kind of fun."

Elijah felt his heart ache. Whatever the little cat's big secret was, it affected her deeply.

He could offer her distraction at the moment.

"It's just a roller-coaster ride, Samantha." Lifting her fingers to his lips, Elijah mimicked the gesture that Ted had made only moments before. "It's a beautiful day. We have the entire tower roller coaster to ourselves. You're going to have the best view possible of the city . . . and it's going to be the second best three minutes of your life."

"Second best?" Samantha's expression was puzzled as she looked over at him. He smirked, holding the elevator door open. And—finally—she laughed. "We'll see. Maybe it'll be even better."

Bratty little sub. With a point to prove, Elijah cupped his hands beneath Samantha's ass and pressed her against the open elevator door with just enough force to make her breath catch. Before she could fully recover, he rocked his hips into the soft flesh of her pelvis and cupped his hand around her throat just before diving in for a hot, hard kiss.

He felt her press back against him, knew that the hand at her throat would send a thread of panic through her. Breath play was against the rules at Veritas, but he knew what he was doing. And he knew that just the tiniest hint of oxygen deprivation could take a sub to heights she'd never before imagined.

He wanted Samantha off guard and aching for him. When he broke the kiss and took his hand away from the slender column of her throat at the same time, he saw his own desperate need reflected in her eyes.

"I think I've made my point." Elijah released Samantha down his body, but he knew that she had noticed his rock-solid erection.

It seemed that he couldn't go even an hour around her without the blood rushing to his cock. He watched as she ran her hands over her lips, swollen from his onslaught, then walked dazedly out of the elevator to where Ted was waiting for them.

It wasn't often that Samantha was speechless, and he couldn't quite hold back his delighted grin as he followed her.

"Holy shit." Samantha held on to the metal bar in front of her so tightly that her fingers went pale white. "Why are we doing this? This is ridiculous. This is *dangerous*."

"Says the woman who plays with fire every day." Elijah sat back in his seat, anticipation zinging through his nerves. The coaster hadn't even started moving yet—he'd asked Ted to give them a few minutes to look out at the view. So far, however, the only thing Samantha was looking at were her knees.

"Look—you can see Alex's casino from here." When Samantha tentatively looked up, Elijah pointed out the massive El Diablo, his friend's hotel and residence.

"Alex owns a casino?" Samantha cast a semidisbelieving stare at Elijah before finally looking out over the city. Though he felt her body tighten against his and heard her sharp intake of breath, she held her own, swallowing hard as she looked at the view spread out below them. "And let me guess. Luca owns an entire city or something, right?"

"Not a city. A small island, yes." Elijah couldn't hold back his chuckle as Samantha shook her head and said something under her breath. She hadn't tensed up at the reminder of his wealth, however, and that was progress.

"Are you ready?" Beneath them the cart began to rumble, inching forward. Elijah grinned as he looked down at Samantha, and was rewarded with a tiny smile in return.

The cart of the coaster chugged up to the first point. It wasn't a long ride, or even particularly scary, at least if you ignored the distance it was above the ground. Elijah cast one long look over the city as they reached the first peak and felt contentment settle in his chest.

Las Vegas, to him, was home. He'd brought Samantha up here to push her, certainly, but also because he'd wanted to share the city with her.

The cart hovered on the top of the first incline. Rather than focusing on the drop, Elijah found himself entranced by the wonder on Samantha's face as she looked out at the city.

"Wow." Her voice was full of awe.

The cart chugged forward an inch, tipping forward. Elijah grinned as the wonder changed to terror, mixed with a heady look of anticipation.

"Fuck!" Samantha screamed as the cart tipped, propelling them down the steep drop. As his own stomach dropped, Elijah forced his head to the side to look at Samantha.

Her cheeks were flushed pink, and her screams were mixed with laughter. She pinned him with those green eyes as the cart whipped around the final loop, momentarily suspending them upside down. She was still screaming with laughter as the coaster slowed and, finally, pulled to a stop back at the starting point.

Elijah unbuckled his seat belt, then hers, turning fully to watch her. Samantha was looking out at the awe-inspiring view of the city, the wind whipping the fire of her hair against the creamy skin of her cheeks.

Elijah felt his heart stutter with a new sensation. When she turned and met his stare, the truth slammed home.

"What is it?" Samantha asked, her brow furrowing. Elijah realized that some of his emotions must have played out over his face, and he quickly smoothed his expression back out.

"I was just wondering what it would be like to fuck you on this roller coaster." Samantha's eyes grew wide at his shocking words, distracting her. It was just what he had intended.

It wasn't fair, demanding honesty from her when he wasn't prepared to give the same. The difference, to him at least, was that there were things Samantha didn't seem inclined to tell him—ever.

And the thought that had just slammed him upside the head was something he fully intended to share with her, and soon.

But first he needed to wrap his head around the fact that he thought he might be falling in love with her.

CHAPTER FOURTEEN

"What a rush." Adrenaline was pumping hot and fast through Samantha's veins as Elijah helped her out of the roller coaster. After attempting to tame her long, tangled ponytail, she stretched and peered out at the city again as Elijah approached Ted.

She didn't have to look to know that Elijah was giving the man a tip for his time. Probably an exorbitantly large one.

He liked to look after people. It seemed to be a bone-deep need inside him.

She was finding that she really liked being taken care of.

"Shall we?" Elijah offered her a hand, steadying her as she stepped down off the platform. Samantha laced her fingers through his and tried to think of the words she needed.

"Thank you." Her voice was quiet. She still wasn't sure what had made Elijah push her to go on the coaster, or why she felt so open and happy now. She didn't understand how he'd known she needed something like this.

But that was Elijah. He knew what she needed, it seemed, better than she did herself.

"Anytime," he replied, his eyes boring into hers. She could see his hunger for her, and Samantha felt her knees tremble.

It wasn't the first time he had looked at her as though he wanted to eat her up. But this time there was something different in his expression—something . . . deeper.

Need and emotion combined into something sharp and poignant, slashing through her like a blade.

Samantha slowed, then stopped, using their entwined fingers to hold Elijah in place.

This time she was the one who initiated the kiss. Standing on the tips of her toes, she placed her palms flat on Elijah's chest. The muscles were taut and warm beneath her fingers as she pressed a kiss to the line of his jaw, then to his cheek, and finally to his lips.

"Mmm . . ." Tilting his head down to meet her, he let her slant her lips over his, teasing, testing. The kiss was like the sun that shone all around them, bright and warm and addictive.

Then Elijah tangled his hand in the length of her ponytail, his free hand splaying across the skin between her shoulder blades. He pulled her to him roughly, their bodies aligning, melting together with the heat between them.

"Mine." Elijah tugged on her hair as he spoke, then pressed his tongue against the seam of her lips, demanding entrance. With a moan she went pliant against him, parting her lips, letting him possess her mouth.

This was what she had been missing her entire adult life: a man who would take control without asking for it.

As she pondered that, Elijah continued to devour Samantha's mouth. Her nipples hardened against the taut planes of his chest, and she rubbed against him like a cat in heat, wanting more.

From far away, she heard the voice of Alicia Keys singing about a girl on fire. Her back pocket vibrated. Her cell was ringing.

With a moan she decided to ignore it and pressed more fully into Elijah. She cried out when he pulled away, looking down at her with a stern expression.

"It could be important. Answer it."

Samantha blinked once, twice, trying to clear the haze of lust that tinted her surroundings. Elijah looked at her, clearly waiting . . . and clearly not inclined to pick up where they'd left off until she answered the call, though the front of his slacks was tented with his arousal.

Impatient, Samantha pried her cell out of the snug back pocket of her jeans.

COLLINS, BETH

A frisson of nerves hit her. Beth rarely called her, although, to be fair, it was because Samantha called her so often that her younger sister didn't have to.

Elijah was right. If Beth was calling, it was probably important.

With an apologetic smile, she turned away from Elijah and walked out of earshot before accepting the call.

"Beth?" Looking back over her shoulder, Samantha caught sight of Elijah's face and froze. His expression was thunderous, and for a long moment she wondered what on earth she had done to deserve such ire.

Then she understood. She'd walked away because she hadn't wanted him to overhear her end of the conversation. She was hiding things from the man who insisted on openness and honesty. The man to whom she had promised to be completely submissive for one month.

"What's wrong with you?" her younger sister replied, making Samantha grind her teeth together. "You sound out of breath."

"Nothing," Samantha snapped, glowering back at Elijah without thinking. "Sorry. You just caught me in the middle of something."

Remembering that Beth wasn't the one she was irritated with, she softened her tone, though the edges of her irritation with Elijah remained razor sharp.

She wasn't a child, damn it. Just because she wanted a strong, dominant man in her life didn't mean that she intended to divulge every burden that she carried to him.

Her sister, her mother—they were no one's business but her own. She didn't intend to talk about them ever, not even if it meant that Elijah would walk away.

If the thought of him doing just that made her heart hurt, well, that was something she would find a way to live with.

"I'll make it quick, then." Beth's voice was tight, not at all the carefree tone Samantha had come to rely on from her younger sister. Her gut clenched with nerves.

"What's going on?" As she spoke, Samantha mentally began calculating. She still had the check from Elijah. It had seemed wrong, somehow, to deposit it, since real feelings had begun to blossom inside her, feelings that went beyond curiosity about the submissive lifestyle.

But if something was wrong at home with Beth, she'd use it without a second thought.

"Are you feeling okay?" Samantha couldn't count the nights she'd lain awake after her sister's diagnosis, certain that Beth would die if she closed her eyes. As they'd learned more about the disease, they'd both relaxed somewhat.

But for years in their teens, Samantha had tested her sister's blood sugar level at the night, just to make sure. When she had seen that Samantha couldn't sleep until she'd done so, Beth had stopped protesting.

It was likely the same realization that kept Beth from snapping back at her, Samantha knew as she tried to calm down.

She would never stop worrying. Forced into the role of mother so many years earlier, even when she had her own issues to work through, she now worried as if it was second nature.

"I'm fine, Sam." Beth's voice held only a hint of annoyance at the interrogation. "This has nothing to do with me."

Samantha relaxed, just a bit, as Beth continued.

"Yesterday I stopped by to bring Mom some groceries."

Beth's tone was hesitant, and Samantha knew that her sister expected to be yelled at for using some of her money on their mother.

Biting her tongue, Samantha said nothing.

"She was pass—I mean, she was sleeping when I got there. Her phone was on the counter when I put the groceries away, and it rang while I was right there." Beth sounded apprehensive. "Sam, it was Stanley. His number is programmed right in, so it can't be the first time he's called."

Samantha felt the blood drain from her face at the sound of the name that she'd tried so hard to forget.

"What the fuck does he want?" she said bitterly, and she heard Beth suck in a breath.

Beth knew that Stanley was bad news—Samantha had drilled it into her head every time the man had come near their family. But her sister didn't know what exactly had transpired between Samantha and the rich man who had once kept their mother as a mistress. Samantha had made sure of it, because she had figured that at least one of them should retain some semblance of innocence.

"I don't know what he wants, Sam. I didn't answer the phone," Beth replied.

Samantha inhaled a shuddering breath, trying to calm herself.

She was an adult now. There was nothing that man could do to harm her, or Beth. If Gemma chose to let the asshole back into her life, that was her mother's own idiotic decision.

"Just tell me if he comes around, okay?" Despite the reassurances that were running through her head, Samantha felt dread balling up tightly in her belly.

Stanley was bad news. If he was calling Gemma, it wouldn't bode well for any of them.

"I'll let you know," Beth agreed. "Love you, Sam."

"Love you too, Bethy," Samantha said absently, her stomach still churning over the idea of what Stanley could possibly want with her mother. She was deep in thought as she ended the call and stuffed her phone back into her pocket.

She shrieked, startled, when she turned to find Elijah standing directly behind her. Though he still looked angry, he seemed to have gotten control over the worst of it.

Nerves tap-danced over her skin. How much had he heard?

He didn't say anything, instead simply rocked back on his heels, his hands in his pockets. He was waiting, she realized. Waiting for her to voluntarily tell him why she'd tried to hide the phone call from him.

The knowledge that Stanley was sniffing around again had drained her, and she didn't have any fight left. She looked up at Elijah with wide eyes and shook her head, her lips pressed tightly together.

"I can't tell you." Though her voice was quiet, it was firm. This was a chapter of her life that she'd tried to put behind her. That she'd *needed* to put behind her, so that she could move on and live her life as a functional adult.

When she looked up into Elijah's eyes again, he most certainly did not look pleased.

"What happens to subs who don't do as they're told?" His eyes darkened, as did his expression, and Samantha involuntarily sucked in a breath.

When he looked at her like that, she wanted to melt and give in to him. But Beth's phone call had left her edgy, not in full control of her emotions. So even though she wanted to look down, to submit, instead she found angry words slipping from her lips.

"I don't have to tell you anything." She cringed as she spoke, well aware of how bratty she sounded, well aware that he could turn and walk away at any moment. Still, she couldn't bring herself to do anything else.

"Don't dare your Dom, little one." Elijah stepped closer to her and threaded his hand in her hair, tugging until her scalp prickled. "You won't like the results."

Her breath shuddering in and out of her lungs, she looked him right in the eyes, defiant and upset. She expected to find only displeasure, to see disappointment. And that was there, certainly.

But so was understanding. When she saw that empathy, a tremor passed over her and the anger drained out through her.

Dropping her stare to the ground, she sank stiffly onto her knees, wanting nothing more than to make it up to him, though she still didn't see how she could force herself to share this part of her past with him.

Damn it, why couldn't he just let the past stay in the past?

Then he cupped her chin, forcing her to look up into his eyes, and she forgot everything except the need to please him.

"I'm sorry," she whispered, and contrition was a tight band around her heart. She was so damn mad at herself.

She'd finally found what she wanted—*who* she wanted—and she couldn't let go of the past long enough to grab hold of it with both hands.

"It's too late for sorry, Samantha."

Her heart pounded as her gaze zeroed in on him. *What*—? *Was he saying*—?

"Since openness and honesty continue to be an issue with you, and verbal warnings haven't worked, let's try something else." Elijah began to slowly undo his belt buckle, and Samantha watched intently as her stomach did a slow roll.

He meant to punish her, right here, right on the rooftop of this hotel with Ted not twenty feet away. He would order her to suck his cock, or to use her hands . . . *something.*

Along with the kernel of fear, she felt an undeniable wash of heat.

"I see that the idea of punishment excites you." In full-on Dom mode like this, Elijah barely seemed to be the same person who had on occasion demonstrated such tenderness. His voice was layered with something that made her want to obey.

"Since you haven't earned the privilege of pleasure, I think I'll withhold it for now." A streak of cruelty colored his voice, and Samantha roused to it.

"Stand and remove your jeans."

Pulled to her feet as though she were a puppet and he held the strings, Samantha looked over Elijah's shoulder at the control booth for the roller coaster. Ted was standing in front of it, hands in his pockets, watching intently but not moving a muscle.

It was on the tip of her tongue to refuse, but a flicker of something in Elijah's eyes gave her pause.

He *expected* her to back down. Thought she would use her safe word.

Damn him! There were parts of submission that didn't come easily to her, but she was here because she wanted to be.

Grinding her teeth together, she undid the button and zipper of her pants. The hint of surprise that passed over Elijah's face had grim satisfaction welling inside her.

Toeing off her sneakers, Samantha slid the stiff denim and soft lace of the clothes that Elijah had provided for her just that morning to the concrete beneath her feet and stepped out of them. Forcing herself to stare at the ground, she tangled the fingers of both hands together and waited. Every nerve in her body was on fire.

"Face away from me."

Wanting with every fiber of her being to look up, to try to discern his feelings from his face, Samantha instead did as she was told.

"Bend your knees and place your hands on your thighs."

Samantha shivered as she followed the instructions. As she rested her sweaty palms on tense thigh muscles, she grimaced at the sensation of exposure.

She felt like a naughty child, about to receive a spanking... which she very likely was. And the most perverse part of it all was that, mixed in with the humiliation, was an unfamiliar deep need.

She wanted to be punished for not obeying orders. Wanted him to give her no other choice than to tell him everything.

She heard the belt whistle through the air seconds before it landed on her backside. A choked cry escaped her as the bite of the leather shocked her senses, making her jolt forward.

"I'm not into extreme pain, Samantha. You know that." Another sharp smack on her ass, another jolt. "And I'm not pleased that you've forced my hand, though that vanilla skin of yours does redden very nicely."

Tears sparkled in her eyes as the third blow landed. Her ass was incredibly sore already, and she didn't know how much more pain she could take. Yet despite the undeniable discomfort, she could feel herself growing wet and needy. Wanting him to fill that aching place inside her.

"I'm doing this because words aren't getting through to you. I'm very nearly at the end of my patience."

"No!" Panic was sharp and flashed bright inside her, and she tried to stand, to turn and face Elijah. But one final lash of the belt landed right over her mound before she could fully straighten, and arousal snapped through her hot and tight, making her moan aloud.

She waited, tensed, for the next blow. Instead, she heard the sound of leather rubbing against cloth as Elijah worked his belt back through the loops of his jeans. The panting of their breath, his and hers, was quickly carried away by the wind on the rooftop.

A single scalding tear spilled over, the wind drying it almost before it had fallen. Samantha shuddered, full of too many emotions, ablaze with arousal that only needed one more small touch to break free.

"Turn and kneel."

Samantha obeyed instantly, dropping to her knees on the hard concrete. It was rough and scraped at her naked skin, but she didn't care.

Over Elijah's shoulder she could see Ted. Somehow, she'd completely forgotten that he was even there.

"Look at me." Elijah's voice was slightly softer, and when Samantha looked up she saw that he was feeling just as undone as she was.

"Tell me what you did wrong, Samantha, and apologize." The expression that lay behind those eyes, as blue as the brilliant sky around them, was less scary than it had been earlier, but Samantha saw that he still wasn't going to take no for an answer.

"I tried to hide something from you. I'm sorry." She meant every word. And more, as she looked up at Elijah, she found that she wanted to share everything with him—wanted to so badly that she could taste it.

Somehow she knew that he could make the nightmares go away. But as she tried her best to form the words and share her burden with him, they still wouldn't come. She'd locked them down so deep that they were entirely petrified. Frantic, she searched Elijah's face. Something flickered through his eyes as he saw that she still wasn't talking, and then his expression became shuttered, neutral.

Dread washed over her. She would have preferred to see the thunderous rage to that blankness.

"Get dressed." He waited, his hands stuffed in his pockets as Samantha drew her panties and jeans back up over her hips with trembling fingers, then slid into her sneakers.

"Let's go." Silently Elijah led her back across the roof and into the elevator. Instead of the casual intimacy that came with holding hands, this time he kept his hands tucked in his pockets, away from her, and Samantha felt as though a wall of ice had grown between them.

Panic had lodged inside her, and she wasn't sure how to make it go away. Well, that wasn't entirely true. She knew how, but the words just wouldn't come.

The ride down the elevator was excruciatingly silent, as was the drive back to In Vino Veritas and Elijah's apartment. He helped her exit the low-slung vehicle, his face still stern.

"Samantha." Elijah spoke only her name.

Hot tears blurring her vision, she turned back toward him reluctantly, though all she wanted to do was run and hide. She looked up at him with wide eyes, swallowing past the large lump in her throat.

"Samantha, I need you to understand something." For the first time since she'd met him, Elijah looked as though he wasn't in complete control of himself. The fact that she had done that to him was not a comfortable sensation.

"There is nothing that you can tell me that will shock me, or turn me off, or make me not want to be with you," Elijah began, his face serious.

Samantha wanted nothing more than to run into his arms, to bury her face in his chest, but that invisible barrier kept her from doing it. She knew they would keep running into this again and again, until she was able to confess her secrets to him.

"You say you want to submit to me. I can help you with that, can push you past so many of your boundaries. But this . . . You need to find it in yourself to trust me—with anything. And if you can't do that, then I'm not the Dom for you."

Samantha sucked in a breath of searing Las Vegas air as the words Elijah *hadn't* spoken rang through the air.

You need to open yourself to me fully, or we're through.

Stunned, panicked, she followed Elijah into the elevator that led up to his apartment. She stared at her toes, clad in the new, bright pink sneakers that she'd found that morning, and felt like she was going to be sick.

By the time the elevator had reached the apartment, she'd reached one conclusion. Elijah was the best thing that had ever happened to her. She wasn't about to just let him walk away.

As they exited, Elijah turned toward her, his mouth open as if he was about to say something. Though she suspected she was breaking all kinds of submissive rules, she interrupted, needing to say what was in her head.

"Please. Give me a minute." Not daring to look up into his eyes, Samantha looked down at the floor as she instinctively dropped to her knees, laying her hands in her lap, palms up. She had seen other submissives doing this at the club the other night, and it seemed like the thing to do at that moment.

"My sister called to tell me that someone . . . someone from our past might be back in our mother's life. That's all it was." Samantha swallowed past the unease that the very thought of Stanley brought to coat her throat. "This person . . . I can't say he ruined our family—that was on my mother's shoulders. But he sure didn't help. I've spent a long time trying to forget he even existed.

"I wanted to tell you earlier. So badly. But after so many years of shoving it away . . . it's like it's frozen inside me." Steeling herself, she looked up, looked into Elijah's eyes. He was regarding her thoughtfully, though she couldn't gauge the expression on his face.

"I don't know how to say I'm sorry in this world," she whispered, shifting uncomfortably on her knees. "But I am. I'm sorry I didn't just tell you this. And I'm sorry that I can't tell you more. Please understand. Reliving it . . . it just might kill me."

Nothing could have stunned Elijah more than when Samantha dropped to her knees in front of him. Though he hadn't taught her the position, she had sunk to her knees as if she'd been doing it her entire life.

And when she apologized . . . it was the most beautiful thing he'd ever heard.

Still he couldn't overlook the fact that she wasn't confiding in him completely. Why couldn't he make her understand that there was nothing she could say that would turn him away?

"I'm tempted to push you right now, little one." He studied her body language as he spoke, noted the sudden and complete tension that racked her frame.

She was terrified of revisiting whatever it was her memory held, and that made it a hard limit, at least for now. It would be detrimental to try to convince her to open up any more right now.

Bending at the waist, he offered her his hand, helping her up from her knees. Catching the side of her face in his fingers, he turned her toward him until she had no choice but to look right at him.

"Thank you for telling me as much as you did." Wrapping his arms around her, he lifted her up until he balanced her entire weight. She sighed and buried her head into his chest, and the contentment that wrapped over him was strange and new.

In his bedroom, he gently placed Samantha on the bed—noting that she winced when she landed on her bottom—then crossed to the bureau. He extracted a thin, silky slip and a pair of sheer panties from the clothing he'd bought her. He contemplated a pair of sky-high, sexy-as-sin red pumps, then decided she would go barefoot for the night.

"Put on these items, and only these." Crossing to the bed again, he placed the lingerie in Samantha's lap. She looked at them, then at him, and he watched as her nipples hardened beneath her cotton T-shirt.

"Are we going to the club?" Her voice was soft and contained the faintest hint of a tremor.

Elijah glowered down at her, watching as she sucked in a breath and looked down at her sneakered feet. The pink tennis shoes were adorable on her, but the way he was feeling, nothing but naked skin and restraints would do.

"Do not ask questions. Do not speak until I give you permission." He wasn't normally so formal with his subs, but he was in a mood. "Dress in what I have given you. Meet me at the elevator in precisely ten minutes."

He noted the tinge of pink that flushed her skin, the shine that came into her eyes as he took control away from her. *Now* it was time to push her, though it likely wouldn't be in a way that she expected.

He crossed his bedroom, pausing at the door to look back at Samantha. With her pink cheeks, bright eyes, and messed hair, she looked entirely fuckable, and he wanted nothing more than to tear her clothes away, flip her over, and drive himself into her from behind.

But he had to wait.

He nearly groaned as his cock hardened, taunted by the images of what he was about to do to her.

"I'm taking you to Veritas."

He was Dom enough to be pleased by the way her eyes widened and her skin paled.

"But . . . you already . . . the belt . . ." She looked so young and innocent as she stammered, and Elijah felt a stab of guilt. He wasn't going to push her to tell him what she was hiding that night. But it was still his responsibility as a Dom to address the issue.

He'd become more attached to her than he cared to admit. And she was here of her own volition. If this—whatever *this* was—was to go any further, all of her baggage would have to be dealt with. Not now, but soon.

"The belt was for hiding the phone call from me." Though his emotions were fully engaged, Elijah felt his cock stiffen further at the memory of Samantha, bent over for his hand, nothing but the bright sky around them. "I'm proud of you for starting to open up to me, so you'll be rewarded tonight as well. But there's more that you're keeping back. I'm not going to push you to tell me, but I'm upset with you. That means that you require another punishment."

Elijah registered Samantha's startled inhalation as he left the room to give her the allotted time to dress. No doubt she thought that another punishment was grossly unfair, but at this point in their relationship he would be remiss in his duties to do anything less.

And there was one thing that would likely give her some comfort if she knew—not that he was about to tell her.

If she was receiving punishment . . . that meant he was about to be punished, too.

CHAPTER FIFTEEN

S hivers worked their way down Samantha's spine, over and over again, as Elijah led her from his apartment and around to the entrance of In Vino Veritas.

She knew—somehow she knew—that tonight she was going to be taken further into the BDSM scene than she'd been so far. She was terrified.

She couldn't wait.

Images flashed through her head, a never-ending stream of color, as she remembered some of the scenes that she'd taken in at Veritas and, back in Cabo, at Pecado.

A woman bound to a cross-shaped structure, naked and open for anyone to touch her.

The hiss of a flogger, slicing through the air before kissing the tender flesh of a submissive.

Hot wax, poured in delicate patterns over bared skin.

She shivered again as they rounded the corner, unsure whether it was from nervousness or excitement, and Elijah took her upper arm gently in his hand.

"Tell me what you're thinking right now." He had been strangely quiet ever since she'd apologized to him. She wasn't quite sure what to make of it.

"I'm wondering what you're going to do to me in there." From the corner of her eyes she saw Julien. She opened her lips to greet him, but a stern shake of his head from Elijah reminded her of the rules.

She wasn't to speak until he gave her permission.

She had never felt more like she belonged to him.

"Are you nervous?" Elijah stopped right in front of the main doors, his hands resting on her shoulders. Samantha could hear the sounds of cars pulling into the driveway, of others arriving for their evening of wine and play, but Elijah was looking down at her as if she was the only person in the world.

Her knee-jerk reaction was to play the defensive, to retort that nothing scared her, not even whips and chains.

Yet she didn't want to lie.

"Yes, I'm nervous." She flicked her tongue out to moisten her suddenly dry lips, and saw Elijah's eyes following the gesture. "I don't think you'll hurt me. But I'm scared . . . scared of the unknown."

Since moving to Mexico, her life had been a comfortable routine. She'd done the same things over and over again, never stepping outside her own little bubble.

Then she'd met Elijah, and her world had turned upside down.

"I like it that you're nervous." Elijah smiled at her, and it was the dark, wicked smile that he reserved for playtime. "But I don't want you scared. Maybe this will help."

Samantha watched as he pulled a length of what looked like silk from his pocket. Pink silk—it was the scarf he'd used to restrain her before.

Heat washed over her as Elijah carefully placed the folds of soft silk over her eyes, tying it behind her head.

"I've got you." Elijah took her hand and pulled her gently forward. Samantha could tell when they passed through the main door of Veritas, could mark their movements as they worked their way down the hall, bypassing the wine bar.

She knew when Elijah opened the door that led into the play area, could hear the influx of sexy music and the equally enticing noises of people experiencing pleasure.

But the scarf over her eyes allowed her to remain removed, just a hint, from the surroundings as Elijah led her across the playroom floor. Her nerves had settled a bit when Elijah finally led her to a stop.

She shifted, her bare feet sticking to the varnished floor, as he undid her blindfold with sure fingers. Samantha blinked in the light as the silk fell into Elijah's hands.

Though the room was dimly lit, it seemed bright as the sun after the darkness behind the blindfold.

The expression on Elijah's face ensured that she would look—*could* look—at no one but him.

"Samantha, do you understand why we're here?" His words were serious, sexy. A frisson of excitement skated over her skin.

She nodded, wanting to please him.

"We're here so you can—can punish me." Her voice didn't shake, even with her nerves, and it was a triumph.

"And tell me why you're being punished."

Samantha felt she should be scared, as if his words should make her want to run. Instead, she heard nothing from him but quiet patience and acceptance.

In that moment she truly felt that she could tell Elijah about her past—and the words were on the tip of her tongue.

She hesitated a beat too long, and the urge passed. In its place, however, was the desire to please him in some other way, even if it meant accepting further punishment.

"You're going to punish me because I . . . because I still have secrets." Her voice sounded far calmer to her own ears than it had in years.

"I'm sorry," she added, unable to keep it in. "I really am."

"I know." Elijah smiled at her, half with that wicked intent, half with . . . was that *affection*? Caring? "And it's more accurate to say that tonight is about proving to you that you can trust me with anything."

His words made Samantha's heart stutter in her chest. Confused, she looked down at her naked toes. From the corner of her eyes she caught Elijah's arm waving, gesturing to someone.

She was too nervous to look up to see who.

"Samantha. This is Luca Santangelo. I don't think you've met him yet." Samantha looked up to find the giant of a man who usually stood guard behind the bar watching her intently.

He was wearing black leather pants, a matching vest open over a well-muscled chest, and nothing else. The same tattoo that ringed Elijah's biceps, and supposedly Alex's as well, was on Luca's arm.

Though she appreciated the beauty of the ink on Luca, the dark artistic swirls, it didn't give her the urge to run her fingers over it the way she felt when she saw Elijah's.

"See anything you like, subbie?" Luca smirked down at her from his massive height.

Samantha sucked in a breath, suddenly nervous. "Apologies, Master Luca."

Her apology to Elijah was only too fresh in her mind, the one she still wasn't sure he was going to accept. Her heart hurt with the notion that she'd failed him, but she didn't know what else she could do. She hadn't been a part of this world long enough to understand all its hidden secrets—she didn't know if she ever would.

"She apologizes very prettily, E."

Samantha stared at her bare feet as Luca spoke. She knew she was mouthy, knew she could be difficult, but in that moment all she wanted was to be able to tell Elijah everything, to share the burden, and for Elijah to truly forgive her.

Why wouldn't the words just come? Was she afraid of his reaction?

Samantha recognized Elijah's feet as he moved to stand in front of her. He placed a finger under her chin and tilted her face up until she was looking right at him.

"She does indeed, Luca." Samantha felt a wild swell of hope surge through her, though Elijah's expression was still inscrutable. "I still have a lot of work to do with her, but it's a definite start."

Samantha felt tears begin to prickle at the backs of her eyes. He was giving her a second chance. She'd never been so relieved.

She would deal with working up the courage to share her secret with him as soon as she could. Right in that moment all she wanted to do was focus on him. Whatever he wanted, she would give him.

She wanted to make him happy.

"Are you thinking of giving the good little subbie a reward?" Luca's rough, gravelly voice was worlds different from Elijah's, which always reminded her of hot buttered rum.

She didn't look at Luca as he spoke, because he didn't matter to her. Her duty was to Elijah, to do what he wanted her to do. When he smiled, and she knew that she had pleased him, she felt as if she was floating on air. Then the words sunk in. "A reward?" she asked, confused. "I thought I was going to get a punishment."

"Yes, I do believe the little cat deserves a treat." Elijah's lips curled into that devastatingly wicked grin that Samantha had come to realize signaled that play was at hand. He spoke as if she wasn't there. Normally that would have made her mad, but she was too unsettled to feel angry.

Her pulse began to speed up.

"It seems you like that idea, Sammie Cat." Grinning down at her, Elijah caught her wrists in his hands and pulled her over to a spanking bench.

Samantha had to work hard not to frown. She knew what the bench was for, but she wasn't sure she cared for the idea of being spanked or lashed while Luca watched. Especially not while the skin of her backside was still so tender.

She turned and caught Elijah watching her very carefully. She stared back for a long moment, then schooled her face into an innocuous smile.

Whatever he wanted to do to her, she would take. She had a point to prove, and she trusted him not to do something to her that she couldn't handle.

"Good girl." Elijah spoke quietly as he pressed a hand to the flat of her back. "You're going to like this, I promise."

As he spoke he turned her so that she faced away from him. She felt him kneel behind her, stroking his hands down the insides of her thighs until he reached her ankles.

She heard the soft snick of metal, felt its chill against her skin as her ankles were bound to the legs of the bench. With the bondage came the now familiar surge of relief.

She was in Elijah's care. She could just let go.

"Luca, could you help me, please?" Elijah left Samantha standing, bound to the legs of the bench, as he lifted his toy bag and set it on the top of the structure that stretched out before her. He sorted through it slowly, allowing her plenty of time to study each item.

A bottle of lubricant. Something that looked like a long, slender lightbulb. A small metal vibrator that resembled a bullet. A foil packet of condoms. A small pillow.

"Luca, could you lift Samantha's skirt, please?" Samantha trembled with anticipation as the hulking man grinned down at her.

She hadn't paid much attention to him before, but he was really good-looking, in an animalistic kind of way. The fact that he was about to participate in this scene made her look at him in an entirely different light.

"With pleasure." Luca moved behind her, and Samantha instantly felt small and fragile. The top of her head barely came level with his shoulders as he smoothed his hands over the sides of her breasts, over her waist, and down over the curve of her ass.

With smooth fingers, he gathered up the clinging fabric, bunching it around her waist and revealing the sheer thong that Elijah had made her dress in.

"Look at that ass," he said admiringly. Samantha shivered, knowing his eyes were on her. "It's a pity E says you're not into pain. That ass would be gorgeous if it was all pink from my whip."

Samantha cast an alarmed stare at Elijah. At the same time she was mollified by the fact that he had clearly spoken to his friend about this scene already, and had set boundaries.

And he'd been observant enough to notice that she didn't much care for the whip—or the crop, or the palm of a hand.

She could have kissed him for it. Later, she would.

"Bend her over the bench for me, would you, Luca?" Large hands pressed against Samantha's back, urging her down until she lay along the top of the bench, the padded top pressed into her stomach. "And no, she's not the sub for your sadistic tendencies, I'm afraid. But I think you'll enjoy some fun with her anyway."

She shifted, a bit uncomfortable as Elijah bound her wrists to the remaining two legs of the table. But then he gently slid the small pillow from his toy bag between her chin and the wood, adjusting her so that she faced forward, could see everything happening directly in front of her, though she was able to rest her head in comfort.

"Stay just like that, Sammie Cat." Elijah grazed her cheekbone with his knuckles, then moved out of her line of vision. She heard him conferring with Luca in hushed tones, and though she strained to hear, she couldn't make out what was being said.

The anticipation was driving her mad.

"Go ahead, Luca," Elijah said before strolling back into her line of view. He walked a few feet away from her, turned to face her, and planted his feet.

From behind her, Samantha felt the fabric of her panties being slowly peeled down her bottom.

"What should I start with?" Luca wondered aloud. "I have a vibrator that will make your pussy cream, and I have a plug to get you ready for my friend's cock. Decisions, decisions."

His dirty words made her entire body clench, and she heard him laugh.

"Responsive little subbie, E. Lucky for you that you saw her first. I bet I could make her like a bit of pain."

"Indeed it is lucky for me." Elijah's words were quiet but serious.

Samantha looked up at him, felt a surge of helpless lust and some other emotion swarm through her.

"I think I'll start with the plug," Luca said. Moments later Samantha felt something cold drizzle over the cheeks of her ass.

"No!" Frantically she tried to raise her head, to look at Elijah. They hadn't discussed *that*. And *that* did not sound like fun at all.

She bucked on the bench, unable to move very far because of the restraints, and was astonished when she felt heat surge between her legs.

Rather than reassuring, when Elijah moved to stand in front of her and called out her name, his voice was stern, his face displeased. She quivered, then looked at the ground, not wanting to see disappointment in his eyes.

He placed one firm finger beneath her chin, then lifted her head so she had to look at him.

"Samantha, do little subs get to say no?"

A retort was hot on her tongue. She had to bite it back, swallow it down, knowing by now that if she continued to protest, the men would devise something that she might like even less.

"I asked you a question." His finger tapped beneath her chin, causing her teeth to snap together.

"No. Sir," she added when Elijah raised an eyebrow at her.

"Thank you, Sir," she said in a sickly sweet tone that she hoped covered her sarcasm. She just couldn't stay silent.

They were about to put something in her rear end. She wasn't looking forward to that. Yet since she was tied down and helpless, she supposed she would have to grin and bear it.

"This will warm up soon enough," Luca said matter-of-factly as his fingers trailed through the slickness of the lubricant. Samantha flinched as he massaged it into the crevice between her buttocks, his fingers finding and pressing against the tight rosette of flesh that lay hidden there.

"Aah!" Samantha cried out when he pressed hard, his finger demanding entrance. Though her body clenched in protest, his finger worked its way through the tight ring of muscle and slid inside her, waking nerve endings that she hadn't even known she possessed.

"Oh my God." She wasn't sure that the invasion felt good exactly, but still she squirmed on the bench as Luca worked his finger in and out of her, her eyes on Elijah the entire time. He was watching her with an almost lazy expression on his face as he slowly undid the zipper of his leather pants, revealing a cock that was semihard and growing more erect by the moment.

Luca's finger slid out of her bottom, and to Samantha's incredible surprise she whimpered at the loss of sensation. Then something larger, harder nudged against her opening, and she knew what was about to happen.

Oh, shit.

"When I count to three, push back against me," Luca advised her, rotating the tip of the plug against her opening. "It's going to burn, but I promise that after a minute it will feel so good."

"I . . ." Samantha's voice was shaky, and she didn't think trusting a stranger with a penchant for pain was the brightest idea—not that she had a choice. But she was also more turned on than she'd ever been in her life. She knew there was no judgment here, but the fact that her body was thrilling to something so forbidden felt wrong somehow.

And yet she was wet—wet and aching for more. And all the while Elijah stood in front of her, idly stroking his cock as he watched his friend working an anal plug inside her, as if he had all the time in the world.

"Three!" As she'd been instructed, Samantha pushed back against the plug as Luca pushed forward. Her eyes widened and she sucked air in through her teeth as the burn he'd spoken of came.

She whimpered as the intrusion worked itself inside her, stretching her, the heat reminding her of her hot glass. And then the plug was fully inside, the base nestled against her skin. She slowly moved her hips, found that it made the plug shift in ways that both hurt and awakened, and she decided to remain still.

"God, you're hot," Luca said as he pulled her panties back over her ass. "I can't wait to be inside your mouth."

Samantha looked at Elijah as a wave of heat rolled through her. He smiled back.

"Use the vibrator on her now, Luca." Elijah slid his pants a little bit lower on his hips, and Samantha eagerly drank in the sight of his flat belly. "Go ahead and make her come."

"What a pretty sub." The new voice was female and unfamiliar. As Samantha heard the vibrator whir to life from behind her, felt the first electric press of it against her clit through her panties, she saw a woman dressed in Domme gear and a muscular young man with a collar and a leash approach Elijah. "Look at that flush she's getting from having you watch her. That's a testament to your ownership, Elijah."

"She's very responsive," Elijah agreed, and even through the pleasure centered at her clit, Samantha felt her spirits sink. He hadn't said anything about ownership. Not that she wanted to be owned—not exactly—but she knew she wanted to be Elijah's even after this month was done.

His eyes on her, Elijah inclined his head to the big, beautiful blond Domme.

"Mistress Cathryn, do you think I might borrow your sub for a few minutes?" He never looked away from Samantha, and her heart began to pound even faster, as she understood that he had something else planned for her.

"Certainly, Elijah. Danny would love to serve you in any way he can." The young man she had called Danny gazed up at her with an adoring look as she tugged on his leash.

Elijah nodded, then slid his pants lower on his hips, revealing the entirety of his cock.

"Samantha once told me that she fantasized about watching two men together. I would like to play out part of that fantasy for her."

Samantha jerked against her restraints as the words sank in. Her body clenched with anticipation, then sagged with disbelief.

What? He wanted to play out her fantasy for her? Samantha opened her mouth—to say what, she had no idea—but Luca chose that moment to slip the vibrator from outside of her panties to the inside of her slick vagina, and she cried out wordlessly instead.

Elijah waited a long moment as Samantha stared up at him and thrashed on the bench, the vibrator making coils of need swirl tightly inside her. She understood he was asking if this was truly what she wanted.

"You would do this . . . for me?" she finally managed, gasping out the words. "But . . . you . . . I didn't know you were interested in . . . men."

Was he? He had never said so one way or another when they'd discussed their fantasies.

He cast her a wicked grin as Mistress Cathryn nudged at her sub with her boot, urging him down to his knees in front of Elijah.

"I'll always choose a woman as my sub," Elijah told her, handing a foil packet to Danny, who accepted it and held it with his teeth. "But I'm not averse to finding pleasure in a situation like this, where the end result is a fantasy fulfilled for you."

Oh. My. God. Samantha wasn't sure she could believe what was about to happen.

"Put the condom on my cock, sub," Elijah commanded Danny, never tearing his eyes from Samantha. To her he said, "If at any point you decide you don't want this, you just use your safe word. Okay?"

"Yes." Breathless, she nodded. And then her entire body tightened in anticipation as the sub named Danny peeled the foil back from the condom.

"Slowly. Make sure my sub can see."

Samantha sank her teeth into her lower lip as, with theatrical gestures, Danny pinched the tip of the condom, then rolled it over the head of Elijah's erection.

Samantha's eyes eagerly drank in the sight of the stranger's trembling fingers, rolling the latex down the rigid length that she ached to have inside her.

Elijah kept his eyes on her, watching, she knew, to make sure that this was what she wanted.

Oh, she wanted it. There was no doubt about that.

She watched as Danny smoothed the condom the rest of the way down Elijah's shaft. The condom secured, the other sub sat back on his heels, his head bowed, awaiting further instruction.

A lightning-quick bolt of jealousy shot through her. She wasn't upset that Danny was touching Elijah—no, that was the single most erotic sight she'd ever encountered.

But Danny was so graceful, seemed so comfortable in his submission. Samantha yearned to be the same way.

"More?" Elijah asked her.

Samantha shuddered, then nodded, breathless.

He bent his head, said something to Danny, something Samantha couldn't hear.

Then the male sub tentatively began to stroke his fingers up and down Elijah's cock.

Samantha watched as pleasure rippled over Elijah's face, a look she well knew by now. Her womb clenched with escalating need as she watched the other sub's strokes grow faster.

Though his face had flushed, Elijah never took his eyes from her.

"No, Danny." The sharp voice of Mistress Cathryn broke through the thick heat, and Samantha flicked her stare over to the woman. Though the woman carried quite a bit of excess flesh, she was still surrounded by a sexual . . . *energy*, Samantha supposed she would call it.

She could see the appeal the Domme held for the male sub. But Samantha wanted only Elijah.

"Danny, I do not give you permission to touch yourself." Mistress Cathryn's voice was sharp. The male sub sat back on his heels with a high-pitched whine that reminded Samantha of a puppy.

She watched as his fingers clenched on Elijah's erection. At the same time Luca pulled the small vibrator out of her pulsating vagina and began to work it in and out in small, hard strokes.

Samantha was hit with a tidal wave of lust. When she opened her mouth to speak, her words were desperate.

"Elij— I mean, Sir. Oh, please, Sir." She was suddenly envious of Danny again, the sensation so fierce that it scared her.

She wanted to be the one making Elijah's breath come faster. She wanted her fingers on his cock, her name on his lips.

"Please what, sub?" With a wicked grin cast her way, Elijah rocked his hips into Danny's grip.

She squirmed. She didn't want to say it out loud.

"Better hurry up, little subbie." Elijah groaned lightly, then rocked his hips forward again. "If you don't beg me before Danny makes me come, then I'll leave you to Luca's mercies. And I'm quite certain his mercies will include a flogger."

Somehow, though she wasn't fond of pain, the mental picture only heated her more. From behind her Luca chuckled, tugging on the base of the anal plug as he continued to work the vibrator in and out.

"I would be more than happy to have you in my care, little one. I have an urge to lock you in the stocks and to teach you what the kiss of my cat-o'-nine-tails feels like." Slamming the vibrator deep inside her, Luca slid his large fingers over the engorged nub of her clit. "It's my favorite flogger. So don't beg on my account."

Samantha couldn't think. She couldn't *breathe*.

Her entire being was focused on reaching that peak that Luca held so frustratingly just out of reach.

"Fuck." Samantha's gaze was torn back to Elijah as he moaned out loud. Though the male sub was moving slowly, so slowly, Samantha couldn't be sure that Elijah wouldn't come at any moment.

She wanted his orgasm for herself.

"Please, Sir." The words stuck in her throat and nearly choked her. Begging was hard. She wouldn't have done it for anyone but Elijah.

"Please, Sir. I need you."

Instantly Elijah placed his palm flat on the male sub's forehead, keeping him from drawing any closer. He pushed gently and the sub released his cock, by now so hard that it pointed straight up to the ceiling.

"Thank you for the use of your sub, Cathryn." Elijah sounded as if he was thanking the woman for borrowing a quarter, though his face was flushed with arousal. "He has talented hands."

"He sure does." The woman smiled cheerfully, nudging her sub in the rib cage with the pointed toe of one of her thigh-high boots. "Come along, then, Danny. I fancy a spell with the bondage chair."

And then they were gone, leaving Samantha alone with Luca and Elijah.

Elijah stalked toward her like a mountain lion who had sighted its prey.

"Trade places with me, will you, Luca?" Samantha's eyes were on Elijah, even as she cried out against the single sharp spank that was laid across the right side of her ass.

"You're a lucky man, Elijah. Her ass is shaped just like a heart." Samantha felt Luca's fingers leave her flesh, and, again, she whimpered at the loss of sensation.

She had to clench her muscles to keep the small vibrator from falling out.

"Isn't it pretty?" Samantha listened and watched as Elijah rounded the table, disappearing from view just as Luca came into it.

"I bet your mouth is just as hot and wet as your pussy." The massive man grinned down at Samantha as he unlaced the front of his leather pants. "Let's find out."

She watched warily as he freed himself from his pants and sheathed himself in a condom. His cock was in keeping with the rest of him—big.

"Open."

Samantha had only a second to wonder what Elijah was doing when the head of Luca's cock nudged at her mouth. Without thinking she parted her lips as commanded and welcomed him in.

"That's right," Luca murmured, his eyes fixed on her with that dominant look of possession that Samantha already knew so well from Elijah. "Suck me off, girl. Make me come."

The dirty words sent a dark thrill through her. She was savoring the sensation of her mouth being filled, of the new taste that was Luca, when Elijah slid two fingers past the elastic of her panties and inside her.

She cried out around the cock that filled her mouth. Elijah's fingers worked their way into the hot, wet space between her legs, clasping hold of the vibrator and withdrawing it.

Samantha tried to protest when he removed the vibrator, but she couldn't say anything—not with her mouth full. As Luca pushed farther down her throat and Elijah tugged at the thin material of her panties, Samantha realized just how powerless she was in that moment.

These two men could do anything to her—anything they wanted. And she wouldn't be able to do anything about it.

There was a sharp edge to the pleasure that swept through her as the notion took hold, but more than that she felt herself finally—finally—get into the moment.

She couldn't do anything but take what they gave her. And that was just fine with her.

"Don't come yet," Elijah warned her seconds before ripping her panties right off. She groaned around Luca's cock, which made him moan and thrust farther into her mouth.

She tensed every muscle in her body as the waves of pleasure approached a crescendo. She wanted to do what Elijah said—didn't want to disobey.

She was red faced and panting by the time she'd gotten herself under control . . . just in time to feel Elijah's fingers trace a rim around the entrance to her rear. They were slick with lubricant, igniting sparks of sensation that turned her body the same consistency as molten glass.

"Push back." Samantha felt helpless as she felt the head of Elijah's cock press against her impossibly tight back opening.

She screamed around Luca's erection as Elijah slowly worked his way inside her. The burn was hotter than when she touched her sculptures before they'd cooled, but entwined with the unfamiliar pain was an overwhelming pleasure.

She found her mouth slowly closing, her teeth nipping at Luca's flesh. He grunted out a warning, wrapping his fingers in the ropes of her hair and tugging to get her attention.

Then . . . finally Elijah was all the way in. He stilled for a moment, giving her time to adjust to his size. She wiggled as much as she was able to, trying to find some relief, a moment's respite from the wicked burn.

Then Elijah began to move inside her tight flesh in motions that were slow but steady, and all she could do was take it.

At the same time Luca thrust in and out of her mouth, hitting the back of her throat with every firm thrust. She felt saliva pool against her tongue, felt sweat trickle down her back, knew she must look horrible, but the look on Luca's face told her that he thought she looked just fine.

And though she couldn't see Elijah—she wished she could—she could picture his face as clearly as if he was standing in front of her. She knew he was watching her, reading her body language, taking in every detail of her response with that eagle-eyed stare of his.

He would be looking at her like she was the only woman in the world.

She wanted to be the only woman in *his* world.

She barely noticed when his hand slid from her hip to splay over the gentle curve of her belly and lower. But when he slid his hand between her legs and started the vibrator again, pressing it to the hard nub of her clit, she felt her nerves go off like a series of rockets.

"Beautiful." Elijah spoke softly to her, his voice low and thick with need. Samantha's body tensed, tried to arch, to move away from the onslaught of sensation. The pleasure didn't dissipate, instead marching relentlessly onward until mentally she checked out, her mind unable to deal with the ecstasy.

The men continued to play her body like an instrument, pulling sensation after incredible sensation from her flesh until she was as limp as a ragdoll.

Behind her, Elijah's thrusts increased. Centering the vibrator directly over her clit as he stroked harder inside her, he spoke through the thick silence that had fallen over all three of them.

"Now, Samantha." Quickly his thrusts became harder, more urgent. "Come for me now."

The next time he circled the vibrator around her clit, she felt the shuddering waves again begin to build. In front of her, Luca's grip on her hair loosened, and he thrust fully into her mouth as the waves of sensation washed over her.

Luca came with a shout, and Elijah with a silent, hard press of his hips against her ass. Through it all, Samantha rode out the bliss that racked her flesh.

Minutes passed, or it might have been an hour, before Samantha felt her thoughts begin to gather into some semblance of clarity. Luca pulled his still semierect but softening cock from between her lips, and Samantha watched idly as he tugged the condom off and disposed of it. Tucking himself back into his leather pants, he signaled to a plump young woman wearing nothing but a spiked collar, a thong, and thigh-high boots. After speaking a few words to her, the young submissive scurried off, returning with a blanket, a soft cloth, and a bottle of water.

Samantha felt Elijah begin to trace his fingers over the small of her back, the tender sensation making her shiver after the onslaught of pleasure. He stayed joined with her as Luca gently wiped her lips, then knelt down and unfastened the cuffs that bound her wrists and ankles.

"Thank you." Samantha stretched out her mouth—her jaw was going to be sore the next day. Not that she'd mind—it had been worth it. Elijah's friend looked down at her with apparent satisfaction.

"Thank *you*, little sub." Luca tapped her under the chin, his expression a bit wistful. The look seemed out of place on the big, powerful man, but Samantha couldn't find the strength to think on it any further.

Opening the fuzzy blanket and laying it across her back, Luca handed the bottle of water to Elijah with a nod. "You're a lucky man, E." With one more smile at Samantha, he left, a sheen of sweat making his muscles shine in the dim light.

"I am, indeed," Elijah murmured from behind her as he pressed a kiss to the base of her spine.

"Mmm," Samantha groaned softly as, with a hand flat on her back, Elijah slowly pulled out of her tight flesh. She wiggled, tried to stand as he moved forward to toss his condom in the trash, and found that without the spanking bench beneath her, her legs refused to support her.

"Don't try to move." Though the expectation that she would listen and obey was clear in Elijah's voice, the tone had mellowed from the urgency that it had carried before they'd come into Veritas.

She murmured a sleepy affirmation as Elijah wrapped the blanket around her, then lifted her up. Carrying her across the playroom floor to a soft couch, he sank down onto an overstuffed cushion with her on his lap. Tucking the ends of the blanket around her, he opened the bottle of water and held it up to her dry lips.

"Thank you." With thirsty gulps, Samantha drained the bottle, then settled back into the comfortable cradle of Elijah's arms. She allowed herself to relax for one long moment before her thoughts began to turn around in her head again.

"That boy—Danny—you . . . he . . ." Samantha hid her face against Elijah's chest as she tried to find the right words. "His Mistress gave him to you to do whatever you wanted."

"And you're wondering if I will ever give you away in the same way." Elijah stroked a hand through her hair, damp with sweat. Unable to speak, she nodded her head against his chest.

"Being temporarily given away to another Dom or Domme just happens to be one of Danny's favorite kinks," Elijah said matter-of-factly, startling Samantha enough that she looked right into his face.

"Seriously?" But there was something tickling at her memory . . .

The questionnaire she'd filled out at Pecado. One of the questions had asked if she was interested in being given to another Dom, either temporarily or permanently. At the time she had been certain that no sane person would do such a thing.

She was beginning to see, to understand. People in the BDSM community may have had different kinks, but there was no judgment. Just because she couldn't conceive of doing something didn't mean that it didn't turn on another submissive.

And it was all okay, so long as it was . . . What had that sheet said again? Right at the top, there had been a logo.

Right.

Safe, sane, and consensual.

"I'd love to hear the thoughts buzzing around that brain of

yours." Elijah slid a hand inside the blanket, past the thin silk of her dress to cup a breast. "These girls were woefully neglected tonight. I'll have to make amends later."

"Can I have a bit of time to recover first?" Samantha knew she sounded apprehensive—and she was. Her body felt like mush, and her brain wasn't far behind. Elijah and Luca had used her well.

Elijah chuckled, and she looked up to find his lips curled in a smirk. "Too much man for you to handle?"

She tried to scowl at him, though she wasn't really upset. "Actually . . . I was wondering if there was someone I could talk to, to ask some questions. A *girl* someone," she added, just to be clear.

"Remember what I said about trust, Sammie Cat?" Elijah's expression was neutral, but Samantha blanched, not wanting to give him the wrong idea.

"It has nothing to do with trust, Elijah. It's more about perspective. Since you are neither female nor submissive, you can't give me the perspective I want." Sitting up tall in Elijah's lap, Samantha craned her neck and looked around the playroom. "Is Maddy still here?"

"Maddy went home to be bedded by her fiancé." Samantha felt a wash of heat and struggled to contain it. She couldn't possibly handle round two—not right now, and probably not even tonight.

"Oh." Samantha was disappointed. She had liked Maddy, and Kylie too, though she'd gotten the impression that the other redhead didn't know much more about the BDSM lifestyle than Samantha did herself.

"But there is someone who appears free at the moment. She's a nice girl, and she's been in the lifestyle for a couple of years now." Setting Samantha on her feet, Elijah tugged the blanket from around her shoulders and gave her a nudge toward the sitting area, where it seemed that the single submissives tended to congregate.

The only woman there at the moment was about Samantha's height, with curling hair and the most gorgeous cappuccino-colored skin that Samantha had ever seen.

She also looked familiar, and Samantha found herself glaring before she could stop it.

"She's friends with that other woman—that nasty one who hit on you in front of me." Placing fisted hands on her hips, Samantha glared at Elijah, upset that he would suggest such a thing. "No way."

"Angie is nothing like Charlotte." The reprimand was clear in his voice: *Don't question me*. "And though I do like this guard kitty side of you, I'm asking you to give her a chance. She's friendly, she can be trusted, and I think she'll be happy to answer any questions you have."

"How do you know she can be trusted? If I'm allowed to ask." Samantha bit her lip as jealousy washed over her. It was no business of hers what Elijah had done before her—just as, to her mind, she didn't need to tell him anything about her own past.

But the sudden thought that Elijah could have been—probably had been—with other women who were in this room right now didn't sit well. Hell, maybe he had been with Kylie. With Maddy. They were both beautiful women—what was to stop him?

"I've never done a scene with Angie." Elijah's lips curved into a grin as he spoke, and Samantha felt her cheeks flush. He knew, the bastard—he knew exactly what thoughts were running through her head. Knew that she was jealous.

What's more, he appeared to like it.

Mortified, Samantha allowed herself to be gently pushed in the direction of the gorgeous raven-haired submissive.

"Go. Talk to her. I'll have one of the serving subbies bring you a drink." Elijah gently pushed her away.

Samantha froze. "I—I don't—I mean—"

"I'll stay close."

Damn it. How had he known what she was going to say? It was uncanny, the way he seemed to pluck thoughts right out of her mind before they had crystallized.

"Go," he said again, and Samantha found herself walking toward Angie. When she was nearly to the sitting area, she looked back over her shoulder. She had assumed that Elijah would have already moved to the bar, would be engaging in a chat with Luca, who was again polishing glasses, or with one of the other regulars who crowded close, eager for one of their limited allowance of drinks.

But instead Elijah was standing right where she'd left him. The blanket he had just pulled from around her shoulders was clutched loosely in his hands, and his feet were planted shoulder width apart.

The expression on his face was one of . . . possession. Sheer ownership. There was no other way to put it.

It frightened her, and at the same time excited her. Turning away from the ferocious gaze, she scurried the rest of the way to Angie, though her mind kept trying to decipher that look.

She knew one thing—that was for sure.

She was in way over her head. But somehow that wasn't necessarily a bad thing.

CHAPTER SIXTEEN

lijah took a seat on one of the high stools at the bar as he watched Samantha make her way across the play area to Angie. He could see by her body language that she wasn't eager to talk to her.

He supposed he could have waited, could have let her talk to Maddy as she'd requested. But Maddy didn't know much about the world of BDSM beyond what she and Alex did—she'd been a neophyte who'd never had even a thought of submission before Alex had scooped her up.

No, Angie was a better choice. Despite her deplorable taste in friends, the woman was a good person.

"Another one bites the dust, huh?" Grinning, Luca slid a tall glass of ice water down the polished surface of the bar. Turning to the rack that held the owners' private supply, he selected a bottle and held it up for Elijah's approval.

"Vintage Romanée-Conti. Nice choice." Elijah nodded his approval, and with the ease of long practice, Luca uncorked the expensive red from Burgundy, France.

"Send a glass to Samantha, will you?" Elijah signaled for Rani, the pretty brunette submissive who was on serving duty that evening. She had been the one to bring the blanket and water over to them after their scene earlier.

"Sir," Rani said as she approached, keeping her eyes on the ground. Elijah handed her the first glass that Luca filled, and was about to send her on her way when Luca handed over a second one.

"One each for the two ladies in the subbie area." The bigger man poured two more glasses and passed one over to Elijah before lifting his own for a taste.

Elijah eyed his friend thoughtfully. He'd long ago gotten over the visual paradox of the big, rough-looking man sipping fancy wine; beer might have seemed a more appropriate beverage for him. But he'd never seen Luca share that fancy wine with a sub, let alone someone he'd never—at least to Elijah's knowledge—scened with.

"Is there something I should know?" Elijah asked, looking over to Angie, who by now was sitting next to Samantha on a low couch. It would have been impossible to miss the spark of possession in the other man's eyes, even if Elijah hadn't been feeling the exact same thing for another woman. "I saw that she tried a scene with Levi earlier, but I don't think it worked out. Why don't you go play once they're done talking? Julien can come inside and man the bar."

Luca snorted, then returned to polishing glasses. "I'm not fixing to hook up with a woman who's barely legal."

Elijah narrowed his eyes at the women. "Angie is twenty-four." Not experienced enough for his liking, but certainly not a child.

"Too young for me," Luca said flatly, then charged the subject. "Are you fixing to keep this one, then? You've never brought a sub from outside to Veritas before."

Elijah let his eyes trace over the classic profile of his redhead. The first time he'd laid eyes on her he'd thought she looked like a goddess, and that impression hadn't changed.

"I want to." It felt good to finally admit it out loud. "She offered me a month of submission in return for introducing her to the lifestyle. I didn't think she'd really be able to submit, but she does, beautifully—at least, in the bedroom and at the club."

Luca leaned over on the counter, propping his weight on

his elbows. His stare followed Elijah's intent gaze at the two beautiful women.

"And after Tara, you're worried that if you try to keep a sub who isn't submissive in every way, you'll wind up getting hurt and, worse, hurting her."

"True enough." Elijah winced and chugged at his wine. It sounded so blunt, when put like that. But as always, Luca had put his finger right on the heart of the problem. "She has a secret in her past that she refuses to tell me. And in total honesty, I'm not sure that I can get it out of her without damaging something inside of her."

Luca studied the women for another long moment, then tipped back his head and swallowed down the rest of his wine.

"There are a lot of rules," he said as he set his glass on the back counter of the bar, next to the other dirty glasses. "But there's nothing to say that you have to hold hard and fast to each and every one if they're not working for you."

Those simple words cleared a fog in Elijah's head.

"If you want her, if it's working between you, then go for it. She's nothing like your ex." Luca nodded, then turned away from Elijah to take a drink order from Rani. Elijah reached for the bottle of Romanée-Conti and refilled his glass. He usually limited himself to one drink while in the playroom, but he was done playing there for the night and was feeling the need to loosen up.

If you want her, if it's working, then go for it.

He would wait for Samantha to finish her conversation with Angie, though he wanted nothing more than to stride across the room, sweep her into his arms, and take her mouth with rough possession.

Once she was done . . .

Once she was done, he would take her back upstairs to his

home. It was time they had a serious chat, rather than circling each other like wary dogs. He was fully aware that it was usually the fairer sex who wanted to have talks about emotions and the future of relationships, but Samantha was a skittish little cat.

His skittish little cat. And fully submissive or not, he'd be damned if he was going to let her go.

Samantha could feel Elijah's stare burning into the back of her neck from all the way across the room. Knowing that his attention was firmly fixed on her, even as he spoke to Luca, made her feel as though his hands were still on her skin.

She couldn't help but feel ridiculous, approaching a woman she didn't know to ask her some very intimate questions. She wished that Elijah had at least introduced them, though she understood why he hadn't.

It was his way of pushing her boundaries, of making her more comfortable with this lifestyle.

Knowing that didn't make it any easier.

To her relief, Angie smiled easily at her and offered a hand. Samantha stared at it for a moment, a bit startled that people observed such normal niceties as handshakes here, in what felt like a different world. It seemed there should have been a secret way of greeting one another perhaps.

It was just another reminder that people from all walks of life were practicing BDSM—teachers, doctors, businesspeople, artists . . .

There was no judgment here—apart from what she put on herself.

"I'm Angie." The small, curvy woman sat on a low couch and patted the seat beside her. She looked up at Samantha expectantly as she tucked a strand of dark curly hair behind her ear.

"Samantha." Knowing that she was acting stiff and awkward didn't make her any more relaxed. She lowered herself to the couch and forced a friendly smile to her lips.

"I hope you don't hold it against me, what Charlotte did the other night." Worry flitted across Angie's face.

"Never." Though she'd been a little grumpy when Elijah had pointed her in Angie's direction for that very reason, her irritation was rapidly vanishing in the face of the woman's friendliness.

"We all make our own choices. We're not responsible for what others do." Shock rocketed through Samantha as she heard her own words.

She'd never said that out loud before, and though she'd been talking about Charlotte . . . well . . . wasn't that somewhat applicable to her life, too?

The pretty, plump girl who'd brought her a blanket and water after Elijah and Luca had turned her brain to mush arrived at that moment with a sparkling glass full of ruby wine in each hand.

"From Master E and Master Luca," the girl said, her gaze trailing wistfully back to the bar where the two Doms sat. "Shit, you gals are lucky. Every sub here would kill to trade places with y'all."

Samantha felt her skin heat even as Angie stiffened beside her.

"I'm not with either of them." Angie looked at the glass of wine apprehensively, as if it might bite her, before pasting a smile on her face and gesturing her thanks across the room.

"I'm—" Samantha cut herself off before agreeing with the other woman. What was she to Elijah exactly? She'd offered herself to him for a month in an attempt to learn more about the pressing needs that she'd been experiencing. Well, and because the chemistry between them was killer. But she knew he was never going to settle for less than all of her . . . And was that something she was prepared to give?

Samantha waited until the serving submissive had gone, then asked, "Are you— Have you—have you ever had a relationship with a Dom? Like a boyfriend or a husband or something?" She had a hard time picturing Luca the Dom as a doting husband. Elijah was easier, maybe because she wanted him so badly.

"Sure," Angie said easily, tucking her arms around a knee. The gesture caused her minuscule skirt to ride up, and Samantha and the rest of the bar could see the bright red of her panties. Samantha was beginning to understand that there were different rules here in the club. "A good Dom is hard to find, though. The idea of control attracts a lot of assholes."

Samantha barked out a surprised laugh. "I don't think that's limited to the BDSM world," she added, sneaking a peek over her shoulder at Elijah. Though he was speaking to Luca and sipping a glass of wine, his gaze was still fixed on her.

It sent a sensual thrill coursing through her body. He was everything she'd ever wanted. How would she be able to live without him after the month was up?

"In a relationship like . . . this," Samantha started, choosing her words carefully, "do you . . . are you submissive all the time? Is that what a Dom expects?"

The other woman leaned back, tucking her legs up underneath her. While enjoying her drink, she appeared to be thinking long and hard about Samantha's question.

"There's no easy answer to that." Angie looked at Samantha over the rim of her glass, the gaze tinted with sympathy. "It's different for everyone. Hell, it's different even with different Doms."

"What do you mean?" Samantha smoothed palms that were damp with sweat over the silky skirt of her slip.

"Well, some couples have a Master/slave relationship, which

is pretty much exactly what it sounds like," Angie began, causing Samantha to shudder inwardly—she wanted a guy who would take control, but nothing that extreme. "And there are lots of other types—weekenders, people who are just into kinky sex, and people who live it twenty-four/seven. But you have to understand that the dynamic between every couple is different, even if they fall into one of these categories. The important thing is that it works for you and your Dom, not that it can be defined."

"Right." Hope was a wild thing rising up inside her. "But . . . it's not crazy to think that a sub could be with a Dom and not be submissive a hundred percent of the time?"

"Not at all." Angie smiled. Then, with a friendly gesture that surprised Samantha, she reached out and took her hand, giving it a squeeze.

Samantha looked at her, startled. Angie smiled back, again with that tinge of sympathy.

"It's rough when you're just starting out. Wondering what's wrong with you, why you want what you do. Wading through a million new rules, a million new concepts. Not to mention dealing with headstrong Doms." Angie rolled her eyes back toward the bar, making Samantha chuckle. "We subs have to stick together."

"Thanks." Samantha let the relief wash over her, but it was followed by tension. She needed to bring this up with Elijah somehow—or did she? Was she allowed? How submissive did he expect her to be? Would he be upset if she tried to talk to him about their future past the one month she had given him?

Screw it, she thought, standing suddenly. *I'll ask.*

But first she had a more pressing need. "Can you tell me where the bathroom is?"

Angie pointed out the discreet doors in the far corner of the room. Elijah had allowed Samantha to bring her tiny purse with her cell phone to the club, which had surprised her until she realized that he was hoping for another call from Beth. Another chance for him to open the door for her to talk.

Apart from her cell phone, the purse had some lip balm, some breath mints. She felt sorely in need of both, so she snagged the bag, still lying beside Elijah's toy bag on the spanking bench that they'd used.

After using the facilities, which were far fancier than any public restroom she'd ever seen—the counter boasted baskets full of shampoo, lip balm, condoms, even tiny packets of lubricant—Samantha paused for a moment at the sink, looking at her reflection in the mirror.

Her eyes were bright, her cheeks flushed. She looked . . . happy. Happier than she'd been in a long time.

Her mind rejected the notion that Elijah was the sole source of that happiness. But she couldn't deny that he'd helped her understand herself, or that—if she dared to admit it—he filled something deep inside her that she hadn't even known was hollow.

From inside her tiny purse, her phone rang. The vibrations startled her and she slapped a hand over her heart, then let out a fleeting laugh when she realized what it was.

"Shit." She pulled her phone from her purse and saw it was Beth again.

Two calls from her sister in one day? It was unprecedented, and Samantha knew it couldn't be anything good.

"What's wrong?" Samantha held the phone up to her ear, adrenaline already beginning to surge through her veins.

"Mom's getting her stomach pumped." On the other end of the line, Beth's voice was weary. Samantha raked her fingers through her hair as her ears pricked up, alerted by a barely recognizable tone in her sister's voice.

"What's wrong with *you*, though?" Samantha realized with a pang that she didn't have many feelings left where Gemma was concerned. It saddened her that her mother had drunk so much that she had reached this point, but Samantha's only real concern was Beth.

"Nothing major." Beth's voice sounded tired, and Samantha felt concern grip her all over. "Super tired. Thirsty. Vision's a little blurry."

"Have you treated it?" Samantha closed her eyes and pressed her fingers to her temples against the sudden wave of stress that washed over her.

She knew that Beth checked her blood sugar faithfully and took the proper amount of insulin. She'd always been good about that, even back when she'd first been diagnosed as a teen. Sometimes blood sugar levels went wonky for no good reason—insulin wasn't a perfect treatment and its effectiveness couldn't always be predicted.

But the danger often rose in response to stress. And Samantha would bet money on what was making her sister sick now.

"Where are you? You're not driving, are you?" Samantha paced the length of the empty bathroom as her thoughts whirled frantically.

She wouldn't head back to Colorado on her mother's account—as far as she was concerned, Gemma had made her own bed, and could lie in it until she died. But Beth . . . she was a different story.

Beth would worry herself sick over their mother, would let herself be manipulated into putting her own life on hold to care for the alcoholic as she recovered. She was already sick from it, and Samantha saw no reason why her younger sister should bear the burden of their mother's selfishness and idiocy by herself.

"No, I'm about to leave for the hospital," Beth replied. Again Samantha heard that warning note, that nagging fatigue riding her sister's words. Panic closed in.

"Don't you dare drive if you're not feeling well," Samantha snapped, raking her fingers through her hair, her heart pounding.

"I don't have a choice, Sam." Beth yawned through the phone. "She's our mother. I have to go."

Worry pushed Samantha over the edge of the cliff she'd been teetering on.

"Take a taxi. It's not safe for you or for anyone else on the road if your blood sugars are off." Samantha's mind worked frantically. She would prefer her sister just stay put until she could get to her, but knew that that wasn't likely to happen.

Beth was too kindhearted for her own good. She would feel the need to be at their mother's side.

At least if Samantha could get to Beth, she could spell her off, give her sister some rest so that she didn't get seriously sick.

"Are you at Three Sisters?" Samantha named the biggest hospital in the small city in which she'd grown up. "I'll be there as soon as I can, Bethy." Wedging the phone between her ear and her shoulder, Samantha dug her fingers into her purse. *There.* The check that Elijah had written her—the one she had felt wrong cashing—was still there, though by now it was creased and slightly tattered along one edge.

Samantha cringed as she thought of how angry Elijah would be when he found out.

But if she told him, he'd insist on going with her. That was just the kind of man he was.

She would rather die than have him see her back in the place where she'd grown up. For someone who valued control so highly, what would he think of her mother's failings? Beth was the only good thing about that part of her life. Everything else she'd worked hard to leave behind.

"Only if you're sure." Beth's voice held a small note of pleasure, which only solidified Samantha's resolve.

She would do anything for her sister. Anything.

Even if it meant possibly losing the man she cared for more than she dared to admit.

Hanging up the phone, Samantha bit her teeth into her lower lip and rapidly ran through her options. Though he was going to be pissed beyond belief, she couldn't tell Elijah. If she did and then tried to leave without him, she wouldn't put it past him to chain her up until she changed her mind.

He would see her the moment she left the bathroom, would intercept her before she was able to make it out the front doors of Veritas.

She looked around the room, her stare landing on the big window. The window was high, but plenty large enough to get through. It was on the main floor, so she'd be safe jumping out.

Looking down at her bare feet and slinky scrap of dress, she realized that she was more in danger of flashing an innocent passerby than anything else. She cringed as she remembered that not only were most of her belongings back in Cabo, but all of the things Elijah had bought for her were upstairs in his apartment—and she had no key.

"Shit." With a bracing breath, Samantha tugged the ornate stool that sat in front of a vanity over to the window and climbed up, levering open the glass as she did.

She would hop in a cab and get the driver to stop at a bank machine. Then somewhere she could buy some decent clothes. She'd look funny until then, but this was Vegas. Surely there would be stranger sights than she.

Bracing her arms on the sill, Samantha hefted herself up and out the window. There was a narrow ledge outside, and she balanced precariously on her knees as she righted herself and prepared to drop down to the ground.

Only her eyes were above the sill when someone entered

the bathroom. The stealthiness of the person's movements caught Samantha's eye, and she paused for a moment to watch.

The slender woman stopped just inside the door, looking around as though expecting to find something that wasn't there. She lifted her eyes to the window, locking stares with Samantha for a brief moment.

Rather than surprise, the woman's face showed sly triumph.

Samantha cursed as she dropped to the ground.

It had been Charlotte, the submissive who had tried to take Elijah away from her the first night they'd come to Veritas. From the look on her face, it seemed she had heard part of Samantha's conversation with Beth—enough to suspect that Samantha was sneaking out—and she'd have to know that Elijah wouldn't be happy about it.

Helplessness washed over her as her toes touched the ground and she felt grass scratching the tender soles of her feet.

Her heart hurt—actually hurt—as she thought of the betrayal she was about to undertake. Her feet slowed as she tried to come up with an alternate solution. But her thoughts kept bringing her back around to the same place.

Her mother had drunk more than usual to land herself in the hospital. An upswing in Gemma's alcohol consumption usually coincided with contact from Stanley. Since he'd called her mother recently, it was a safe enough assumption that the man was sniffing around her again—why, Samantha couldn't understand, but then, their relationship dynamics had never made any sense to her.

But Stanley was bad news, and Elijah was observant as hell. It would kill her to see the all too familiar combination of pity and disgust in Elijah's eyes, of all people.

She was going to be with her sister. That was what she did— she took care of Beth. She could only hope that Elijah wouldn't hate her when she got back.

CHAPTER SEVENTEEN

"Master, I beg your pardon, but I have news that I think you will want to know."

Elijah scowled down at the lithe, nearly naked blonde kneeling on the floor at his feet. His gaze had been so focused on the bathroom door that he hadn't seen Charlotte approach.

He wasn't at all pleased to see her before him. He was sure he'd made himself perfectly clear when he'd handed her over to Luca for punishment earlier in the week.

"You're pushing your luck, Charlotte." He didn't hold back, letting his anger color his tone. He had no use for submissives who manipulated and tried to top from the bottom in devious ways. No matter what Charlotte thought she saw in him, it was never going to happen.

And *where* was Samantha? She'd left Angie and headed to the washroom nearly fifteen minutes earlier.

"I assure you that you'll want to hear this." Charlotte looked directly up at him—forbidden behavior for a sub who was supposed to be repentant—and ran her tongue over her lips. Elijah imagined she thought the gesture was seductive, but as it came from her he found it only off-putting.

"You've worn out my patience, sub." Assuming a bored expression—the worst kind of reaction for a sub like Charlotte, who craved attention—Elijah turned back to the bar and reached for his glass of wine.

Charlotte rose from her knees, popping up in front of him with her hands clenched tightly.

"Samantha went out the bathroom window. She's going to visit her family and didn't want you there."

Elijah's first response was to deal with the inappropriate behavior in front of him, despite the feeling of betrayal that coiled in his belly. He curled his fingers around Charlotte's shoulder, his fingers digging just hard enough to get her attention.

"Luca." He spoke quietly, but felt his repressed anger and, more than that, hurt welling up. "I do not have the patience to deal with this sub right now. She needs to be punished for disobeying my orders, for spying on another submissive, and for behavior unbecoming to her station."

Charlotte sputtered as he continued to hold her but otherwise paid her no attention.

"I can't say I'm overly interested in spending any time with her myself," Luca said. Elijah watched as Luca narrowed his eyes and cocked his head, studying the woman, considering. Finally he raised his hand and gestured in the air. "Mistress Cathryn." Luca waved the blond Domme over to the bar area. She approached with a sway to her hips, her exhausted and happy-looking submissive trailing on a leash behind her.

"Master Luca. Master E." Cathryn cast a wicked grin in Elijah's direction. "Have a good session?"

"Indeed." Elijah knew he needed to deal with Charlotte, but his mind kept straying to Samantha. He didn't doubt Charlotte's words—the woman wasn't creative enough to make up a story like that.

She'd left, then. And the only reason she would have snuck out was so that he wouldn't see her.

He wasn't concerned that she was embarrassed of him, or

what they did together. No, he was quite certain that, if she was being sneaky about going to visit her family, it was to protect the secret that she was trying so desperately to keep hidden.

His mind turned that over as he watched Luca converse with Cathryn.

"This one has developed an unhealthy and harmful interest in Elijah's submissive, Cathryn." Luca growled. None of the Dominants looked at Charlotte, and Elijah could feel the anger radiating off her. Well, he was angry too. He would have found out about Samantha regardless, but the way she had run up to him just to tattle had been designed to hurt.

"E and I are done with her. I was wondering if you would be so kind as to take on the responsibility of punishing this one."

Cathryn's eyes lit up. Her submissive, clearly still feeling the aftereffects of subspace, just smiled dreamily.

"You know, Danny seems to be done for the night, but I think I have another round left in me." Cathryn's eyes raked over Charlotte, who wore a bustier, a G-string, and nothing else. "How do you fancy some time on the fucking machine, girl?"

Charlotte's skin drained of color, and Elijah felt a twinge of sympathy that he quickly quashed.

The fucking machine was one of the most popular pieces of equipment at Veritas. Many submissives begged for it as a reward. Others, like Charlotte, dreaded it, knowing that it would attract quite a crowd, and that any pleasure she found on it would be undignified and very impersonal. The fact that it would be a female Domme and not a male Dom at the controls would only embarrass Charlotte more, since the sub had eyes only for handsome, wealthy Masters.

Given that she had tried to take away Samantha's dignity as Elijah's sub, he felt that it was only fitting.

He didn't say anything as Cathryn led the woman from them. His mind was still on Samantha—what the hell was going on?

Nodding a quick good-bye to Luca, Elijah exited the playroom, his emotions far darker than he cared for them to be.

He had thought they were making progress tonight. Damn it—he *knew* they had. She'd wanted to share everything with him, to submit completely, and he'd had no doubt that she was on the right path.

Charlotte had said that Samantha had taken a call from her family—her sister, surely—and then had climbed out the bathroom window. He was not happy that she hadn't come to him.

It was with sickness in his gut that he realized that this relationship between them was never going to work. No matter what he felt for her. And as he saw their relationship going up in flames, he realized exactly how much it was that he felt.

The little redhead had caught him off guard when she'd entered his life. She'd worked her way into his heart, even when he'd been sure that his ex had destroyed the parts of him that were capable of a relationship.

In short, he loved her. And she'd run from him.

When the great wooden doors at the front of Veritas loomed before him, Elijah gave in to his frustration and slammed his fists into them. From the corner of his eye he saw a small group of Doms and Dommes eyeing him with alarm, but he pushed through the doorway before any of them could approach him.

"You're going to have bruises on your fists."

The voice was quiet, barely discernible, and Elijah thought he was imagining it. But as he turned his head in the direction from which it had come, he saw that his ears weren't playing tricks on him after all.

Samantha stood just outside the doors to Veritas, her arms wrapped around her torso as if she were cold.

She was such a welcome sight, he had to physically restrain himself from striding to her and wrapping her in his arms. After her betrayal, he couldn't just show her such affection.

"Why are you still here?" His voice was flat, at odds with the storm of emotion taking place inside him. She shivered. Silently he unbuttoned his shirt, peeled it off, and handed it to her.

"Thank you." Samantha shrugged into the pale blue button-down, which covered her slip entirely and made her look very young.

"Well?" Elijah hoped she had a damn good explanation.

"I left out of habit. I've spent years hiding this, you see. It's a hard habit to break." She looked at him, those green eyes wide, and Elijah felt his breath catch.

"I told you that you don't have to hide anything from me."

"I know." She said it softly but firmly, and when she raised her chin he saw the pride and stubbornness that were as bone deep in her as dominance was in him. "But I'm not going to lie to you. I'm trying to open up. I knew that if I came straight to you you would insist on coming with me. I need to go back home. And I don't want you to see all of that. I don't even want to visit it myself."

Elijah couldn't have felt more shocked if Samantha had hauled off and slapped him across the face.

"I see." And he did, with clarity.

He should have trusted his first instincts, that she wasn't capable of full submission.

He could have saved them both a lot of heartache.

"Are you going, then?" His voice was cold even to his own ears, and when he saw the hurt pass over Samantha's face he wished he could stop. But self-preservation had kicked in, and he felt himself withdrawing even as he stood there.

She nodded, looking stricken. "Elijah, I have to. I—"

He held up a hand, cutting her off. Anger was a black force descending on him. He wanted to haul her upstairs and lock her in chains in his bedroom until she came to her senses.

Maybe even if she didn't. Damn it, he *needed* her.

But as in all Dominant/submissive relationships, the bottom was the one who held all the cards. And she was telling him no.

"I'll let you upstairs to pack a bag and will call a car for you," he said.

And then he would open one of his ludicrously expensive bottles of wine and welcome the oblivion that would come with booze. He had a feeling he was going to need it for some time to come.

Elijah had gone back to the bar at Veritas, an untouched glass of wine in front of him. He had selected a bottle from the owners' private rack himself, snarled at Luca to leave him alone, and retreated to a corner of the bar.

He wanted to be left alone. But he didn't want to *be* alone, which was why he couldn't handle the idea of drinking by himself at home right now.

Alcohol consumption was closely monitored in Veritas, because drunkenness and BDSM play were a dangerous combination. But with Samantha gone he wasn't planning on doing another scene again tonight.

Forcing himself to lift his wineglass, he sipped at the ruby liquid inside the expensive glass. It tasted sour on his tongue, a reflection of his mood, he knew, and not the wine.

"Two fingers of Jameson's, water back," a rough and familiar voice said to the bartender, and Elijah felt a thread of anger slide through him as Robert, an older Dom who had been one of the first members of Veritas, took the barstool beside him.

Elijah forcibly swallowed his irritation. As one of the owners, it was his job to be polite, even when he didn't necessarily want to be. And Robert was a good friend—he didn't deserve to get pissed on just because Elijah was in a shitty mood.

"Saw you with your sub earlier," Robert said. Elijah tamped back a glower as he turned to look at him. The other Dom was in his seventies, but age hadn't diminished his stature. He was large, though not as big as Luca, and had a way of filling the space around him.

He just wanted to drink in peace and wallow in his anger at Samantha. Couldn't he do that in his own damn bar?

Humming out a noncommittal noise, Elijah stared into the depths of his glass as Luca delivered a glass of whiskey to the newcomer. Elijah watched from the corner of his eye as Robert sniffed the potent fumes, took a long swallow, and sighed with apparent satisfaction.

"Yep, saw you with your sub. Was a mite jealous, truth be told."

"Bit young for you, isn't she?" White-hot possession flooded Elijah, and his fingers tightened on the stem of his wineglass as he turned to glare at the other man.

"You wound me, Master E. I've still got some swagger." The man held up his arms, signaling that he came in peace, though Elijah saw the spark at being challenged by another Dom.

"I'm not trying to move in on your lady. She reminded me of Gladys."

Even at his age, Robert was a powerful enough Dom that he drew the attention of subs twenty years his junior. He hadn't touched any of them since his wife and longtime submissive, Gladys, had passed away the year before.

Though he no longer participated, he still came to the club. It felt like home, he said.

Elijah was inclined to agree—even with the emptiness he was feeling at Samantha's departure.

"The way your sub responded to you was what put me in mind of Gladys. A connection like that is rare."

This time the older Dom caught Elijah's full attention. He turned, his eyes homing in on his target. "What do you mean?" he asked, trying to tamp down the terrible hope. He had no business thinking the way he was. Samantha had made her choice, and any Dom worth his salt abided by those hard limits set by their other halves.

"She was so entirely focused on you. It was gorgeous to see. So submissive to you, even when Big Guy here was in the scene." Robert gestured to Luca, then rubbed a hand over his forehead. "Made me miss Gladys right hard, it did."

It took an extreme effort for Elijah to keep his emotions from running riot over his face. There were hundreds of Doms and Dommes who carried memberships to Veritas. Out of that number, only a handful were experienced enough, comfortable enough in the lifestyle to turn dominance into an art form.

Robert was one of them. He was dominant to his core— had been, to Elijah's understanding, for his entire adult life. A lifetime of experience had given the man unrivaled skills of observation.

And Robert had seen complete submission from Samantha in their scene?

What was he seeing that Elijah wasn't?

Sipping at the wine without tasting it, Elijah regarded the other man thoughtfully, noted that, true to form, Robert was looking around the play area, taking in everything that happened around him.

"I think that sub and I might have parted ways." Elijah chose his words carefully, not liking how they sounded. "I don't think she has what it takes to be fully submissive to me."

Beside him the former soldier snorted inelegantly, finishing his whiskey and sliding the empty glass across the counter. He turned to look Elijah in the eye, and Elijah felt a hint of kinship, Dom recognizing Dom.

"I've been in the lifestyle for fifty-two years." Though Robert's eyes followed the path of a pretty sub with long gray hair as she walked by, he didn't look further, reminding Elijah that that connection between himself and Samantha, between Robert and Gladys, wasn't something that could be found with just anyone. "And I topped a lot of subs before I met my wife. Some are a hell of a lot more work than others, but in my experience those are the ones whose submission is the sweetest. Hell, I scooped up the most ornery one I ever came across quick as I could. And I'm telling you, that pretty redhead of yours was giving in to you in a way that makes me think she would only ever submit to you. No one else."

Robert slid off his barstool, then nodded to Elijah. "Of course, if you own a place like this, you've probably never had to work too hard with a sub. They probably throw themselves at you. And I hate to offer advice when it hasn't been asked for, but you looked like you could use some."

And with that the man was gone, muttering something that sounded like "stubborn young pup" as he stalked away.

Elijah stared after the older man, turning the abrupt, unexpected conversation over in his head.

Robert had had some hard truths for him. And despite himself, Elijah could feel himself heeding his advice. Since Tara, since he and his friends had opened Veritas, he hadn't had to work for a sub at all. Hadn't wanted to, preferring to keep it casual.

Samantha . . . She'd crept up on him because she was different. And he liked it.

Carelessly shoving the glass of wine aside, Elijah stood from his own barstool and walked to the exit, his stride suddenly full of purpose.

They had problems to deal with—that was for sure. And he was still pissed as hell at her—damn it, her words had sliced right through him.

But he was damned if he was going to let her slip away without a fight. It was time to push a bit more.

It seemed that he was about to take a trip to Colorado.

Samantha looked down at the two sleeping women in the small hospital room. One was in a hospital bed that had the rails up, an IV pumping clear liquid into her hand. Her skin was so pale that Samantha could see the bluish veins running just beneath its surface.

The other woman curled in fetal position on a small, lumpy cot. Though her pallor was better than that of the older woman, she still had amethyst smudges beneath her eyes.

It was impossible to miss the resemblance between the two—and between them and herself, she realized. The same large eyes, the same straight nose. Though Beth's hair was pale strawberry to Samantha's red fire, and Gemma's was bleached bottle blond, the three women were still clearly related.

Resentment surged as Samantha looked down at the woman who had given her life. She tried to feel sympathy, love—*something*.

Instead there was only bitterness, bitterness tainted with the bloodred hue of rage. And layered underneath was panic, the clawing need to flee back to what she'd left behind in Vegas.

"Sam?" Beth's voice was hoarse as she sat up slowly and looked around owlishly. "How did you get here so fast?"

"I wasn't in Mexico." Samantha kept her voice deliberately light and her eyes trained on the only person in the room that she cared about.

Beth frowned but didn't press, seeming too sleep muddled to push further.

"Thanks for coming." Rubbing her eyes, Beth lay back down on the tiny cot. To Samantha, Beth seemed to shrink back into the teenager who had needed Samantha's support.

"How are you feeling?" Samantha whispered.

"I'm doing better."

Samantha repressed the urge to throttle her mother. Without the extra stress from her mother's incident, Beth would have been feeling just fine.

Smoothing her messy strands of her hair away from her face, Samantha perched herself on the edge of her sister's cot. They both stared at their mother for a long time, and Samantha wondered if there was something missing inside her, some emotional capacity that would have allowed her to care about her mother.

Gemma had wronged her in so many ways, the biggest of which was something that had radically altered the way she saw the world. But surely she should have still felt *something* for the woman in whose womb she had lived for nine months.

"I wish you'd come with me," Samantha said, staring down at her hands. They were pale, the skin crisscrossed with thin burns from her hot glass.

"I wish you'd come home," Beth replied, and Samantha bit back a sigh. It wasn't a new conversation, but it was one they still had from time to time.

She couldn't move back without facing the trauma of her past. And she couldn't exorcise it without telling Beth what had happened.

"My girls."

Samantha lurched as the cigarette-ravaged voice rasped over from the hospital bed.

"Both of you here to see me. It's about time." Gemma gestured feebly with her left hand, found it connected to an IV, and scowled. She turned the disapproving stare onto Samantha, eyeing her up and down before saying, "You certainly don't look like you've been in Mexico. You spreading lies again?"

Samantha's nails dug into her palms and she narrowly avoided shouting. An extreme reaction like that was what her mother wanted—she *wanted* to play the martyr, the saint whose elder daughter had run away for no good reason.

The woman thrived on drama. Because of that, both of her daughters hated it.

"I'm not here to see you, and I don't care what you believe or not." The latter was a lie. Samantha had once cared very much about whether her mother believed her, and at the time when she'd most needed her to, she hadn't.

"Let's not argue," Beth pleaded, wringing her own pale hands together. Samantha swallowed back the nasty retort that was on the tip of her tongue, ready to fling it in her mother's direction, but she swallowed it down instead, knowing that Beth hated any conflict.

Samantha sat, frozen, her fingers clutching the blanket on the cot as Gemma and Beth chatted, mostly about the things that Gemma perceived as having gone wrong since she'd been admitted—the food, the attitude of the nurses, what the stay was going to cost. Samantha wanted to strangle the woman—if she hadn't tried to drink herself to death, none of them would have been at the hospital in the first place.

She tried to tune the words out, the strange, tense ebb and flow an angry song to her ears.

"—still don't understand what all that nonsense is about," Gemma was saying, scowling at Beth, who looked pleadingly at their mother. "Surely you can just control it with diet. You must not be eating well, if your whatchamacallem levels are too high."

Samantha watched as Beth's mouth fell open for a long moment. Something more potent than irritation lashed through her as she saw her sister open her mouth to respond, then close it again with a shake of her head.

It was unbelievable. After so many years, that Gemma had no idea of anything about her own daughter's chronic illness was unthinkable.

Standing, her muscles stiff with tension, Samantha stalked to her mother's bed, waving her finger in the air.

"Beth is a diabetic, you coldhearted bitch."

Gemma sucked in a wounded breath. She looked hurt.

If the shoe fits, and all that.

"I don't know what that means." Raising her nose in the air, Gemma sniffed, rather like a dog that had examined its breakfast and found it lacking.

"It means that you should have learned all of this years ago, when Beth first got sick. You should have been the one taking her to the emergency room, figuring out what the hell was wrong with her. You should have been the one up with her in the night, checking to make sure her blood sugar levels stayed steady." Samantha fisted suddenly sweaty fingers in the loose cotton of her T-shirt. When she realized that she'd actually said the words instead of just thinking them, she began to tremble.

But it felt *good*, getting it out. Better than she could ever have imagined.

Samantha watched as something uneasy seemed to flicker through Gemma's eyes, so similar to her own. It was quickly covered with the cool composure that Samantha had seen on the older woman throughout her whole life.

"If you've got something to say, then say it, girl." Gemma regarded her coolly.

Samantha looked back, not daring to turn away, and noticed anew that her eyes were the exact same shape and color as her mother's.

No matter what she'd done, she hadn't been able to forget where she'd come from. So maybe it was time to start confronting instead of running.

A trickle of excitement worked its way through her rage. If she could do it, if she could face this, then maybe it wouldn't be too late to make things right with Elijah.

With an uneasy look at Beth—the younger sister she'd tried so hard to protect—Samantha turned back and faced her mother.

"How could you do it?" she asked quietly. Bitterness coated her tongue as the rage and disappointment of years past tried to flood through the small door she'd opened inside herself.

On the bed, the sickly woman shifted fretfully, her eyes darting away from her daughter.

"Don't you dare say you don't know what I'm talking about," Samantha said, cutting her mother off when the woman opened her mouth, not giving her a chance to deny it. From the corner of her eye she saw Beth shift uneasily, and Samantha cringed as she understood she couldn't protect her kid sister anymore.

"I told you what he did," Samantha continued quietly. Though she wanted nothing more than to look away—to run away—she forced herself to study her mother. The years hadn't been kind to Gemma Collins, a woman once so beautiful that she'd attracted scores of wealthy men.

But her mother had traded so much for that ritzy lifestyle, and that was what Samantha couldn't find it within herself to forgive. Gemma had turned a blind eye to Beth's illness, to Samantha's problems, to the needs of the children who depended on her.

"I told you what he did, and you used my pain to manipulate him." Saying the words out loud ripped the scab off the old wound, and Samantha grimaced as it bled anew. "You took money from him to keep quiet, rather than doing what you should have and standing by me."

"That money let me keep you girls fed," Gemma finally snapped, struggling to sit up in the narrow bed. Her skin was nearly as white as the sheets, save for two bright red circles of anger that popped up on her cheeks. "It was the lesser of two evils."

"You could have gotten a job. Could have stopped drinking. Could have stopped leeching off rich men who couldn't keep their hands off your daughter." Samantha heard Beth's startled intake of breath and held up a hand to stave off the questions.

Gemma glared at Samantha, defiance written all over her face. But there was no apology, no true repentance, just anger that Samantha was calling her out.

And then, suddenly, Samantha felt sorry for her mother. The woman would never know what it was like to be with someone she loved.

And in that moment she knew that she would do whatever it took to make Elijah see that they were meant to be together. She would find the strength to tell him everything—if he ever forgave her for running away from him.

"Why is Stanley calling you again?" Samantha no longer cared for herself, but she wouldn't put it past either the man or his on-again-off-again mistress to take out their frustrations on Beth. "What does he want?"

"He loves me," Gemma snapped, her fingers clutching the sheets as she looked from one daughter to the other. "He's come back to me time and time again when my own daughter hasn't."

"You know better than that." Strength was flooding up inside her, Samantha realized, growing with every word that she spoke. She'd never dreamed that evicting the monkey that had sat on her back for so many years would feel so freeing.

"He likes having control over you, but he doesn't love you." Pain stabbed through her when she saw that she'd touched a nerve—maybe she wasn't as numb to her mother as she'd thought. Still she felt the need to finish now that she'd started.

"He hasn't come around for years now. So what is it that he wants?"

"Get out." Gemma's voice was full of venom as she waved a shaky finger at Samantha. "Go. I don't ever want to see you again."

No, definitely not as numb as she'd thought, because she felt each word slicing through her heart.

"Good-bye." She nodded at Gemma, then moved to hug Beth, who cast her a bewildered look and clasped her sister's hand.

"Let's go," Beth said, and Samantha started. Her little sister's face was composed, but Samantha knew her well enough to see the anger that seethed just below the surface.

"You can stay." Gemma gestured in Beth's direction, like a queen who had just had her stomach pumped. "You've always been a good girl."

Beth rounded on their mother, and Samantha was surprised that flames didn't shoot out of her sister's mouth.

"I have spent years—*years*—catering to you because I thought that maybe, just maybe, you lived the way you did because you couldn't take care of yourself." Beth's fingers trembled, and Samantha gave them a reassuring squeeze. "You think I would stay now? I cleaned your house. I cooked for you. I bought you groceries. I mopped up your puke when you got so drunk you didn't even know your name, and I picked you up from bars that you had no business going to."

Gemma's face was frozen, her eyes glassy, her skin waxy.

"And now I find out that one of your johns put his hands on

my sister, and *all you did was ask for more money*." Beth was visibly vibrating against Samantha, and pride washed over her.

"I'm done. We're done." Beth looked at Samantha, with quiet apology in her eyes.

Samantha shook her head—no apology needed. She would have done it all over again if she had to.

"Let's go." Samantha tugged on her sister's arm. She wouldn't have been surprised if the confrontation had sent her sister's blood sugar levels skyrocketing again.

The two young women left their mother without a backward glance. As they passed through the doorway, Samantha felt as though she'd left an immense weight behind.

Halfway down the hall, Beth dug her fingers into Samantha's palm and gestured at a small, sterile sitting area.

"I need to sit down." She lowered herself into an ugly avocado green vinyl chair that had probably sat in the same spot for thirty years, and Samantha looked over her sister with a practiced eye.

Glassy eyes. Pale cheeks. Disoriented look. Unless she was mistaken, her sister's blood sugar had dropped this time, rather than shooting up.

A counter full of trays holding that evening's hospital meal sat across the hall. Not caring that Beth wasn't a registered patient, Samantha grabbed one and lugged it over to the rickety coffee table in front of Beth. After perusing the contents and wrinkling her nose at the mystery meat surprise, she removed the carton of apple juice and the bowl of green Jell-O.

"Here." She handed them to Beth, then perched in a chair across from her sister. Beth eyed the Jell-O with distaste before peeling back the foil lid on the juice.

"Still taking care of me, huh?" Beth sipped at the juice, color washing back into her face.

"I'll never stop," Samantha replied, and she knew it was the truth. The need to take care of her sister was an integral part of her after so many years—and it was why she could finally see how lucky she'd been to find a man as good as Elijah. Someone who would take care of *her* for a change.

God, she hoped she hadn't fucked it up beyond repair.

"About Stanley," Beth began hesitantly, draining her juice and crumpling the plastic cup in her hand.

Samantha shook her head and held up her hand, stopping her sister from speaking.

"It's in the past now, Bethy. Truly." Or it would be as soon as she told Elijah. And she *would* tell him, she suddenly saw. She wanted to be his, in every way possible, if only it wasn't too late. "Let's just move on."

"Move on from what?"

Samantha froze as she heard the words that came from behind her. Her entire being snapped to attention, tuned in to the man whose voice she would have recognized anywhere.

Beth looked up—and up—and whistled with appreciation.

Samantha didn't even flush at her sister's reaction. Instead she turned around slowly to find a pissed-off Dom staring down at her.

"Sir." Her mouth went dry. This mattered, more than she'd ever imagined it would. *He* mattered.

"Sir?" she heard Beth mutter, as if from far away. "I'm not going to ask. But I'll leave you two alone."

"Don't go back in there." Only for Beth was Samantha able to rip her attention away from the one person who could command her attention.

"As if. I meant it when I said I was done." Beth snorted. "I won't go far. We still have to talk."

"Take your Jell-O." The words were automatic, as was listening for her sister's long, suffering sigh. Then Beth shuffled away, leaving Samantha alone with Elijah.

He followed me. Her body itched to sink to her knees in apology, or to leap into his arms and smother his face with kisses. The only thing stopping her was the nurse who now guarded the counter full of food trays and who was eyeing Elijah with undisguised fascination.

Samantha couldn't blame her. Even dressed casually in jeans and a blue-striped polo shirt, he was gorgeous. Powerful. Sexy. Dominant.

"You're here." The words felt stiff. There was a barrier between them, one of her own making, but she had no idea how to go about breaking it down.

"You're mine," Elijah responded, his stare pinning her in place. "Though your actions tell me that you don't feel the same way."

Guilt unlike anything she'd ever felt before washed over Samantha. She shivered, suddenly cold, as she realized what a major wound it was that she'd inflicted into the heart of their relationship.

To hell with the nurse who was ogling her man. To hell with everyone who might see. She wanted to give Elijah everything, and she didn't care who knew.

On trembling legs, she moved away from her chair and crossed to where Elijah stood. He watched her, his expression unyielding, until she dropped to her knees in front of him.

She caught a flicker of shock in his eyes before she dropped her stare to the ground. She clasped her hands in front of her, lacing her fingers together until they went numb.

God, she hoped she wasn't too late. How stupid she'd been. He'd shown her, over and over, that he could be trusted with everything she had.

Now she just had to prove that she would give it to him.

"I'm so sorry, Elijah." The words were pale in comparison to what she felt. Just as when she'd tried to hide the phone call from Beth, Samantha realized that she had no idea how to say sorry in this world. And she wasn't sure she could depend on her teacher to instruct her any further.

Elijah nodded, but terror roiled in Samantha's stomach when she saw that, for the first time since she'd met him, he looked uncertain. "I'm not in a place where I'm prepared to listen to you tonight," Elijah started, and the nerves in her gut rolled over, making her nauseous.

She saw then how deeply she'd hurt him, and it horrified her. She hadn't known she'd had that much power over his feelings, or she would have been much more careful with them.

She'd been so stupid. There was no shame in showing him the less than perfect side of herself. In fact, giving that part of herself to him was empowering.

She didn't have to shoulder her burden alone.

"Are you—are you ending it? Officially?" Samantha whispered. She felt as if the weight that she'd left back in Gemma's room had returned to slam her on the head.

Elijah paused, that stare of his making her feel naked.

"I don't want to." His words were raw and honest. "I see you submitting now, but I don't know if I can move past your actions, which tell me that you don't trust me. This kind of relationship can't work without trust going both ways, Samantha. You know that."

"I—" She had no words. The truths that had seemed so real when she'd spoken to Beth in the ladies' room at Veritas now seemed flimsy bared in the fluorescent lights of the hospital.

What had she been thinking, running from the one man who had given her things she'd always wanted? So he was going to see who and what she came from? She should have trusted that he could handle it. But now—now she was going to tell him what had happened with that bastard.

He'd demonstrated to her that he would accept her entirely,

so long as she was honest with him. And in return she'd thrown that gift right back in his face.

She swallowed deeply, willing herself not to cry.

"Is it too late to tell you?" She laced her fingers tightly together to stop the trembling.

A flash of—could that be pain?—worked over Elijah's face.

"I don't know," he replied, and Samantha grabbed on to the sliver of hope with both hands. "But tonight isn't the time."

Samantha nodded, her teeth biting into her lower lip until she tasted blood.

"I'm going to stay with my sister tonight, at her apartment." Elijah nodded, his face carefully blank.

"Julien booked me into a nearby hotel. The Three Sisters Inn, I believe." Elijah's face was serious, but Samantha had a hard time picturing the wealthy tycoon at the small-town hotel. Just as she was starting to have a hard time imagining their lives ever really fitting together, no matter how hard she hoped.

"All right." She stared up at him, not daring to be submissive in that moment. She was going to fight for this man with everything she had. "When can we talk?"

Elijah looked at her for a long moment, considering. "Tomorrow morning you will come to me. You can tell me what you need to tell me. And then we'll decide if you want to return to Vegas or go back to Mexico, or stay here."

Samantha blanched at the firm tone. Knowing Elijah, she understood that what she professed to want wasn't going to be the deciding factor in that decision, but rather what Elijah perceived that she truly desired.

"I want to go back to Vegas with you." She made her words as firm as she could, but Elijah only raised an eyebrow.

"We'll discuss it tomorrow."

Her mouth dry, she parted her lips to speak, but Elijah

frowned at her, and she understood that he didn't want to hear from her.

Her knees trembled as she stood. Being around him without being able to touch him was painful . . . and she knew that he wouldn't permit her to put her hands on him until he said the words.

"I need to go find Beth. She's had a hell of a day, and she and I need to talk." It was an excuse to escape this painful distance that had crept up between them. For once, Samantha felt more compelled to do something besides taking care of her sister. Maybe it was because Beth had shown her that she was quite capable of taking care of herself by standing up to their mother.

"I understand why you did what you did, Samantha." The connection between them pulsed, a tangible thing. "But I need some time."

"Time. Right." Samantha looked at her fingers, twisted together in a knot as tight as the one in her belly.

Shame flooded through her, a sickly wave. Had she messed it all up with the man who was everything she'd ever wanted? She shook her head helplessly, finally giving in to the prickles of tears.

"I'll see you in the morning." Turning, Samantha headed off in the direction that Beth had gone, her steps halting. It killed her to walk away.

But she'd walk right back in the morning. And she'd be damned if she left him again.

CHAPTER EIGHTEEN

Elijah waited until Samantha was at the end of the hall before standing and following in that direction. He knew he'd given her a lot to think about, and it weighed heavily on him that he'd dumped it on her on a day that had clearly already been long enough.

No matter what she was thinking now, she was still his, and he was responsible for her safety. He would make sure that she and her sister got back home safely.

And no matter what she now thought, the decision that would be made tomorrow was entirely hers. He already knew what he wanted—knew it with startling clarity.

He wanted her, wanted his smart-mouthed bedroom submissive with an intensity that bordered on painful.

But she'd hurt him in a way he hadn't thought possible, more than even Tara had hurt him. He saw now that his ex had only ever played with submission.

Samantha—he had a real chance with her. An opportunity for everything both of them had ever wanted. Everything in him wanted to accept the submission she'd so beautifully offered. But he needed a bit of distance to think, to work through the feelings that she'd roused in him.

Damn it, she'd wounded his pride along with his heart by not trusting him. He was a dominant man, but he bled just like everyone else.

He followed at a discreet distance as she met up with her sister, and the two women exchanged a few words. The family resemblance was definitely there, he noted as he curiously studied the woman who meant so much to Samantha.

What he felt for Samantha was an all-consuming passion. Lust like he had never known before.

And mixed with that were intense feelings . . . feelings that felt a lot like love.

The two sisters hugged and linked hands, moving down the hall to the entrance of the hospital. Elijah saw Samantha stiffen and was on alert before he saw what it was that upset her.

A man in his midfifties whose pricey suit couldn't hide a sizable belly had just entered the hospital. Though he may have seemed fairly innocuous to some, Elijah could see that this man's eyes were nothing but cruel.

Shit. Samantha had frozen, was clearly fighting through terror. Before he could think it through, Elijah was striding down the hallway, his long legs eating up the distance, driven by the primal need to protect his woman.

". . . just go away. Leave all of us alone." Beth's words jangled with nerves.

"Why are you here, Stanley?" Samantha's voice was quiet, but Elijah could hear the core of strength . . . and the trembling behind it. "What do you want?"

"Your mother has something of mine." The man's cold eyes flickered over Elijah as he approached, but he was so intent on his goal that he didn't pay the younger, bigger, more fit man more than a glance.

"You've taken enough from her." Samantha broke her stare from the older man to turn and meet Elijah's eyes as he approached. Yes, there was strength there—his little cat had claws. But there was also anguish and embarrassment. "Now go."

His years as a Dom had taught Elijah how to read people very, very well. In that moment, as Samantha looked up at him with her emotions written all over her face, he understood.

Whatever secret she was keeping, it had to do with this man. The way her body angled away from him, the way the man leaned in toward her with a predatory stance, told him the story he was going to hear from Samantha the next morning.

Pulling Samantha back, Elijah stepped in front of her and her sister and drew up to his full height. He knew damn well how intimidating he could be.

"Elijah!" Samantha pushed at his back. "You don't have to do this."

He appreciated that she didn't expect him to fight her battles. Yet he was going to, as long as they were together.

"Who the hell are you?" The other guy looked Elijah up and down as if he was a bug on the sole of his shoe, but Elijah caught the split second of hesitation before rage that flickered over the man's face.

Rich, Elijah thought, *along with a deep sense of entitlement. Doesn't like being told no.*

"The lady asked you to leave." Elijah allowed his lips to curl in a smile that held no mirth. "So go."

"Or what?" Stanley sneered, turning to Samantha and licking his lips. "It's in your best interest to help me get what your mother has, honey. It's something real personal. Your mom's not a real trustworthy kind of gal, you know."

"What does she have, Samantha?" Elijah felt her efforts to push him away dwindle. He took a moment to pull her forward, to look down into a face that had drained of color.

"Pictures," she said, numb. "I never knew what happened to them. But she must have held on to them, to taunt him with. It would be the kind of thing she would do."

Elijah's rage boiled over. Grabbing the portly man by the collar, he hauled him up to his tiptoes, then leaned down until their noses almost pressed together.

"If you do anything—*anything*—else to hurt either of

these women—in any way—I'll kill you." The words coming out of his mouth sounded as if they belonged to a stranger. Though he had a definite need for control, he'd never been a violent man.

But this man, who had hurt Samantha? He wanted to pound his head into the pavement.

With a final glare to emphasize his point, he set the man back down on his toes, becoming dimly aware of the sounds of people in the background reacting to his temper. He observed, as if from outside his body, Stanley shaking like a chicken who had been caught in the rain.

"You little punk, I'll bury you." Stanley poked his finger right into Elijah's chest, and Elijah narrowly stopped himself from grabbing it and snapping it in half. "You don't know who you're messing with. I'm a very rich man. I have connections you can't even dream of."

So it was money, then—that was what spoke to this bastard. Elijah smiled as cold control washed over him, and he saw Stanley tremble a bit as the cold reached his eyes.

"No matter how much money you have, I guarantee I have more." Elijah felt a current of satisfaction as Stanley's face paled. "I have more connections. I know more people."

Wrapping his hand around the finger that still bore into his chest, Elijah yanked it and squeezed. Stanley tried to pull away, but found he couldn't.

"If you do anything to hurt either of these ladies or anyone they care about, if you try to contact them ever again, I'll come for you." Elijah released Stanley so abruptly that the other man stumbled back. Elijah stood perfectly still, a menacing statue, as the other man sputtered.

"Keep her." Stanley sneered around Elijah at Samantha, who dug her nails into Elijah's back in upset. "Nothing I want anymore anyway. But you can't stop me from visiting Gemma, whenever I want, however I want. She's always pathetically grateful for my attention. And your old lady's a better fuck than you ever were."

With a last glare, Stanley marched off down the hall, his spine so straight that Elijah thought he must have had a stick rammed up his ass.

No way in hell was that fucker getting pictures of Samantha.

"I'm going to call my car. It will be here in just a minute. It will take you two home." Elijah pulled his cell from his pocket, tapped out a text message, then jammed the device back into the denim. He looked down at Samantha and her sister. The startled expression that crossed Samantha's face told him he looked every bit as ruthless as he felt.

He toned it down a bit for her.

"Come to me in the morning," he repeated, then gestured to the glass doors of the hospital. "That's my car. Go."

"Where are you going?" Samantha eyed him warily, even as Beth tugged on her arm.

Elijah met her eyes, thought about making up a story.

Total honesty.

"I'm going to take care of that." He jerked his head in the direction that Stanley had gone, then readied himself for an argument.

He was taken aback—pleased—when Samantha smiled, a predatory curve of the lips, and nodded with approval.

"Thank you." She leaned toward him, then stepped back. Finally she stood on her toes and quickly pressed a kiss to the line of his jaw, flushing as she retreated. "Thank you for everything."

Then she was gone, hustling her sister out the door.

A no-nonsense nurse was approaching Elijah when he turned back toward the depths of the hospital, the look on her face telling him that she planned to evict him from the premises. When she looked up into his face, she faltered, stopped, stared.

"I'll be gone momentarily," Elijah promised as he strode back into the hospital.

"I just have to take care of one little thing first."

S amantha set her hands on her knees and leaned back against the hotel room door. Fatigue was like a heavy blanket, weighing her down, luring her in.

"No." Shaking her head, she tried to stay awake.

The hallway was empty. Nothing to look at, no one to entertain her, to keep her from falling asleep.

"Damn it." For what felt like the hundredth time, she looked in the direction of the elevator.

Still no Elijah.

Resigning herself to waiting, she tipped her head back and closed her eyes, allowing her thoughts to wander.

Elijah had told her to come to him in the morning. She couldn't wait that long. The pressing need to smooth out what was between them made it impossible for her to focus on anything else.

She'd had Elijah's driver take Beth home, then bring her to the Three Sisters Inn. The woman working the front desk was someone Samantha had gone to high school with, and a few minutes of playing buddy-buddy had yielded Elijah's room number.

Now all she could do was wait—wait and try to figure out the best way to say she was sorry.

The chime of the elevator sounded. Groggy by now, she saw him striding out of the lift and making his way down the hall before she could get to her feet.

"Samantha." He stopped cold when he saw her. She swallowed, hard, as she took in his face.

His lip was split and bloodied, and his eye was swollen and beginning to turn black. In his hand he held a data stick.

Samantha had never seen him less guarded. She looked at his split lip, his black eye, the data stick.

Going on instinct, she dropped to her knees, right there in the hallway of the Three Sisters Inn. With her eyes on his feet, she spoke the words that came from her heart.

"I love you."

Elijah growled. Startled, she looked up just in time to see the ferocity on his face as he grabbed her by her elbows, lifted her off her feet, and pressed her against the door.

"Hold on to me." Elijah placed his hands under her butt and lifted, pressing her against the doorframe. At the same time his lips possessed hers.

"Wait," she whispered, pulling back. Elijah growled again as she slid her fingers over the split in his lip. His eyes devoured her expression, absorbing every nuance, and for the first time since she'd met him he seemed hesitant.

"Was this okay?" he whispered.

Samantha's heart swelled.

"Thank you." Gently, she pressed her lips to his, trying to put everything she felt in her heart into the kiss. "Thank you."

They stared into each other's eyes for a long moment, and Samantha felt as though she would burst.

Impatient, she wiggled her hips against his hardness. "Let me show you. Let me thank you," she said.

"Hold this." Elijah thrust the data stick between Samantha's teeth as he fumbled in his pocket while still holding her against the door. Pulling out the key card triumphantly, he opened the door and they half walked, half fell into the small hotel room.

"Bed." Spitting the data stick onto the floor, Samantha's lips roamed over his face, his jaw, his neck. Working her fingers down between them, she tugged at the button of his jeans. "Now."

"One thing first," Elijah muttered, placing her gently on the bed. His eyes never leaving hers, he moved back to where the data stick had fallen.

Lifting his foot, he stomped down on the stick. The plastic crunched beneath the heel of his boot, and he hissed with satisfaction.

When he looked back at Samantha, she saw more of that hesitation, but coupled with it was possession.

No one would hurt her as long as she was with him.

"I need you. I can't wait anymore." Grabbing for his belt loops, Samantha pulled him to her. Her big, gorgeous Dom looked down at her with a hint of amusement as she undid his belt buckle, the button and zipper of his jeans, then impatiently tugged the denim down his legs.

His boxer briefs went along with the pants, and she couldn't hold back a smirk as she realized that her bossy Dom was still and quiet, letting her do as she wished for once.

The smirk slid from her face when she looked back up and found that Elijah's rock-solid erection was directly in front of her lips.

The silence in the room was thick, heavy. She looked up at Elijah as, slowly, she wrapped her fingers around the base of his shaft, then slid her lips over the head of his cock.

"Samantha." Elijah groaned as she swirled her tongue over the tip of his penis. His salty musk spread out over her tongue.

She wanted more, wanted to give more. She needed to show him how she felt.

Tightening her grip on the base of his shaft, Samantha worked her hand up and down as she began to suck, hard and fast. Her cheeks hollowed out as she pulled on him with her tongue. She heard his quiet moan as he relinquished control and gave in to her attentions, tangling his fingers in her hair and tugging.

The bite of pain spurred her on. She moved her hand faster, sucked harder. She cried out a protest when the hands in her hair pulled her back, out of reach of his cock.

"Strip." Elijah's voice was a harsh bite.

Samantha stood, obeyed as quickly as she could as Elijah tugged his shirt over his own head.

Then he laced his fingers in the cheap cotton T-shirt that she hadn't had a chance to remove yet and ripped the garment right off her.

Heat flooded through her as Elijah clasped her around the waist and moved her up to the head of the bed. When he lay down flat on top of her, she almost gave in to the pleasure, almost let him take control.

"No," she said. Pressing her palms flat against his chest, she pushed until he rolled onto his back. "I need to do this. I need to show you."

"Samantha." Elijah bit out the word, frustration evident in his taut features. Feeling like an animal, Samantha bared her teeth at him, shifting until she straddled his hips and his cock brushed through folds that were already wet.

"I want you. I want all of you." Bending, she pressed a tender kiss over his heart. The fierce heat in his blue eyes blazed as she righted herself, and she felt her heart stutter in her chest.

"Take me, then," he said. His fingers found her hips and dug into her flesh, hard enough to bruise, and Samantha thrilled to the bite of pain. "However you want."

"Like this." Reaching down, she took his erection in her hand. Pressing it to the heat of her entrance, she slowly took the head of him inside.

"Goddamn it, Samantha." Elijah's body was tense with the effort of keeping still, of letting her have control.

The big, bad Dom was hers, and she never wanted to let him go.

Silently she sank down on him, taking his cock fully inside her. She cried out as he filled her, feeling overwhelmed, though she was the one in charge.

Below her Elijah trembled, moving his hands from her hips to tangle their fingers together.

"Mine," Samantha said as she began to move, sliding up just a fraction, then back down. Elijah raised their entwined hands, each of them leaning into the touch as Samantha rose and fell, just enough to create friction, but never so much that she wasn't completely full of him.

Elijah's eyes went wide a moment before he stilled beneath her.

"What's wrong?" Leaning over, she searched his face. "Am I hurting you?"

"I'm not wearing a condom." Elijah's voice was strained.

Samantha didn't break the connection that drew hot and tight between them.

"I know." Her words were taut with emotion. "I trust you."

The sound Elijah made then was full of possession, rumbling from the depths of his chest. Before Samantha could even inhale, he had flipped her back over and was looming above her.

His eyes blazed into hers fiercely.

"Mine." He echoed her earlier words before plunging as far inside her as he could go.

Samantha cried out, then lost herself in the sensation as Elijah took over her body. Pleasure drew hard and fast, and her cries became incoherent when he reached a hand between her legs and rubbed over the hard nub of her clit.

She lost herself seconds before he clasped her by the hips, lifting her off of him just before he came, savoring the sensation of his heat lashing over her belly and thighs, marking her in the most primal of ways. It felt different—so much more intimate.

And then, before she knew what was happening, he slid his fingers between her legs and pulled a second, harder spasm of bliss from her body, and she couldn't think about how she was feeling at all.

"I was married once." Elijah's voice could have been coming from anywhere in the room. They lay in the pitch-black darkness, her frame sprawled on top of his, his hand stroking idly over her back.

She stilled, waiting.

"Her name was Tara. She was beautiful, fun, and best of all submissive. Alex and Luca wanted her too, but she chose me."

Samantha felt as though she should be jealous, but strangely felt nothing but calm.

"What happened?" she asked quietly. She didn't want to break the spell.

"We were both young, and we thought that love was enough." Elijah seemed to be lost in thought. "It turned out that we weren't as well matched as we'd thought. I can see now that she wasn't really interested in submission at all, and it turned out that I needed . . . more."

"Which is why you were so concerned that I wouldn't be able to fully submit." Samantha's throat suddenly felt tight. "Elijah, I've told you what I want. I want a man who will take control without asking for it. I want a man who will take care of me, feminism be damned. But I don't know if I can run around thinking of you as my Master."

"I can't deny something that's so much a part of me. I'm dominant. It's who I am." Elijah traced the lines of her shoulder blades with one hand while the other cupped the back of her neck. "But I think I was wrong about you. You make me work harder for your submission than I've ever had to work with a sub before. But it's so much sweeter when you do submit to me. A strong woman giving herself to me is the sexiest thing I've ever experienced.

"When I said that I needed someone who was truly submissive, I didn't mean that I needed that kind of relationship twenty-four/seven." His fingers worked the knots of tension at the base of Samantha's skull, and she arched beneath the touch. "I think we can find a way to make it work together. As long as we trust each other."

And that, Samantha knew, was her cue. Drawing in a shuddering breath, she steeled herself to tell the tale that she hadn't spoken of since she'd told her mother, who had then turned around and used her daughter's trauma to gain money.

"My mom was—is—a professional mistress." Samantha grimaced at the sound of the words. "She has a taste for expensive things, but has no desire to get an honest job to work for them. So she trades sex for financial support, for jewelry and clothing and cars."

Beneath her Elijah was silent. Though it hurt, she continued.

"Some of the guys were okay. Most of them ignored Beth and me. We're pretty sure that we have different fathers, but neither of us has ever met our dads, not that we can remember."

The more she told, the easier it got.

"My mom started . . . seeing . . . Stanley when I was fifteen and Beth was twelve. He made me uncomfortable from the start, the way he'd watch us. But he didn't do anything until I was sixteen."

She'd been counting down the days until she was old enough to take Beth and leave.

"They came home one night, both drunk as hell. I could hear them having sex, couldn't sleep over the noise. When they were done, I was relieved, and finally went to sleep.

"But I woke up a couple of hours later and found him in my room."

Closing her eyes against the visual, Samantha reached out blindly for Elijah's hand. He laced his fingers in hers and held tightly.

"You can imagine the rest," she said quietly, willing the pain to fade from memory. "It happened a few more times. He took pictures."

"How did you get him to stop?" Elijah's voice was full of repressed fury. Samantha felt a wave of satisfaction that someone was so angry on her behalf.

"I took a kitchen knife and caught him with his pants down in the bathroom one afternoon." Grim pleasure accompanied the recollection. She would never forget the look on his face as she'd held up the butcher knife, determination and desperation in her every muscle.

"I told him that if he ever touched me again, if he ever even *thought* about touching Beth, I'd sneak into their room while he was sleeping and cut his cock off. I meant it, too." She gnashed her teeth just thinking about it. "That afternoon I tried to tell my mom. She denies it now, but I know she believed me. But instead of trying to protect me, she used it to get money out of him. Money and the pictures. He left, and she started drinking more. He's popped back up now and again—I think because he likes tormenting her. The pictures . . . I didn't know she'd held on to those. Another bargaining chip, I guess."

The whole story out, Samantha fell silent. Instead of terror that Elijah would think less of her, though, she felt relief.

It was out. She couldn't control it anymore.

She squeaked when Elijah rolled her onto her side, facing

him. In the blackness she could just make out the stubborn line of his jaw.

"I think even more of you now that I know this." Strong fingers traced over her jaw, her lips, and Samantha nuzzled into the touch like a kitten. "You survived, and you made something of yourself. And now you've faced your fears. You're the bravest woman I know."

Samantha closed her eyes and said a silent prayer. Yes, she was brave—so brave that she spat out her next words before she could chicken out.

"So, are we . . . okay?" She trembled as the hand tracing over her cheek stilled. "I'm so sorry I left. So sorry."

Elijah was silent for a long moment, less than a minute, but enough for Samantha's mind to head down a dark, winding path.

When he wrapped his arm around her waist and drew her in close, her heart began to beat double time.

"I know you're sorry, Sammie Cat." His hand was splayed out over the small of her back, and she arched into the touch. "So this is what we're going to do."

CHAPTER NINETEEN

The last four weeks had been the longest month of Samantha's life.

"Three weeks and six days," she muttered to herself as she parked her new previously owned sedan in front of In Vino Veritas and slid out of the driver's seat.

She was there a day early. She couldn't wait anymore, and she didn't care what Elijah said about it.

"Miss Samantha." Julien grinned at her as she approached the front door, her palms slick with nervous sweat. "You look lovely."

"Thanks, Julien." Samantha looked down at the red miniskirt and bustier that she'd chosen specifically for their color. "Uh... is everything set up?"

"The crate is in the entryway, and I've kept him busy for the last hour." The man's eyes twinkled with mischief. "You're sure you're set on him? Because I'd be more than happy to step into his place."

"I'm absolutely sure." Samantha's nerves hummed with anticipation. She'd seen the sense in Elijah's proposal that they spend a month apart, even as she'd protested. Loudly.

He'd wanted her to take time away from him, away from sex, to make sure this was what she wanted.

She'd used the time to pack up her things in Mexico and move both herself and Beth to Las Vegas. She and Elijah had spoken, texted, and e-mailed, but it was all a pale substitute for being with him in person.

"You're ready?" Julien pulled his phone from his pocket, and Samantha nodded as butterflies began to dance in her stomach. "I'll text him, then. You go on in."

Swallowing past her nerves, Samantha pushed through the heavy front door of Veritas. In the place where she'd once told Elijah that they needed a piece of art stood a wooden crate, the nails pulled out, waiting for the sides to be pulled off.

The lobby was otherwise empty. She'd asked Julien to discourage people from loitering around there right then.

Tugging at the hem of her bustier, she walked to the crate, her impossibly high heels echoing on the stone floor. She tugged one of the wooden sides away, letting it fall to the floor with a crash.

The crash muffled the first of Elijah's footsteps. As soon as she recognized the sound, she whirled, eyes wide, desperate to lay eyes on him again.

"Sammie Cat." God, the man looked good. Rather than one of his more laid-back polo and jean ensembles, he was dressed in a fancy custom-tailored suit. The top two buttons of his shirt were undone, and he was missing his tie.

He looked good enough to eat.

"Hi." Of all the things Samantha had expected to feel, shy wasn't one of them. But after a month of phone calls, she wondered if his feelings had changed, now that she was here in the flesh.

"Come here to me." His voice was gruff. He held out his arms as she hesitantly crossed the space between them.

And then she was enfolded in his powerful strength, the smell of him in her nostrils, and nothing had ever felt more right.

"Fuck." Elijah pulled back, looked her in the face, then claimed her lips in a fierce, hot kiss. When he finally released her, she laughed, slightly out of breath.

"It's good to see you, too." Grinning up at him, she tapped her fingers on the side of the wooden crate and waited.

"Is this . . . ?" Elijah's worlds trailed off with anticipation as he stepped back to look at the crate. With the one side that Samantha had removed, the wooden box stood open, the sculpture upright and draped in cloth, waiting to be revealed.

She tensed, suddenly terrified, as Elijah tugged on one end of the cloth. His opinion mattered more than anything.

"Oh, Samantha." Elijah's voice was full of awe. She watched, still nervous, as he raked his fingers through his hair and circled the sculpture to take it in from all sides.

She looked with him, trying to see it as he did.

The glass was similar in shape to that first sculpture at his exhibit, the one that had brought them together. That sculpture had been packed up and shipped to Elijah's home, and was presumably upstairs right then.

This one was more suited to be displayed at Veritas. It had the same contrast of masculine and feminine, the same burning sensuality.

But where the first sculpture had been made with Samantha's unexplored desires in mind, this one . . .

This one was submission fully realized. A deep, passionate red, the swirls of glass spoke of the beauty of a strong woman giving control to the man who had earned it.

"It's called *Submission*," Samantha said quietly, her words nonetheless echoing off the high ceilings.

"Are you absolutely sure?" Elijah turned to her, eyes burning.

After a month of mental practice, Samantha sank to her knees with far more grace than she once had. Settling on the cold floor, she waited, her eyes on the stone, her palms facing up.

The gesture said what her words could not.

"Stand up." There—*there* it was, that total dominance. God, how she'd yearned for that over the past few weeks.

She hurried to obey his order, wobbling only a bit on her heels. The fierceness that she saw on Elijah's face when she looked up took her breath away.

"I bought this the day you flew back to Mexico." Digging in his pocket, Elijah pulled out a braided white gold necklace, the chain as thick as one of her fingers. "I've carried it with me ever since, hoping that you would come back."

"There was never any doubt." Samantha stared at the necklace greedily. It was beautiful, and exactly, uniquely her, with the large pendant made of the palest green glass. But it wasn't the object itself that drew her so much as what she hoped it represented.

"If I put this on you, it means that you're mine. In every single way. Is that what you want?"

Samantha reached surreptitiously for the skin on the inside of her elbow and pinched.

"Ow." She rubbed the spot to soothe the sting, then looked up to find Elijah frowning at her. "Sorry. I just wanted to make sure that this was real."

Some of the same emotions that she was feeling flickered over Elijah's face. He dangled the necklace from his fingers, letting the gorgeous metal and glass catch the light.

"Last chance." His words were light, but Samantha knew him well enough by now to hear the trace of apprehension behind it.

Narrowing her eyes, she grabbed for the necklace, scowling when a now grinning Elijah held it out of her reach.

"Mine." Samantha put everything she felt into the one word, looking up into the face of the man that she loved.

He spun her gently, then finally, finally settled the necklace around her throat. The ball of glass settled into her collarbone as if the piece had been made for her—and knowing Elijah, it probably had.

She trembled as his fingers danced over her bare skin, settling the necklace into place, then securing the clasp. He spun her back around, then traced his fingers down the line of white gold.

"Mine," he agreed, and after staring at each other for a long moment, they both broke into grins.

"Want a drink before we go play?" His fingers skimmed from the necklace down, dancing over the swells of her breasts. Samantha felt her body tighten—she wanted to go play *now*.

The last month had taught her that some things were worth the wait, so she smiled and took Elijah's hand.

"Know anywhere I can get a decent glass of wine?"

ACKNOWLEDGMENTS

A big thank-you to the usual suspects for all their help with this book! To my super editor, Kerry Donovan, without whom this book would . . . well . . . suck. To my agent, Deidre Knight, who inspires me daily. To Suzanne Rock, the best critique partner in the world. To Sara Fawkes and Avery Aster, as well as Barbara J. Hancock, D. L. Snow, Juliana Stone, and Amanda Vyne for cheering me on (and listening to me whine). To my husband, Rob, for getting the kidlet out of the house so that I could get some work done. For my parents and the staff at their business for letting me hide out in a back office when the getting-the-kid-out-of-the-house thing didn't work so well. And finally, thank you to Brenda Novak, who has supported me through my son's recent diagnosis of type 1 diabetes, and who helped me translate the medical terms into understandable language for this book.

Lauren Jameson is a writer, yoga newbie, knitting aficionado, and animal lover who lives in the shadows of the great Rocky Mountains of Alberta, Canada. The author of the serial novel *Surrender to Temptation*, she has published with Avon and Harlequin as Lauren Hawkeye and writes contemporary erotic romance for New American Library.

All I wanted was to feel sexy.

Grimacing, I pulled the confection of openwork silk off of my shoulders and down. What had I been thinking? A girl with some curves—namely, me—couldn't wear ruffles. This whole endeavor was a terrible idea.

My bangs were sticking to my forehead with sweat as I tugged the lingerie back over my head. I contemplated dropping it to the ground and stomping on it in frustration, but repressed the urge and hung the lingerie back up, nice and neat, on its plastic hanger.

That was what I always did, after all—shoved my real feelings away, smiling prettily when I wanted to scream.

Frustrated and close to tears, I eyed the last item that I'd brought with me into the dressing room at Magnifique, the fancy lingerie boutique that I'd passed by on my way to work every single day for the last year. That item was also lace, but instead of being heavily ruffled and made for a woman with the build of Barbie, it was a deep indigo, made of soft silk, and sophisticated instead of cute. It would skim the body and accentuate curves.

This one had to work. It just had to. How was I ever going to convince my ever so proper boyfriend to make love to me in a position other than missionary if I couldn't find something to entice him with?

Inhaling deeply and avoiding the sight of my naked flesh in the mirror, I tugged the slip off of its hanger and over my head. It felt lovely, the material moving in a sensual glide over my skin.

With my eyes squeezed shut, I turned back toward the mirror, sucked in my tummy, and, after a lengthy internal pep talk, peeked at the reflection staring back at me.

"Oh." The woman in the mirror smiled with surprise and pleasure at the same time that I did. Smoothing a hand over the length of my now-messy blond ponytail, I scanned the image nervously, looking for the flaws that I saw every day—the swell of my stomach, the slightly too heavy breasts, the hips that were a hint too wide.

I saw none of them. The incredibly sheer lace kissed my curves rather than clinging to them, and this made my waist, my belly, and my hips all look just right. My breasts rose enticingly out of the low neckline, and the hem of the little slip hit midthigh, covering my butt yet hinting at more.

I looked . . . Well, I looked hot.

It was a strange sensation.

Before I could convince myself otherwise, I stripped off the slip and put my office clothes back on. The knee-length skirt, blouse, and cardigan sweater were all solid black—bright colors made me feel fat. The monochromatic look worked just fine for the office, however—Cambridge–Neilson and Sons, the law firm where I was an administrative assistant.

The law firm where my boyfriend, Tom, was a junior partner. The slip that I was buying was in an effort to please him. *No,* I corrected myself as I brought it nervously to the front counter, it was about pleasing *me.* About looking—and feeling, I supposed—sexy enough to entice Tom to be a little more adventurous in the bedroom.

To possibly, maybe, encourage him to do some of the deliciously naughty things that I thought about nearly all of the time. Dreamed about, too.

"Your total comes to two hundred dollars and seventy cents." I'd been playing it cool until that moment, acting like I bought expensive lingerie all the time, but the sum that the tall, slender brunette salesgirl announced very nearly made me choke.

Two hundred dollars? For that little scrap of lace?

I couldn't afford it. I should have just let it be. Did I really want to spend that much in order to please Tom?

The salesgirl, whose nametag read BERNADETTE in swirling cursive, saw my wistful glance at the swath of midnight blue that she was wrapping in silver tissue. I forgave her the stylish boots and the fresh salon haircut when she gave me a kind smile and said, "It's expensive, but we're all worth it, aren't we?"

I thought of how I looked in the slip, and then thought of someone looking at me while I wore it. Of his dark eyes taking in the way the blue set off the pale cream of my skin, of the way my nipples flushed through the soft lace.

Yes. I had to have it.

"It's fine. I'll put it on credit." Rummaging through my

large leather satchel, I finally found my wallet. It caught on a cardboard envelope as I pulled it out, and the print that I had just picked up from the photography place next door slipped out and onto the counter.

Bernadette glanced over, and I saw her study it for a moment longer than necessary. "He looks familiar."

I turned to study the picture, too. It was of Tom and me posing rather seriously at the beach. It had been a rare unplanned moment in our courtship, on a business trip to Los Angeles, when I had begged him to pull the car over so that we could watch the sunset. Surprisingly, he had agreed. With the sun setting behind us in a riot of glowing shades, and the angle clearly showing that the picture had been taken by one of us with a cell phone camera, it should have been a romantic shot. Instead, we looked so incredibly austere, so at odds with the sunset and the ocean, that the whole thing seemed rather silly.

Still, it was the best picture that I had of us together. I was going to frame it and keep it on my desk at work. We had been dating for over a year, after all.

"Hmm." Before I could reply, Bernadette snapped her fingers, even as she expertly nipped my credit card from my hand and ran it through her point-of-sale machine. "Yesterday! He was in yesterday. Big spender." When she caught what I'm sure was my surprised expression, she clapped a hand over her mouth and giggled sheepishly. "I probably shouldn't have said that. Now I've ruined whatever surprise he had for you."

"Surprise. Right." Brow furrowed, I took the candy pink–and-cream-striped bag that she handed me, nodding my thanks before walking away.

I was quite certain that she was mistaken. I would have let it go at that, but the woman's statement niggled at my mind all the way back to work, and then as I sat at my desk, slowly pecking away at the handwritten letter that one of the lawyers needed typed up.

Never had Tom bought me expensive lingerie. He'd never bought me candy or flowers, either, for that matter. He just wasn't that type of guy and, foolishly, early on in our relationship, I had told him that grand gestures weren't important to me.

I hadn't lied—they weren't important . . . exactly. But a soft inner part of my heart still craved some kind of sweet gesture from time to time—something that told me I was being thought of when I wasn't there.

I was fairly certain that I wouldn't ever receive one of these gestures from Tom. Yes, Bernadette was mistaken.

But another thought formed in my mind as I worked my way through the afternoon. What if . . . what if . . . ?

No. Tom wouldn't do that. Tom loved me.

"Hi, Devon." One of the senior lawyers chose that moment to walk by. Though quite possibly paranoid, I was convinced that she gave me a pitying glance, barely masked by her small smile. That was what settled my mind.

Begging off early with the excuse of a headache, I hurried down to my car.

I would just go home—the home that I had not yet moved into, actually—and see Tom. Once I saw him, all of this silliness would fly out the window, I was sure.

And, I thought as I looked sideways at the Magnifique bag on my passenger's seat, maybe I could model my new slip for him.

I almost felt as if I should ring the doorbell. Tom had given me a key the previous week, after we had decided that my moving my meager belongings into his place was a sensible idea, but I hadn't yet used it. I suspected that I'd been clinging to my independence—I loved my little studio apartment, the one that I'd already given notice for, but Tom had pointed out that it wasn't nearly big enough for two people. Plus, his was closer to the office.

A shorter commute just made sense, after all, even to me. Sleeping in two separate rooms when we weren't having sex did not make sense, and never would, no matter how many times Tom told me that it would provide better sleep for both of us. The mere thought made me grind my teeth together.

I would rather have a less than perfect night's sleep, with my partner by my side, than the alternative—sleeping down the hall from each other like a couple who had been married for far too long.

I wasn't going to give in on that issue.

Sighing heavily, I once more squelched the urge to knock at this place that was now supposed to be my home, and instead turned my key in the dead bolt. I had to fiddle with it, the way you do with new keys, before the lock gave way.

"Hello?" I didn't raise my voice. The apartment was dim and quiet, and though I hadn't expected his presence—he was at a lunch meeting—I almost felt relieved that he wasn't home, that I didn't have to ask the difficult question.

I could take a few minutes to orient myself. Maybe sit down and think of some ways to brighten up the utilitarian bachelor's apartment, so that it felt warmer and more welcoming to me.

Before I was even out of the entryway, I heard it. Faint at first, but steadily growing louder, and unmistakably coming from the direction of the bedroom.

"Oh. Ohhhh."

Confused, I cocked my head at the sound of the female voice and took a few steps down the hall. Then, when Tom's voice joined in the chorus of sex sounds, my mouth fell open, and I felt as if I'd been punched in the stomach.

Tom was indeed home. He was home, and unless I was very much mistaken, he was having sex with another woman in the bedroom where I, his longtime girlfriend, was rarely permitted to sleep.

Bernadette had been right.

Adrenaline shot through my veins and made me feel sick. Suddenly intent on ferreting out the second piece of evidence to back up the riot of feelings that was surging through me, I scanned the apartment until I saw it wadded up on the floor beside the couch.

A bag from Magnifique—the tissue paper ripped by eager fingers. Feeling as if I was going to throw up, I picked up the bag and shook it out.

Whatever Tom had purchased the day before was gone— probably on the floor of his bedroom—but the receipt was still there.

Four hundred twenty-three dollars for a bustier, garter belt, and stockings, all size extra small.

Extra small. Well, that definitely wasn't me. Tears of humiliation sprang to my eyes and clouded my throat as I stared at the area of carpet around the discarded bag. There, right out in the open, were more details that I couldn't ignore. A single nude-colored pump, with PRADA stitched into the sole. Two wineglasses, a film of red still coating the bottoms.

That was it. I was done.

For a moment I thought that I might fling open the door to the bedroom, might confront them both and be self-righteous in my indignation.

But I couldn't gather up the courage. No. I knew myself, and I knew that I was more the kind of woman to apologize for disturbing them than to rain hell on their cheating heads. I had been raised that way, to be proper and polite at all times, and it was a tough habit to shake.

In the end, with rage and unfairness and humiliation all warring through me, too many emotions to deal with, I did the only thing I could think of.

I scribbled a note that said—very properly, of course—my good-byes, and left.